Mystery Emerso X
Emerson, Chuck.
The Franklins : trenchcoat
investigation /

34028084789834
FM $17.25 ocn872273023
03/11/14

DISCARD

Presented to

**Clear Lake City - County
Freeman Branch Library**

By

Friends of the Freeman Library

Harris County
Public Library

your pathway to knowledge

The Franklins

The Franklins

TRENCHCOAT INVESTIGATION - ONE

CHUCK EMERSON

One Drum • Houston, TX

The Franklins Copyright © 2013 by Charles Stephen Emerson, Jr..

This book was produced using PressBooks.com, and PDF rendering was done by PrinceXML.

Much of this novel takes place near a body of water called Clear Lake found in the Texas counties of Harris and Galveston. However, this is a work of fiction. Names, characters, places, and incidents are products of the author's imagination or used fictitiously. Any resemblance to actual events, locales, or persons, living or dead, is entirely coincidental.

+

Copyright 2013 by Charles Stephen Emerson, Jr. All rights reserved. No part of this publication can be produced or transmitted in any form or by any means, electronic or mechanical, without written permission.

+

DEDICATION
My son, Stephen Charles Emerson
(known theatrically as Tzoul Shine)

+

Special Thanks to these kind and patient Beta Testers who made it all the way through an earlier version of this novel and gave considered, insightful feedback (in reverse surname order):
Elizabeth Zajic, Emma Tran, Andrea Tantillo, Marina Olson, Pam Howell, Randy Edwards, and Guy Avellon

+

Please visit my web presences
www.ChuckEmersonTX.com
www.Facebook.com/ChuckFiction

Chapter 1

Second Friday in April

Closing time on Friday had arrived when that should-have-known-better brunette burst between me and the door I was closing.

"Hey, what are you doin'? Get back out here."

"Your name Trench?"

"We're closed. Gonna have to ask you to leave."

"Are you Mr. Trench?"

"That's the name on the door."

"Get in here and close the door. Sit down."

Was it my office or hers?

"You have a minute. I know you do." She stepped her tallish frame over to my desk, stopped, looked back at me like I was disappointing her.

Intruder stood about five-seven in a teal sleeveless tennis blouse, white shorts and tennis shoes. Nicely toned and sculpted, probably in her early forties, her milk chocolate hair hung straight and thick to her shoulders framing good looks and light blue eyes.

With nary a wrinkle in her blouse and shoes snow white, it was clear Intruder had not been playing tennis that afternoon.

I shut the door, forty-five with a buzz cut, maybe three inches taller than Intruder and tipping the scales at two-and-a-quarter. And that fe-male had just pushed me aside.

"What did you say?" I said as I reached my high-back chair.

"We close at five. It's after. Rate doubles."

Intruder placed her small purse next to my out tray, said, "We'll deal with that in a moment. Sit down."

"No. I'm standing and you just stand right where you are, tell me why you are here."

Intruder matched my stare, brow a deep set of furrows, said, "I saw your listing – in the lobby."

"What were you looking for when you discovered *my* listing?"

"Some good help."

"With what?"

"A crime."

It was time I gave some crap back to her.

"The already committed type – or do you wish to hire a consultant to help you commit one – without getting caught?"

"You're a rude sort."

"Hey, I once had a woman walk in this office, not much older than you. Wanted me to off her husband. Very dramatic. Convinced me the guy needed to die."

"Did you kill him?"

"I gave her the name of a good psychologist. Which kind of crime are you talking about?"

"No murders."

"No? You bust in here when I'm leaving for the weekend and you can't even make it interesting? What's up with you?"

Her dislike for what I'd just said was written all over her face. "I'm trying to find where the profits from our food business have gone."

"You saying some money's missing?"

"You catch on quick."

"Maybe what you need is a business consultant – maybe an auditor. A CPA. There's also a mixed breed called a *tax attorney*. Now, if you think a private investigator might be expensive, wait until –"

"Those firms charge three hundred an hour and up. I know."

"Hey, then I'm a bargain at *one* hundred."

Intruder showed additional displeasure but did not speak.

I gave her half a minute, said, "So you got a beef with your husband," I said. "That's not news in this office."

"Okay, hear this, then."

"I'm waiting."

She set her jaw, stared me down some more, harder, said after a good minute, "I think my husband's dishonest. A crook. A thief. A liar."

Chapter 2

Friday

The anger in her words was deep.
"And you know this how?"
"I damn well know it."
"What do you know?"
"He's skimming cash from the restaurant business – *our* restaurant business. Probably a little at a time."
I nodded like I was an old hat at finding skimmed cream.
"Sure does. Adds up every day." A thought popped in my mind. "You know what, though?"
"What?"
"I'm standing here wondering why you're complaining. If he doesn't get caught, you're reaping a huge benefit in tax-free cash, maybe an early retirement. If he does get caught, *he* goes to jail. The feds probably don't find half his stash. You get the protected assets under Texas law. If y'all are still talking when he gets out, he digs up the money the government didn't find, you two get reacquainted in Belize. Maybe you should open a Swiss account now?"

The anger in her eyes told me she didn't care much for my perspective. A moment later came a cough, one of those short, dry ones they teach in finishing school, the kind that's supposed to let you know that what you just did or said would be dealt with harshly.

"Mr. Trench, you view yourself as a professional, correct?"

I worried where she was going with that. Maybe I should wait to see if she coughed again?

I waited a three-count. No cough. "Okay."

"What, in your professional opinion, might be the motivation of such a behavior?"

"Skimming cash?"

"Yes?"

No brainer. "Well, it's The American Way: tax avoidance."

"Name three more."

I had to think a minute. A short one. "Money for gambling debts."

"Good one."

"Money for his mistress's apartment."

"You're rude, but that's a good one. That's two."

"Money needed to pay the Mob for protection."

She shook her head, like a nun who knew a second grader was lying. "Mr. Trench, the Mob doesn't work in Clear Lake."

My office was located near the southern edge of Clear Lake City, a large residential development twenty miles southeast of downtown Houston. Seven small cities touch the Clear Lake's waters, as does the Johnson Space Center. Over two hundred thousand people call it home. "Clear Lake" grew quickly in the '60's in response to the construction of NASA's Manned Spacecraft Center which was later renamed in honor of President Johnson.

"Ma'am, which of the four is it – or is it something else?"

"That's why I'm considering hiring you."

"It could take a lot of time to find out. Might need to hire some help. How many restaurants?"

"Eight."

"Nice." I could see the billable hours escalating on Excel. "Have you seen any suspicious package pickups or drops?"

"No."

"Have any of the employees come to you with suspicions?"

"No. They don't talk to me much."

No wonder!

"Then where did you get this idea?" I said. How do you know he's skimming?"

"I just had a burr under my saddle, I guess, so I hired a tax attorney. She charged me thousands of dollars to review our tax returns, financials, and the restaurants' books. She told me gross sales were down the last twelve months compared to the prior five years, even though the economy was up and restaurants in our area had been able to raise prices."

"How is payroll? I had a case where the owner hired a shadow."

"Someone to follow the owner around?"

"No. The person didn't exist past the shadow his fraudulent withholding form made on the stockroom floor."

"The tax attorney said playing games with payroll is harder to do since the Patriot Act, especially the last few years in Texas what with ICE feeling its oats. She suggested the skimming."

"You have no proof." Statement, not a question.

"Just pages of reports and graphs. The CPA-attorney is quite convinced."

"To justify the money she charged you, of course she's gonna put on a good show."

She didn't reply and I stepped to the window and looked out on the patch of grass that allowed the owners to call my office building a *garden office complex.*

I said, "You still haven't shared with me your best-guess motivation for any skimming."

No answer.

I continued looking out the window, giving her indirect privacy. It's gotta suck if she spent significant bucks and still didn't know.

Chapter 3

Friday

After a few minutes, still staring out the window, I decided to conduct myself as a professional and be understanding, never mind her cutting into my weekend.

"Ma'am, what do you think it is? You're a woman. His wife. Women usually have some intuition about such things."

It took her a good two minutes to reply.

"Mr. Trench," she said, her voice wavering, "I think I'm probably in denial about something."

With sugar you get....

"Not seeing the forest for the trees...?" I said.

"Spring says I'm a drama queen."

"And who might Spring be?"

"Our daughter."

Ah! More fodder.

I turned to face her. "How old's Spring?"

"Seventeen. Oops, eighteen."

A fun age.

"Lots of knowledge and very little fear?" I said, like an expert.

"Except when it comes to dating. You have kids?"

Busted, I was.

"Nieces and nephews. I try not to spoil them."

"Mr. Trench, never mind Spring. My intuition tells me my husband is up to no good. Like you said, women have a sense of such things."

"So, are you asking me to take you on?"

She stood, moved toward the far end of the window. It was her turn.

I stepped back around behind my desk chair and waited.

In two or three minutes, her head turned ever so slowly toward me and she said, in a Junior League sort of way, "You mentioned a moment ago, I believe, that you charge one hundred dollars an hour,"

"Plus expenses," I said with an empowered nod.

With a look that could be called only one thing, condescending, she came over to my desk, sat in the left chair, set her shoulders back, crossed her legs, and said, "Now, tell me, Mr. Trench, do you bill out forty hours *every* week?"

"Don't need to."

She didn't say anything out loud; no words. Her eyes, though, they sent dry ice bullets in my direction.

"I have a pension," I said, hoping I had served an ace. "United States Navy retirement."

"So this Trenchcoat thing is a sham, nothing more than a glorified hobby!"

A mean return of serve.

"No. Not with my overhead – got a house to pay for. This office doesn't come cheap."

"I thought all investigators lived in their office."

I let the air settle a moment to deflate her attempt at humor before saying, "My retirement check allows me the latitude to pick and choose the gumshoe cases I want. While I strive to give quality, dollar-friendly results to my clients, I also want to enjoy the work."

"Cost-friendly results goes without saying," she said. "I need some professional assistance. I'm also a businesswoman, familiar with negotiations at *every* level."

"Good. Let's – "

"The assistance I expect I'll need will require large chunks of time."

"Right. Well, let's – "

"Should I determine that it would be wise to retain your services, I will negotiate that hourly rate – down."

"I'm afraid – "

"Mr. Trench, you're not very busy. I've investigated *you*."

The building directory thing was a sham.

"I don't need Spenser," she said, "or Elvis Cole, or C.S.I. Miami for that matter. I'm here, Mr. Trench, because what I require is no more than *average* competence."

A clear insult, spoken with that condescension seasoning again.

I stood, reached my hand out to shake hers goodbye.

< >   < >

"Sit down. You haven't had a new client in weeks."

"This meeting is over," I said, hand still outstretched.

"Sit down, Mr. Trench."

How did she know about the lull in gumshoe work? The flow of electronic look-ups for background checks, skip traces, missing child support deadbeats and such had streamed at a decent, steady pace for a couple of years, but she was correct: nobody had asked me to be their gumshoe in a couple of months.

I wondered if an ill wind had blown through the lips of one Lynnette Schnabel, our Executive Suite receptionist. She was supposed to be discreet. Or maybe another private investigator had dug up my business information. Why wasn't this witch retaining him – or her?

"Mr. Trench, sit down!"

Damn woman. Retiring from the Navy meant I didn't have to take direct orders anymore, much less get yelled at.

"Ms. – what *is* your name?"

"Not needed. I'll pay cash."

We did another stare-down for a moment, then I leaned forward a bit. "The IRS likes to see names in my case files, like, you know, the client's."

"Ahhhh tell you what, you may call me *Mrs. Franklin*. For the time being."

I withdrew my hand, debated whether she might be a plant from the state licensing office and behind on her weekly quota. Maybe she was so bad off she needed to sucker me into a violation on a Friday afternoon.

One way to safeguard the situation: evidence.

I sat down. Slid my middle right hand drawer open, rummaged around like I was looking for something and tapped the record switch on the MP3 digital device laying in the rear tray. The always-on Bluetooth microphone I had fastened beneath the six-inch desk overhang had worked really well when I'd tested it. It was time for the real thing.

"Mr. Trench!"

"Just looking for my receipt book."

"No receipts. This is a cash transaction."

"Fine." I hated carbon forms, hated pressing hard with a ballpoint pen. "But I'll need a Ben Franklin right now. If you're not carrying much cash, there's an ATM in the lobby. And that only gets you a half hour today and you've fifteen minutes left."

"Mr. Trench, I am not accustomed to – "

"Look, I was about to head out the door when you showed up. I have plans." Okay, so I lied. She didn't sound like she was dealing from the top of the deck either. "Perhaps I won't find your requirements within the scope of this agency's mission statement."

Mrs. Franklin scooted back in her chair and recrossed her legs.

I frowned.

She didn't say anything right away.

"Mr. Trench, your *usual* operations , amount to zip. Nada. Nothing. No new detective work in weeks, remember?"

"Navy retirement, remember?"

"Mr. Trench, you're not getting a hundred."

"Then this meeting is over," I said as I stood yet again.

"Shut up. Sit down. Listen," she said, harsh as a witch in an old B movie.

I held my ground.

She stood back up and returned to the window.

Chapter 4

Friday

Maybe five minutes later, she said, still looking out the window, "Mr. Trench, I am willing to give you eighty an hour, maximum five thousand a week."

A week!

I could end up tailing that guy for days, all day and night, run up way more than five thou in a week. Easy. He'd eventually demonstrate a pattern that would allow me to avoid being parked out at the curb all the time, so the bill would go down over time. But that could take a while.

In my excitement, I had almost forgot one item.

I sucked it in, said, "Plus expenses."

"Yes," she said, glancing back at me. Not a comforting sight. "Let's limit them to another thousand a week. Anything more, you have to fax me for approval, in advance."

A dame with her own fax number.

Then my brain farted.

"You know what?" I said.

"What?"

"I didn't ask – you didn't say – I'm guessing you don't work outside the home." Once out of my mouth, I knew it sounded really lame. I slid into *even dumber* with, "You umm didn't get off work early on a Friday to come see me, I don't think?"

"How... observant."

I sucked it in yet again, forged ahead. "What's your gig – what do you do?"

She left the window. Sat. Leaned forward and folding her hands, placed her pinkies on the edge of my desk. "I work a card table."

A dealer at the casinos in Louisiana?

I punted. "Tarot?" It sounded funny when I first thought of it.

"Not hardly."

"Casino in Lake Charles?"

"Not likely."

"Ummm, what then?"

"Bridge. I chase all the details, hope my partner can keep up."

"Country club or ladies club?"

"Bay Oaks. Others you wouldn't recognize."

I let her go on that.

"So you like puzzles?" I said.

"Yes, except when it's part of my own life."

"I hear that."

"Mr. Trench. We digress. You haven't agreed to my terms."

I was supposed to be the bad ass setting terms. My reminding her about expenses was as much saying "yes," wasn't it?

And did she really have the money to pay me?

"Mrs. Franklin, it's customary to obtain a retainer on this much work. I'll need two week's worth of estimated billings."

Her responding facial expression was coy, almost over to the flirt side. After a moment, she said, "I think I follow you. Just don't go flying off to Rome on your expense account unless –"

"Unless I clear it with you – fax you, first."

"Right. Wait here. I'll be right back."

She grabbed Prada and paraded out. Potty break?

< >   < >

She returned a few minutes later. Gliding in the door, she said, "Lexus parked; locked."

Parked? Locked?

"I was temporarily stranded," she said.

I guess she read the question on my face.

"I had a friend drop me by here. My Lexus wasn't ready at the dealer's when we went by. She couldn't wait for me – had to go get her son. Dealer agreed to deliver the Lexus here, by six. I went to check."

I hadn't heard that one before. Didn't quite believe her but gave her an "A" for creativity.

"A good thing," I said. "Another thing. This husband of yours got a name?"

"Ben. Benjamin Franklin."

Seriously?

I said, "You just pulled my leg clear out of its socket."

"You think I pulled your leg, do you now, Mr. Trench? I do not kid or tease."

"Okay, then... and you would be...?"

"Mrs. Ben Franklin."

"Your *name*?"

"Candice Faith Pence Franklin."

I guessed she wasn't big on nicknames.

"Follow along, please," she said, sounding like a second grade teacher. "I'm ready to count."

She pulled a banker's envelope out of Prada and counted Ben Franklins. She stopped at fifty. I had asked for twice that.

I said, "And the first week's expenses?"

"You fax me those weekly."

Dammit.

"So we're doing, basically, the max total hourly fee for a week, in advance, and the expenses in arrears, each week. Correct."

"Yes. Cash, as you see."

I decided not to push for the second week. My mind had already purchased an overhaul for my boat's engine.

"Don't forget to give me his Social Security Number before you leave."

She gave me a *smarter than any woman you've ever tangled with* look for a good ten seconds or so before saying, "I've done you one better. It cost me less to work up this info ahead of time than to pay you to go find it yourself. Dealing with that tax attorney taught me a thing or two."

She dove into Prada again and extracted a number ten envelope, from which she removed an 8.5 X 11 sheet of twenty-four-pound paper, lunar blue – the really dynamic shade I'd seen on a shelf at Office Depot. She unfolded it, relaxed the creases, and let it float gently onto my blotter.

The beautiful page was scarred with black laser toner in regular, bold, and italic serif fonts. A quick glance told me the sheet contained every statistical data point that Equifax or Experian would have on Benjamin Ivan Franklin. The reverse mapped out family history back two generations and out to third cousins.

One thing took me as strange. Under "spouse" my client's name showed only as "Mrs. Franklin." Did I really know anything about, Candice Faith Pence Franklin?

"And what is your Social Security Number and date of birth," I said.

It took another ten minutes to get that information out of her. Drivers license number, another five.

Chapter 5

Friday

Mixed emotions warred within me on the drive home to Seabrook.

Mrs. Franklin's description of my business activity had been a bit darker than fact. True, I was happy to have a cash customer, someone who could pay a fair investigator's fee for a good period of time, but my business then wasn't far from where I'd hoped it would be when I'd opened up shop five years earlier.

So, yeah I was happy about the five g's but, as I headed home east on the NASA Pkwy., I couldn't hold onto the happy thoughts. They ran away every time one of Mrs. Franklin's questions echoed in my head: "You have kids?"

Technically I'd told Mrs. Franklin the truth. I didn't have any kids. My kid wasn't going to turn sweet sixteen that coming summer.

Kara had died eight years before, about two years after her mother divorced me over the "deplorable life of an enlisted sailor's wife" and joined her folks in Florida. I had no choice but to continue doing the Petty Officer First Class thing down at the Navy's Mine and ASW command in Corpus Christi, Texas.

When my wife divorced me, I couldn't really argue with her taking daddy's little girl to grandma's in Florida. I went T.A.D. (temporarily-assigned duty) often as a member of the Naval Security Group. Trips came at irregular intervals and lasted varied periods of time. The secrecy of the missions was another one of her complaints. I couldn't discuss them with my wife and she had her suspicions.

I figured the divorce wouldn't be all bad: I could spend my thirty days annual leave every year with Kara. It was the one item I insisted on in the whole divorce decree.

Kara's death wasn't anybody's fault; just one of those *very unfortunate elementary school accidents.*

Kara was where she was supposed to be, up on the sidewalk waiting for grandma to pick her up after school. The crossing guard was where he was supposed to be, holding the STOP sign beside his head. The school's faculty and administrators were where they were supposed to be, too, on that bright, sunny afternoon, up on the sidewalk greeting parents as they picked up their youngsters.

From what the police pieced together from witnesses and the physical evidence...

the crossing guard saw no more children approaching the crosswalk and lowered the STOP sign.

a student's mother driving a Suburban saw the STOP sign go down and applied gentle pressure to the gas pedal. She was, as always, paying close attention to the goings on around her. She was a good mother. She knew kids. She had two buckled in right behind her.

the Suburban moved forward at under five miles an hour. The mother soon saw a boy darting back towards the school building from her left. He was sure to cross her space momentarily, so she twisted the steering wheel hard to the right.

the SUV and its tall off-road tires hardly noticed the short curbing or Kara.

Kara and I only got to spend one summer month together.

< >   < >

That Friday evening I took a look at the lunar blue sheet Mrs. Franklin had provided. It certainly was an extensive one-page compilation of data on Benjamin I. Franklin, better than any other client had ever provided. I did wonder what he looked like, though. She had neglected to provide any photos of Ben, never mind video files or their web download locations. She did note that hubby didn't have a Facebook page. How did she know? He could be on there as Alfred E. Newman or George Pectorals. I didn't think it likely, but a good gumshoe has to explore all the crazy stuff, too.

I decided I didn't want to reinforce her concept that I had little else to do, so I saved the photo shortage for the next morning. We had scheduled a meeting at the IHOP on NASA Pkwy..

I asked if IHOP was one of her husband's restaurants. She didn't think my question was the least bit funny; said the last thing they would own would be a franchise.

So, none of the eight restaurants were franchises. Important information. Skimming would be easier from a ma-pa operation: no national franchise inspector to come by, comparing known national parameters and ratios against local books to make sure corporate was getting their contractual pound of flesh.

Chapter 6

Saturday

Two large coffees sat steaming when I walked up to a two-person booth near the IHOP kitchen at eight thirty. Mrs. Franklin had arrived early.

"Sit down, Mr. Trench," she said, flipping a page of a monster photo album, two inches thick. "Enjoy some lousy coffee."

"Don't mind if I do. Where is it better?"

"Whole Foods, inside the Loop."

I slid in and grabbed the cup without lipstick on the rim. "To Saturday!" I said, raising my cup.

Mrs. Franklin turned another album page.

< >   < >

"So," I said, "have you thought of anything else that might help clue me into the truth, any cave I should explore?"

She looked up with a rested pair of eyes. "Nothing much in here," she said, her chin dipping toward the photos. "I'm not going to let you have the whole album. Maybe a couple photos. Just wanted you to see that Ben can fool even me."

Where had that remark come from? I let a moment pass, said, "How so?"

"You know how you men get in trouble for not recognizing a woman at a function when you were introduced to her six months before, even if she's cut her hair and dyed it?"

I'd been there. Guilty as charged.

I said, "Makeup has something to do with it, doesn't it? Magic is what I used to call it. Ben is a guy so hair dying doesn't fit."

"Not necessarily." Her words had arrived like a text message, dressed in no sentiment, no lilt to her voice, no color, no temperature. I didn't like it.

Mrs. Franklin looked up, caught my hesitation. "Ben volunteers as a clown during the holidays. Learned theatrical makeup in college. Has maybe a dozen wigs. Can literally walk right past me at the mall and I won't know him."

"He tested you on this?"

"Says he did. It was early on in our marriage so I have no reason not to believe him."

"He was honest once?"

"To a fault." Those words did have temperature and color, betraying a deep wound I figured, perhaps from a flash back to times steeped in perfection for its own sake.

"Since you fear he's strayed from the straight and narrow," I said, "do you suspect he's ever *hidden* in a disguise for reasons our local sheriff might find, you know, objectionable?"

"Like dealing drugs?"

"That could be one use of a disguise."

"I'm sure he is doing something illegal right now."

"In a disguise? What kind?"

"I have no idea."

"Have you checked his theatrical stuff, his makeup? You said he has twelve wigs."

"Yes, of course. You think I'm stupid?"

"Didn't mean –"

"We have eight restaurants, Mister Trench. He could hide the goop in any one of them."

Yup. Probably has "owner only" access to at least one storage room.

"And the money has to be going somewhere," she said, her tone more like a whine.

"Okay," I said sitting up straight. "Name the poison – the racket – the gig, Mrs. Franklin."

"If I knew that I wouldn't need you." Clients. Ya gotta love them.

I reached a hand toward her. "Let's see the photos."

She spun the album one-eighty, flipped back to the front and led me through the pages. I laid a paper napkin off the bottom edge of each page where I saw a photo I thought would be useful. In the end, I'd marked seven. She told me I could have two, then relented and agreed to temporarily part with a third.

"I'll get copies made at Office Depot. Get these back to you this afternoon." Why she wouldn't let me copy a dozen or two never became clear.

She refilled her cup for the second time. "Another point I neglected to make yesterday."

"Sure."

"I don't want you coming by the house. We must meet in public places or not at all."

We weren't suspected of having an affair...?

"I don't follow," I said. "Why not your home?"

"The neighbors like Ben more than me."

I sat back and chewed on that. "You're saying they like money more than, say, personality?"

"Money's not it. They keep asking me to volunteer for committees."

"Then your problem – our problem – would be...?"

"He's slicker than Teflon-coated ice."

Chapter 7

Saturday

I'd dealt with some real bastards in the Navy but had never heard "slicker than Teflon-coated ice" before. I was speechless.

"He can make you like him," said Mrs. Franklin, "even while he's twisting a dagger around in your shoulder."

That was severe. I punted. "How about my office? Can we meet there?"

"Perhaps."

Nothing like a reticent client.

"How about you take ten minutes to orient me to the public behavior persona of your modern day Ben Franklin?"

"Would you like to hear him talk?"

"Not without watching his face, movements, demeanor."

"No problem. Let's go out to the Lexus."

Now it had been a long while since a lady had invited me up to her place or dropped the extra hotel key in my suit coat pocket. A very long while. But never in my life had I been invited to share a woman's Lexus.

Of course, very married Mrs. Franklin – I remember making a mental note right then to ask for her permission to use her first name – hadn't meant anything even remotely personal or intimate. It turned out she wanted me to sit in the second row of the SUV and watch home movies on an LCD screen.

Ben was not what I expected, ladies man with dark hair and powerful build. Screen showed tallish yet lanky, freckled and sandy-haired – and a bit too serious. Looked like he didn't know how to play, even with his kids.

After the first clip, I said, "How long have you had the digicam?"

"We bought the first one when they came out, maybe fifteen years ago."

"How far back you got these videos?"

"Of Benjamin?" she said mostly to herself. A wrinkle worked its way across her brow over the next minute or so. Then she said, "I'd have to say that the oldest would be ten years ago when I finally learned how to work the camera."

She had seemed quick witted, so the camera learning thing confused me.

She must have noticed the fog in my eyes. She said, "Benjamin wouldn't let me work the camera. Said it was a man's place. Then we got one of the first ones with the fold-out mini screen on the side."

"Those were damn expensive."

"But spread like wildfire. I told him they'd finally got it right with the video cameras. Anyone could work them. Ben had nowhere to go with that argument. He couldn't hide behind the camera. Had no excuse to not be in the movies. And the kids were older and wouldn't settle for less."

I sensed that a power struggle was behind her wondering about skimmed money. "You and he don't get agree on several fronts?"

"You would be correct."

"What's the biggest?'

"He won't admit the company's mine." I had expected a pause and couple of frowns but her response had come in less than a nanosecond.

Why wasn't that on the lunar blue?

An oversize burr under her saddle, clearly. But where had that been the day before? "What do you mean? You said he had eight restaurants."

"He does. But Shrimp-Steak, Inc., the corporation that owns the individually organized restaurants – owns all the stock – the corporation that got the funding when *we* started it all, lists me as the majority shareholder."

"Back fifteen or more years."

"Right at fifteen."

I knew exactly what the deal was. "You took advantage of federal set asides for businesses owned by women and minorities." I had picked up a lot of small business practices working with a CPA on a couple of divorce cases.

"Yes *we* did...." Mrs. Franklin stopped talking. Was it anger or regret? I didn't know but it sure was something.

After what seemed like five minutes but it was probably fifteen seconds, she took one of those short deep breaths, said, "Ben was doing catering when I met him. Was still doing it when we got married. He did it back when everybody wasn't. Today even a hot dog stand advertises catering service."

"Hot dog under glass."

"Funny."

"I work at it."

"Please, Mr. Trench. Those preferential points for women and minority-owned businesses did wonders, won Ben lots of work – heck, we fed the coast guard for a while. He couldn't have built the business without my name on the top of the letterhead. He truly hated catering, even though he was so very good at it. Too much ass kissing, he always said. My gender – and a chunk of my aunt's money – enabled him to make the money to get into owning and running restaurants, which was what he wanted in the first place."

Sometimes I get these huge hunches. I gave her a moment to reign in her anger, then said, "Is there more?"

The tendons on her neck jumped out. "Spring says he married me to build his business."

A new twist. Daughter does know.

"So what do you need me for?" I said. "Why don't you call a board meeting – initiate an audit? Demote him – what is he, President and you're Chairman of the Board?"

Chapter 8

Saturday

I waited for her to respond. The tendons in Mrs. Candice Franklin's neck held taught, stretching out like the supports for the Eiffel Tower. It took a minute for her to turn back to me.

From there I gave her another minute, then said, "Why haven't you taken over if you no longer trust him? If what you tell me is accurate, it's your company, even if Texas is a community property state."

"You don't have any kids?"

Where was that going? "No. Not...now."

"Not married?"

"Was." It had been almost ten years.

If I didn't get a permanent squeeze real soon, I could probably kiss my prostate goodbye in the very near future. At least my urologist thought so. *The bizarre shit my mind jumps to during important conversations – I'm nuts!*

"Check with the parents of your nieces and nephews," said Candice. "Sometimes you let things ride so that the kids don't grow up stretched tighter than catgut on a first-chair violin."

I let that sift through my mind a minute. "Okay, so when were you planning to step forward? Your kids could be old enough. Son is what, twenty-two, daughter eighteen last month? My sister says her fifteen year old is more mature than I am." *There went another bizarre interrupt-a-thought – and I said it out loud. Sheesh!*

"For a hired hand, you sure seem to take a broad stance."

"I found a long time ago that if I know the politics and the bullshit going on under the surface, I can figure out what the truth is a hell of a lot faster."

Mrs. Franklin locked eye contact with me for a good minute. I locked back. Said nothing. Waited.

She said, "You're probably right."

"Hard to say that to a guy?"

"Especially one that thinks he knows everything." No way she was talking about me.

"I can refer you to a female shamus. We have a couple in the area."

She smiled. "I met them. They're more codependent than I am."

I'd heard that word once before. Thought I just might look it up later that weekend. Didn't happen.

"You're the one paying the freight," I said. "One thing, though."

"Yes, Mr. Trench?" She was still formal.

"Your name. Candice. Would they call you Connie for short?"

"I will not accept short shrift. I am Candice. Candice Faith. That's the short and long of it, as my grandmother used to say." She laughed. She did!

After we both smiled directly into eye contact, I said, "Okay, I still want the lowdown on what you think Benjamin might have as a motive for the money. If he really is skimming, there has to be a reason. The business has been profitable, right?"

"Always. It's profitable even though he's skimming."

"I'm giving you that for the moment. What would he need the money for?"

She smiled. Popped out with what, for her, would be a short giggle. "He's always said he wanted his own tropical island."

I had been looking off into nowhere when she said that so I was pleased to see a small upturning of her lips when I glanced back at her. "You can kid around, too?"

We came up with: retiring; starting a new family; running for Congress; and buying various toys like a Bentley, a Dodge Viper, a four thousand square foot condo in Vail, and a thirty-five foot cabin cruiser.

As the game's energy dwindled, it became clear to me that nothing fit into the bit stream of her intuition. If Candice had that strong a sense that something *was* going on, if she was willing to put out five grand a week to find out what was going on, then she would recognize what it was when the concept surfaced. Yup. She would.

We needed to brainstorm soon. Meanwhile, it was time I followed Benjamin around town. Got my own sense of his persona.

"Where is he, this hour on Saturday?"

"Charlie's, I think. That office is bigger."

"He visit each one every day?"

"No. He picks and chooses, random fashion. Keeps the managers guessing, he says. That way he doesn't have to visit each one. I'm sure he never gets to more than four. I know of days he's worked only two. Every once in a while a manager is ill and Ben has to take on a good part of that load. Besides, gasoline, even in a company vehicle, is still too far over three dollars a gallon not to make a businessman think twice about chasing around town."

"You sound like you have a sound head for business."

"I told you, I'm the president." Her tone had edged toward playful but the echoed doses of resentment and plain old anger were still there.

"Well, thanks for the photos. I'll get them copied, like I said."

"Tomorrow – let's make it Coffee Oasis. Same time. The coffee's better."

I stood. Shook her hand. "You're on." Rusty's coffee bar was five minutes down the road from my house.

Chapter 9

Saturday

I'm not one for sitting on stakeouts. They just aren't fun or glamorous like on the cop shows or in the movies. Sitting, waiting for someone to do something – anything – is about as boring as life gets. Besides, if your suspect is the right bad guy, he's more likely to be watching out for The Man. So, sitting on stakeout is like erecting a large neon sign. And in Southeast Texas the steam bath inside a parked car can easily get over a hundred, even in early April. No fool sits for hours in their car in Houston. Nobody – well, there is commute prison, aka afternoon rush hour.

I'd been parked a bit down Highway 3 from Charlie's Steak, Seafood and Spirits, in front of a barber shop, for ten minutes. Needed a cooler and less conspicuous crow's nest to stalk my prey. Benjamin drove a Dodge Charger SRT8, 2012. Bright red. Had the bigger hemi. Candice had made a side notation: "45th birthday present to self." Birthday present or not, there had been no red vehicle in the lot when I drove by and I had a decent view of the only ways in or out.

I started up my Sierra Gold Metallic 2004 Subaru Forester XT and went looking for my favorite color, red. The XT wasn't red for professional reasons – like stakeouts and full-time all-wheel drive with a turbo engine. It could go anywhere, and fast, if you didn't mind ugly.

I turned west on NASA Pkwy., then did a U-turn and came back, turning right down Highway 3 past Charlie's. No red machine on big rubber wheels. Benjamin clearly had better ideas how to spend his Saturday morning. I parked back in front of the barber shop to think.

Why would Benjamin be working on Saturday? Candice had not been long on compliments of Mr. Franklin, and had made no remark about his being a workaholic. What I might have in Benjamin Franklin was an owner who treats Mondays and another day during the week as his weekend.

I consulted lunar blue sheet for Candice's cell phone number.

"You already have an emergency, Mr. Trench?"

"No, Mrs. Franklin, I don't. One thing I was wondering – you got a second?"

Static played hell with my pollen-ravaged ears for a moment, then I heard her say, "... and not much more than that. Isn't the blue sheet enough?"

"Oh, it's great. Wish all my clients would do the same. I just need to know which days he considers his weekend. You know, restaurant business is good on Saturday and Sunday."

"Mondays. Golf Tuesday and Thursday afternoons."

"No two days in a row?"

"No. He goes in Tuesday and Thursday mornings. Only Hurricane Alley is open on Monday."

"Sports Bar?"

"You might be a detective after all."

"Not so far. No Charger in Charlie's parking lot."

"You sure? He just...."

Candice's voice had all but vanished in the static. Almost like she'd done the digital version of fainting. "You there, Mrs. Franklin?"

I waited another maybe ten seconds. "Mrs. Franklin?"

"Yes. Yes, I'm here," she said, her voice a bit gurgly. "Sorry."

"You were about to say something about Benjamin?"

"Yes. I just spoke with him, maybe ten minutes ago. He said he'd arrived at Charlie's about, oh, it would be twenty minutes ago, now, I guess. You say he's not there?"

"Haven't been inside but I don't see a single Dodge four-door or any red vehicle anywhere close. Does he have a reserved covered parking spot? Is there an alley or something in back?"

"No alley. No covered parking."

"Gotcha."

"I'll give you another address – just a minute."

I turned up the fan on the AC and waited. There was very little cloud cover and Mr. Sun was about to cook me, what with the Forester's large windows and what they called off-black upholstery. If it had a weak point, it was the AC. Unlike so many Toyotas and Hondas, the Forester was still made in Japan. How hot did it get on that island, really?

"Here it is. You ready?"

Actually, I wasn't. I'd sat there twiddling mental thumbs, hadn't bothered to take out my note pad and pen. I faked it. "Sure. Shoot it to me." Always had a good memory for numbers.

In less than two seconds, she read off an address a couple of miles away, then said she had to go.

The street name didn't sound right but the hundred block made it one nearby. I scrounged a pen from the glove box, wrote the number on my palm but didn't need to ink my hand any further. The street name would stick with me. Who ever wanted to live on Helm Street? The only helm I ever knew was on a ship.

As I pulled from the curb, another point raced across my mind: if it *was* residential, then that explained the hurried manner in which Candice gave me the address. Benjamin was supposed to be at work. At Charlie's.

What kind of surprise would I get up on Helm Street?

Chapter 10

Saturday

The Charger was on Helm Street, parked in all its red magnificence in a concrete residential driveway facing the street. Its prominent rear end sat just inside an open garage door. The other half of the double garage (single door) shaded a Buick sedan of that neutral brown-tan color, the one they make when they're not painting all Buicks gray. The tan brick-veneer house occupied the middle of a block in a middleclass subdivision, probably built in the mid sixties, back in the time when several builders constructed houses on any given street – not like today when one builder develops a whole subdivision and houses all look the same. Yeah, I hate that.

I coasted by and parked three doors down, across the street in front of the only ugly lawn, under a huge oak. This tree was so stout, so robust it put the Forester in shade so deep I figured no one could see inside the windows.

I readjusted my driver's side and review mirrors, doing the stakeout thing in reverse. I retrieved a steno notebook from under the passenger seat while I conjured up reasons why Benjamin would back the Charger into the driveway, half into the garage.

Had he loaded or unloaded something, an item he didn't want anyone to see? The rear bumper looked like it was far back enough to where the garage door would land on the rear window if lowered. Or was he parked nose out to provide a quick escape? Of course, there are people on this planet who do everything on the moment's whimsy, no rhyme or reason to any action. Candice had given no indication that Ben had the slightest bit of whimsy, though.

Like I mentioned, sitting in cars, watching and waiting is a real pain. Well, it's even more tedious backwards. Five minutes later, pain's dagger slashed the left side of my neck at the shoulder. Was my telephoto digital SLR in the trunk? Had to be a better way to watch Ben.

A good while later as I readjusted the rear view mirror and was about to turn on the ignition, Benjamin made his escape. No, that's not the right word. You can't be escaping if you have a smiling, unarmed escort holding your arm.

Following Ben to the Charger was a very slender blonde unit, tresses long and stringy. Her shimmering midnight blue micro dress caressed an absolutely wonderful ass. Standing on just one too-high pump, other calf up ninety degrees like in the movies, she planted a big wet one on his cheek as Benjamin attempted to open the driver's door. I was too far away to tell if that public kiss or the next thing she did made him blush. She grabbed his left ass cheek, gave it a good, firm shake. Repeated. Damn!

Benjamin soon exited the driveway, turning right, away from me. I was going to lose him. I turned the key with an eye on the side view mirror but lost him as Helm curved slightly. Restraining an urge to bolt, I calmly placed the Forester in drive and eased from the curb. At the end of the block, I flipped a mental coin and turned left and then left again and headed to the end of the block one street over, hoping to catch sight of Benjamin at the next cross street.

No such luck. No Charger in red or any other color. I drove up to El Dorado Blvd., a major east-west artery in the Clear Lake City subdivision, and looked both ways. No bright red anything. Damn. What next? I flipped several mental coins.

A horn bounced me into the now. My mirror treated me to the mid-thirties gaunt face of the stringy blonde – in the tan Buick? That was so wrong. She evidently had places to go, tooted at me twice more. Modern day cheap car horns are so wimpy, stupid sissies compared to my dad's old GMC truck. Now there was a horn.

I shrugged my shoulders and raised my arms in an exaggerated fashion, then opened my window and waved for her to pass on by. I got a clear view, her sun-torched countenance glaring at me and mouthing words as she passed by, words I figured her mother didn't know she knew. She looked mid-thirties in profile view and a bit flat-chested. I noted the Buick's plate in the steno book, saying thank you, Ms. Rude, then counted to ten before following her.

Chapter 11

Saturday

Sun-torched blonde had made a right on El Dorado and then drove the long block down to the traffic light at Space Center Blvd. I followed and saw her move into the left turn lane, poised to head north on an artery that could take her up to the Spencer Highway in Pasadena, if she stayed on it. I slowed, worried she would figure me for a tail if I entered the left turn lane right behind her. Should I charge straight through on the yellow and come back around?

My decision was made for me. An idiot in a U-Haul rental truck cut in front of me, hit his brakes and entered the left turn lane with a sudden stop, half his truck in my lane. By the time the amateur had negotiated the truck through the intersection at the next signal change, red stared at me again.

I made like a jack-rabbit north but Stringy's head start proved too much. I reached the Fairmont Pkwy. in Pasadena, a good five miles and no tan Buick on the road. I headed back on home.

About halfway back to my place, Mrs. Franklin called.

"Yes, boss," I said, adjusting my Bluetooth headset.

"I like a man who knows who's boss." Did she intend humor?

I was temporarily speechless.

"Mr. Trench?"

"Yes, Ma'am."

"After your visit to Helm, I imagine you have some questions."

"I might. Is my orientation class going to meet again today?"

"Good guess. Meet me at Coffee Oasis in fifteen minutes. You *can* do that?"

For five thousand a week, I wasn't going to complain or mention that I'd already visited the god of espresso or that we were scheduled for Coffee Oasis in the morning. "Yes. I can."

"Very well. See you there. I'll drop Spring over at the mall or something."

That hadn't sounded quite right. "She doesn't have her own car?"

"In the shop. She trashed the clutch."

"Right," I said, thinking she liked to drive. Baybrook Mall and Seabrook sat at opposite ends of NASA Pkwy..

At the next red light, I wondered what had transpired since Mrs. Franklin did the hasty telephone hang up thing. The issue drew something other than a direct connection in my head, but did lead to the Helm house and a question mark in bold.

My mind then stumbled from Helm to Mrs. Franklin and buyer's remorse. Was she meeting with me to cancel my activities? Heck, that could happen. The sooner we met, the less working I'd be doing for no good reason.

Chapter 12

Saturday

Mrs. Candice Franklin sat legs crossed at one end of an oversized, overstuffed dark chocolate sofa at Coffee Oasis, simply stunning in her tennis outfit. Her socks, top, and sun visor glowed in fluorescent fuchsia. Her shorts and athletic shoes all but invisible in snow white. She had looked great in my office but I had never figured her a Barbie. That afternoon Barbie had competition.

"Sorry I forgot to ask you if you wanted something," she said instead of hello. "I have a Jasmine Tea coming." She seemed more polite, even wearing fuchsia, not the same woman as the day before.

"I'm all coffeed out." I said, as I dropped down on the other end of the sofa. "What's up?"

She fiddled with a cuticle for a moment, then said. "I suppose you're wondering –" She stopped. A painful cuticle?

I watched her fiddle a good thirty seconds, then said, "Wondering is how I solve cases. I never make entries in the judgment file until after I'm clear of the case – and sometimes never. Private investigators often get pulled long before all the mysteries are solved. If the investigation is terminated because of a, shall we say, unpleasant discovery, folks can call the police and have the guys in blue take over. Why not? The police don't invoice."

She abandoned her cuticles for a small smile in my direction. "Yes, I suppose they don't. I just don't know how to approach this."

I decided to get tough with her. "Mrs. Franklin –"

"Candice."

Right then, I knew she wasn't going to fire me. I took a quick deep breath but exhaled slowly, as prescribed by the Nav's medics.

"Fine. Great."

"You look like you want to say something...."

"Yes. I wanted to say that one sure way to spend more bucks on me is for you to not tell me the whole story. And I get to bill for these little meetings."

Just then the barista brought her Jasmine Tea. She fussed with it for a moment, then placed the tea on the coffee table in front of us and said, "You're right. I'm just running up my own bill. It's all just so not... not... Did you enjoy high school?"

I've never been big on large buildings with a lot of people inside. "Must have. My high school grades weren't so hot but good enough for my dad to let me get a part time job, to buy a car. I got a good deal on a 1980 Plymouth Volaré, two-door. It was an example of American engineering gone haywire. They were introduced without all the engineering completed on the carburetors. The one I bought was from the last year Chrysler made them. I figured the bugs had all been worked out by then."

Candice smiled. "I see. I was going in another direction."

Sometimes I talk too much. That was one of them. "Go on, please."

"It's just that life has gone well for me compared to many, many others, yet it has not followed the path that I thought existed when I graduated from high school."

"Life isn't like they taught us in high school," I said, happy to interject one of my favorites.

"You, too?" See seemed surprised, yet smiled. "It's not so much what they taught us," said Candice. "It's what has happened and what just *is*."

I nodded slowly, as if I understood.

"You see, that address you visited, it's, well, a place I know he goes and he doesn't know I know. It's like our little secret except that he thinks it's a secret from me but really I'm keeping my knowledge of it secret from him – I know, I'm rambling. I think I just said the same thing twice."

She had. I said nothing, but did add a small smile to another slow nod.

"Once, I borrowed a friend's wig and sweatshirt and another friend's car and followed him around for a day, about ten months ago. I think it was a Wednesday. I was way past angry when I saw that ugly blonde. The ratty hair. That girl – she's a candidate for osteoporosis, she's so skinny. Can't understand what she's ...."

I like 'em skinny. Candice was near perfect, certainly in great shape, fantastic, especially given her age and such. I sat back a little and nodded some more. What's a guy to do?

"Like I said, I was angry, but I discovered I wasn't sad. I didn't cry. I didn't even tell the girls in my Bunco group about it for two or three months."

I had the urge to ask her what she said when the women who loaned her the wig and the car asked about her adventure – managed to control myself, though.

"What really amazed me," said Candice, "was that I could still have sex with him. Now, did you listen carefully? I said sex. Not love making. The love hadn't lasted long in our marriage. It's hard to love a workaholic. They'll never take time for the gentle and long warm-fuzzy activities."

I sat there amazed that one day she could withhold so much and the next talk about her sex life.

"Say something!" she said.

Another direct order from The Boss. I leaned near her, said, "Being enlisted Navy and getting sent out temporarily somewhere for two weeks, sometimes two, three months with little notice didn't do my marriage any good. By the time she left, I would have left me, too. So, I understand and won't judge. And you're the one paying me. Confidentiality goes without saying."

She sat bolt upright, then stood and excused herself. I watched her walk toward the facilities.

Had I tripped over some imaginary threshold by inserting the "paying me" part at the end? Probably, I decided. It was guy talk. Guys understand "who's the boss" better than women. Girls always want to meet and discuss, form a committee or something.

Chapter 13

Saturday

Candice returned with her head down a bit, like a shy sixth grader walking up to recite in front of the class. Her gait was as even and steady as ever. No clues there. Since she didn't announce the meeting was over, I watched her get settled back in the sofa and sip some tea.

In a couple of minutes she said, "Sorry. I've been so nervous. Stuff's been held in all too long. Spring's been on me about it – you know, T.M.I. She says I have a Ph.D. in T.M.I."

I wanted to laugh but didn't. I was touched by this.

The afternoon before, Friday, I had figured Candice for a ball buster, a very angry about-to-be-ex wife. That Saturday afternoon, I sat at the other end of the sofa from a caring soul who probably had seen many years with shit for a husband.

I thought it would be nice to let her know I was sympathetic. "Say, how long has – how long have you been earning points for saint of the year?"

It worked. She smiled, let go a rush of air.

I waited a minute for her to say something. When she didn't, I said, "Go ahead. I'm guessing there's a lot to the story. Go on."

"Thank you, Mr. Trench, I –" She excused herself to get another tea. I protested that I'd get it for her but she would have none of that.

My cell phone took the opportunity to ring. I found the red END key.

When she returned, she said, "I like their coffee so much better than Starbuck's. I just can't do the coffee caffeine in the afternoon and decaf has always been a family joke. It's what a cow does when she has a baby. Get it?"

I did. I laughed.

She fidgeted tidying up the coffee table in front of the sofa for a bit, then said, "Okay, where I left off was – I think I was trying to say that life, especially relationships, aren't like they taught us in high school."

I returned to nod mode.

"So, when I spied on Ben a year ago, Drake was a sophomore in college and Spring a junior in high school. I wore the wig in May, I think, just before school let out. And you know what? Right after, when I drove back to Kristen's to return her car, I felt a sense of satisfaction, like my intuition had been validated. It was a powerful, calming feeling. It didn't last – the calm.

"When I woke up the next morning, I had a different feeling. I'm still not sure what it was. Then after two days of not being able to figure out just how I felt – what I felt – I had no idea what to do about it, I mean, the stringy blonde. You know: should I confront him – or her – or perhaps just let my lawyer tell his lawyer which restaurants I wanted. Or maybe get my own lover. Or what? I didn't know which way was up. And I wasn't crying and I wasn't thinking of the best way to murder him, either. Maybe that was more confusing than anything. It was more like I didn't care."

It was time for me to earn my money. "You sure that blonde's a lover?"

"Well, I know sex goes out of a marriage to some extent with everyone, but Ben was never an active newlywed with me. My first husband was such a bundle of hormones, used to go after me so often, I would stay sore –" Red had raced into her cheeks. She stopped.

I guessed she must have told that story to *the girls* many a time and had forgotten she had a male member of the species in front of her right then. I hoped it meant she had finally gone upside of the idea of trusting me, being comfortable with telling me all the gory details.

She choked a bit, said, "I am sooooooo speaking out of school."

That was another down-home saying that didn't fit the marble statue who had hired me yesterday. "Mrs. Candice, may I ask you where you are from?"

"That's an easy one: everywhere. Army brat. Lot of places in Texas but I swear we never stayed anywhere for more than two years. The Army doesn't do that to families any more, my friends tell me."

Right then the barista brought her beverage.

Chapter 14

Saturday

Candice took a sip, said, "Now, you had asked me a question: is the stringy blonde a lover? As far as I can tell, yes. He's not stopped visiting that house. Probably twice a week, maybe more."

I was glad she'd put us back on track. "Could it be something else, like drugs? A wardrobe-gifted bookie?"

"I should think not. Why would you say that?"

"There's this general understanding in my business that affairs rarely last more than six months. Sometimes a year, but not often."

"Oh, you don't know Ben. He isn't large on new adventures. The search for a lover had to be very nerve wracking for him. Even if I was so horrible he had to use Viagra. Sometimes I think she fell in his lap. Anyway, however they got together, he's the kind that, if he found something he was comfortable with, he would stay with it. Look at our marriage."

I nodded.

"For a long time I told myself the girl had chased him. If that were true, she's not doing a very good job of closing the sale."

"Another reason to think it's something else."

"I don't borrow the wig every week or anything, mind you, but I have kept up on the situation, admittedly in a circumspect fashion."

I still didn't have my mind "wrapped around" that situation or the stringy blonde or Mrs. Candice Franklin. I took another tack. "You're not worried he might catch something? Give it to you?"

"I – don't want to go there. Ben is so conservative, he probably uses a rubber to masturbate."

That shut me up – and good.

"I was rude," she said. "I'm sorry. Like I said, you don't know Ben."

"Why, after a year of these frequent rendezvous, did you just now decide to hire me – and you say my purpose is to find out what he's doing with the company money? Are you thinking he's paying her rent?"

"If he is, it's in cash. I can look at the books anytime I want – and I have. Hired the tax accountants, remember?"

"Right. Now me. You wouldn't have the woman's name or anything?"

"No. Sorry. I don't even know where she works – that's not true. I've followed her. I know the building she works in. She's in retail in some fashion, I think. Never went inside to investigate, find out her name, or anything."

"That's my job. You have the address?"

"It's inside the loop on West Gray, near Shepherd. That new stuff they built where they tore down that historical shopping center." She fumbled around in her purse for maybe half a minute before saying, "It's not on the blue sheet, is it."

It wasn't a question but I picked up the ball and ran with it anyway. "No ma'am. If it were I would have called you about it last night."

"You read every letter, every number on that page, I imagine."

"Yes. Twice."

She tossed her shoulders as if to throw off a chip or something. "I'll get that for you. Your e-mail is on your card," she said, nodding to the Z10 on the table in front of me.

"And, continuing to do my job," I said, "are there any other *unusual* aspects to your husband or to all you all's relationships or business dealings? Any more surprises? Any curve balls?"

"You're angry. I've wasted your time."

"No, Candice, you've wasted yours. Or call it Mr. Franklin's money."

She stared at me, chewing on the inside of her lower lip.

"Mrs. Candice Franklin, I'm only as good as my information. Kinda like a computer: garbage in; garbage out."

That hit home with her. Her mildly nervous, often flippant or giddy personalities reverted to the strong, assured businesswoman of yesterday afternoon. "My responsibility. My error. I know better. You are correct. I will have you a third reference page in time for coffee tomorrow."

"And we are doing breakfast coffee?"

She smiled in a strange sort of way. "You would prefer ice cream on Sunday afternoon?"

What a great idea. "You bet. Two o'clock? Marble Slab on Bay Area?"

"That one is too cramped. How about the Slab next to that deli in front of Cinemark?"

"Works for me."

"Very well, I must be going."

"Candice, a couple things. I don't have a friend with a scandal web page or an old high school buddy who's a reporter for the *Chronicle*. In many ways, what you tell me *is* privileged. What isn't, I have a lousy memory for. You understand?"

She nodded she did.

Chapter 15

Saturday

I was on autopilot heading toward Seabrook on NASA Pkwy. when I realized I hadn't visited Benjamin in his work environment. I also needed to stop at Office Depot to get the photos copied. I did a U-ee and headed back to Charlie's Steak, Seafood, and Spirits on Hwy. 3. The lunch rush would be long gone.

I parked next to the Charger! Ben Franklin had returned from the scene of the crime – well, whatever that was on Helm. I placed a call to Walmart customer service while I took surreptitious photos of the license plate and windshield stickers. Smart phones. Yes.

Charlie's lunch rush was late or was that normal for Saturdays? There were folks all over the place. You have to wonder, though, when a restaurant specializing in seafood is located next to another establishment named Thai Seafood: is there enough business to support both?

I was seated in a small booth near the front door. Benjamin shot in and out of the kitchen three times before my glass of water with limes appeared. Charlie's itself was nice enough, décor a cross between early T.G.I. Friday's and Johnny Carino's.

Mr. Franklin looked a bit thinner than his photos and kinetic in everything he did. With movements stiff and jerky, his walk more closely resembled a circus clown on stilts than a successful businessman. Long legs and the coordination denied.

And Benjamin appeared anything but fresh. About halfway through my entrée, he came out of the kitchen looking like his hair had gone through a wind tunnel, then missing the long, clean apron he had worn earlier. His eyes were bloodshot. I could see the red from where I sat, never closer than six feet.

Lunch, however, was fresh and tasty, right off the boat. I would be back.

A gnawing in my elbows grew deeper and deeper as my plate emptied. Somehow I was short on basic information – lacked a firm foundation and didn't have my waders with me to go stomping through any swamp.

It was my first full day of the case. Ben Franklin was anything but what I expected. A third party had been introduced – and it wasn't a banker or fence. And Candice Franklin had shown me two extremely opposing personalities.

I entertained grabbing Benjamin and suggesting he needed to sit down. "Come, sit at my table. Take a break." Wasn't gonna happen. Next idea, please.

With my waitress something less than talkative – the good ones don't work on the weekends, do they? – there was a short supply of inside informants.

Lacking any clear plan, I decided dessert might inspire me and ordered Murphy's Irish Stout. They didn't carry it but had Guinness Stout on tap. Yes! A pint gave me another half hour rent on my vantage point near the door. I'd could sit and watch and see if anybody as interesting as the stringy blonde came to visit.

Down to about two swallows of stout, my thinking was that nobody interesting ever came in the place, just lots of older couples, probably from Webster or Nassau Bay, out for a chatty lunch.

As I tipped the glass for the last swallow, the front door burst open and a body builder type charged in, beads of sweat rolling down the sides of his shaved head. He stormed around the restaurant challenging the wait staff and bus boys for Benjamin's location. And Baldy wasn't low key about it. "Where is he right now?" was most common, followed by a shout, "You tell him I'm out here – you better."

Up till Baldy's arrival, no segment of time longer than five minutes had elapsed without Benjamin making a swing through the restaurant, from the kitchen, around a few tables, on over to the greeter's station and back to the kitchen. Maybe the staff hid him in the walk-in freezer?

All in all, I figured the entertainment was worth another stout.

I sipped my second pint ever so slowly but my additional investment paid no return. After ninety total minutes of sitting in Charlie's, I discovered the chair was engineered to encourage patrons not to overstay. My behind and thighs reported "hard surface below." I took the hint, tipped based on my newly-acquired contract, and headed outside. The Forester no longer had a Charger for company so I headed on home to Seabrook via Office Depot.

One thing kept ricocheting around inside my head all the way home, the last thing that Baldy said as he exited without his prey: "You tell Ben I'll make it hurt permanently, where he likes it best, if he doesn't contact me this afternoon!"

Chapter 16

Saturday

Around four o'clock I stepped out my sliding glass door and strolled across the grass down to the channel, the rear property line of my house. I stood on the bulkhead and looked left and right, seeing who was out on their boat. Most everybody. It was Saturday.
I spit in the brown stagnant water.
Again.
I didn't spit often. Spitting meant I was unhappy.
< >   < >
I knew I should be working.
But there was this problem.
One part of me wanted my business simple, like those skip traces. Just log on the computer, Mr. I.T. Tech, and make a buck. The other part of me craved cases with live bodies, complex people with lots goings on confusing things. Fact was, at that point, I had five years in business and very little experience with live bodies.
At that very moment most of what I had from Candice Franklin, including the delineations on lunar blue, were unstable

wisps of fog. Not live bodies. Live bodies are vibrant. They give off energy. They move around. They leave tracks. They dare you. They hide from you.

Fog is, well, a fluffy mask.

I had a wife who came to me for help: said her husband was skimming off the top of the family business; she didn't know for sure or why; knew he had a one-year mistress and had seen her; cared about the money; the husband, not so much. Her lunar blue info was, well, what I could find on my computer. It was its own confusion, its own mystery.

And, hell, Candice said she was still sleeping with her husband.

< >   < >

I felt no burr under my saddle, no electricity in my veins.

The Golf Channel had started to look interesting.

< >   < >

I waved to a neighbor paddling back in his kayak. He waved back.

What a great life. You get white hair, you buy a kayak.

< >   < >

What was I complaining about?

I should just bill the lady for my time and expenses, not worry about it.

I couldn't just do that.

I popped the Z10 out of my pocket and tapped to Candice's cell.

"Sorry to bother you," I said before she spoke a word.

"You – you have something – already?"

"Just a question: which restaurant do you guess Benjamin would be at about now on a Saturday?"

Silence.

"I ran by Charlie's after we talked," I said. "He was there. And there was this *friend* of his, bald head, more muscles than Superman, maybe forty, not over five eight, suit coat size forty-six, maybe forty-eight. You know him?"

Silence.

"I guess not," I said, wishing that cell phones had the clear connection of the old landlines. Used to be you could often hear the caller breathe, hear what was going on around them. "Could you tell me, then, where the big dine-out bucks fly from now until say eight?"

A cough. "You remember," she said, her tone on the angry side of cordial, "I told you he was unpredictable and irregular on purpose, to keep the managers on their toes, on edge for their jobs?"

"Okay, yes."

"So, since I haven't seen him since he left the house today, I don't know."

"Can you rule out five or six?"

She did, after a minute. Four. That left me with four.

"I think I'll see where the Charger parks this evening," I said. "You have a nice one and I'll see you tomorrow for ice cream."

The line went dead.

I wondered if she were with *her* lover, given the age of her daughter and the time of day on Saturday.

That lover thought rumbled around that empty cavern I call my brain until it ran out of gas – which was quickly. Just couldn't mesh "lover" with "Candice."

Still, something with her whole case just didn't mesh for me. I could not prove it, had not one good logical reason as to why, but the discord was there. I felt it.

After a run through the shower, I steered the Forester south down Texas 146 out of Seabrook over the Kemah bridge. Galveston

Bay was hazy as usual. I turned right just south of the bridge and headed west on FM 2094. Took another right at the second light, onto Clear Lake Shores Drive, the entrance to the small island community by the same name.

A very fine restaurant was one block down, Magnum Steak. I was probably too early to make any new friends but early enough to avoid waiting in their "Oh, it is Saturday and you have no reservation" line.

And once again I was glad I had a small SUV with full time all-wheel drive. It had rained much of the week before and parking was still mud.

I made three slow trips in, out, and around the area.

No Charger.

Hunger left me for some reason, so I headed west on FM 2094 into League City, a town whose name never has been explained to my satisfaction.

Had the nouveau riche of South Shore Harbour lured Benjamin?

Chapter 17

Saturday

Benjamin housed Harbour Seafood and Ribs in one of the spiffy strip centers just west of South Shore Harbour Blvd on FM 2994. No stucco for those guys. Deep red brick high on three sides with covered walkways guarding eighty percent glass fronts, the three similar retail buildings lined up in a row heading west. The cement paving in the rear delivery area was as tidy as the parking area for the customers in front, so determining if the Charger was around was quick and easy. He wasn't or was already wise to me and not driving red.

I know, I know, you're thinking I should call each restaurant and ask for him. Hang up before he comes on the line.

Well, no. I didn't want Benjamin getting any ideas that might spook him out of any of his habits, idiosyncrasies, routines or routes. I wanted him off guard and lazy.

Benjamin probably took his non-customer calls on his cell phone anyway. Calling that would surely goose his gander. "Hi, Benjamin Franklin, where's your tired ass right now?" Yeah, that's the ticket to a successful investigation.

His cell service was on an account billed to Shrimp-Steak, Inc. Candice noted on lunar blue that she didn't have the login password to that account. Otherwise we could have used the subscriber locator service. Her phone was on a family plan with the kids.

I needed to determine if he was actually skimming and, if so, how he handled the cash – had to be cash. People get careless after they've gotten away with something for a while. If I watched Benjamin often enough....

In the meantime, I'd never actually met the man so watching him could give a sense of his personality outside a madly busy restaurant.

< >   < >

While I drove the half hour over to Friendswood and Michelle's Fine Dining, I turned on the CD player and picked up Stephen King's *11/22/63* where I'd left off on Thursday. This was an old trick of mine. If something needed to escape my subconscious, it would eventually jump right past the narrator's words.

I lived in Seabrook because of the water, the brackish but relatively calm Clear Lake, the bayous and Galveston Bay. I figured the folks in Friendswood didn't like water or they wouldn't live twenty miles from it. Friendswood had a reputation for money and standoffishness and that wouldn't mix well with small fishing boats anyway.

For Benjamin to have successful concerns in such varied locations as Clear Lake Shores and Friendswood for fifteen years spoke to his incredible acumen as a restaurateur. It also told me skimming some cash off the top would be a piece of cake for such a sharp operator. *But was he?* Or was business really down at all eight locations?

Candice played daytime bridge so Benjamin had her overhead plus a daughter heading to college in the fall and a son already there. Tuition, books, fees, lodging and respectable cars. I figured he ought to be working harder to ramp up his business to pay for all that. Of course, he could have socked away so much over the years that he now could afford to slow down and enjoy life. Well, a workaholic's life.

None of this type of question was answered on lunar blue pages one or two. Would Candice's third page contain some answers or direction? I couldn't know that until the next afternoon.

< >   < >

Friendswood thinks the maximum speed limit inside a city limits should be thirty-five-or-less and they mean it, so I poked along FM 518 for a while before I reached Michelle's.

The lot was decent enough but a dumpster appeared to block the path to the delivery entrance. I parked in an outer slot and was considering a walk behind the building when a bright red Charger pulled up and parked next to me. How was the lighting? I turned my head to the right, ostensibly to deal with my cell. Didn't want my ugly mug stored for later recall.

I counted to thirty after I thought I heard the Charger's car door thump shut, before turning back around. A man in slacks and a light shirt was just entering the building under marginal lighting. Was that the guy from Charlie's? Couldn't tell.

I hoped I was in luck, but moved the Forester to be safe. Then I figured to give Stephen King a half hour of my mostly undivided attention while I waited and watched to see what Benjamin Franklin did next.

About ten minutes later, the man came out. I cursed myself for not following the procedure I learned when I worked Shore Patrol for three years: verify information. The lunar blue was a bit too dark to be read in the parking lot lighting, so I opened the shallow compartment on top of the dash and extracted a slender Maglite.

There were at least two red Charger's in the Houston area, it seemed: Benjamin's and the one dining at Michelle's this evening. License plate didn't match lunar blue.

Chapter 18

Sunday

I was anxious to meet with Candice on Sunday afternoon. She might have real information for me to chew on, lunar blue page three. And she did not disappoint, was right on time for ice cream. I stood and waved to her from a table I'd managed to commandeer when I arrived early, farthest from the I-45 feeder. The Marble Slab was packed and noisy – great for conversation privacy, delivering sensitive information.

She handed the third sheet to me when I returned with her waffle cone, chocolate dipped and overflowing with strawberry shortcake ice cream. I viewed the new twenty-four pound paper with the laser printing in a whole new light. It glowed fluorescent lemon. I had grown fond of lunar blue. It would also be hard to misplace fluorescent lemon and I guessed that was still the point.

"This was difficult for me, Nate. You forced me to stop and think. Then I started to feel. I really should have done this investigation stuff several years ago."

I went into nodding mode and did so, slowly.

"Never mind that. You owe me a good night's sleep."

I've had a few markers pinned to my ass over the years without my consent, but that was the first sleep deprivation lien.

The sorrowful look in her puffy eyes made me go easy with my reply. "I have to work with my clients a bit harder sometimes to get them to do what they need to do for themselves. I hope you can reach a point where you understand that."

She dipped her head, once.

"I struck out at the plate in the restaurant hopping game last night."

"Ben moves around. I told you."

"And that's why I needed this information. Shall we finish our ice cream first or do you want to watch my face as I read it now?"

"You decide."

I hate it when I give a lady the option and she won't take it. Absolutely drives me nuts.

I snuck a breath. "Mrs. Candice, you are the client. What would be more comfortable for you, especially after missing your sleep and all?"

"Neither."

I had no idea what to say to that. At least it was a straight answer. She had wanted a meeting. She said that. I remembered quite clearly.

"I know I told you differently," she said. "I'm embarrassed to reveal what I think the real reason was."

I was still lost. "Help me out here, Candice."

"No one has taken me out for ice cream since college."

My mind went *tilt*. I know I didn't answer but have no idea what my facial expression was.

"And since you're more or less on my payroll," she said, turning in her chair toward the display freezer, blocking my view of her eyes, "I must have figured I could just get you to do it."

I was a detective, an investigator by trade – did signal intelligence work for fifteen years and Shore Patrol before that. Never, never in a blue moon would I have guessed what she said. No way. Did not see it coming. A slight crush on me, me, maybe? But, a butler, a servant, a yo-yo on a string? Never.

"Are you angry with me, Nate?" She still wasn't looking at me.

Were we filming in black and white? She was acting like some daft heroine in a bad thirties movie.

"I'm a private investigator. The private means 'not public.' Information and activities are confidential. True, I do delve into my clients personal, private motivations sometimes to help solve a case. But I don't date them. I can't. Never mind what you see in the movies. It's suicide for both. And, besides, I have the kind of life that's not conducive to a traditional family's activities."

She turned her head back around, a severe look in her eyes. "I'm not asking you to marry me, Mr. Trench. I'm asking for your considered company."

Marry? What the hell?

Did I want to keep the client? "I see," I said.

Women. What ever are they thinking? I was clueless as to what was going on. And what the hell was meant by and expected of *considered company*?

""Do you understand?"

I wanted the client – the money. I had to show some professionalism, seemed to me. "All I know is I'm a private investigative service. I'm not an escort service."

That seemed to make her angry. Her lips pursed so tight, they turned white. She did not speak. I guessed her jaw was locked tight, too, tendons in her neck showing.

Maybe what I saw in her eyes was an anger sheltering a long-term hurt. Maybe not. Either way, that sort of thing wasn't my department. I decided to steer things back to business. "Shall I read the lemon page now?"

She stood. "I had better go."

"Mrs. Franklin – Candice?" I stood. Too late. She and her small bag were halfway to the door.

I sat back down still looking toward the front of Marble Slab, intending to finish my ice cream while reading the fluorescent yellow page. When I glanced down to retrieve it, I discovered I had a more immediate chore: Mrs. Franklin's cone. She had dunked her strawberry shortcake upside down on the table top.

Chapter 19

Sunday

I got the mess cleaned up and then enjoyed a fresh amaretto ice cream waffle cone – but not the fluorescent lemon: no new amplifying or helpful information about her husband's business or behavior outside the home. Candice's latest "paper" mostly raised more questions. I had her money, the retainer. She could fire me – or apologize.

Without any pressing personal leisure activities – the NBA playoffs didn't begin until Monday evening and the tide was way low – I figured I might as well check out what was really cooking in Shrimp-Steak's kitchen, in case I was still in Mrs. Candice Franklin's employ.

As I walked to the Forrester I got smart and recalled the wonderful Freeman Library was but five minutes away, I drove over there to see if all their free internet terminals were in use. I wanted to print out a custom map of the area that encompassed the locations of all eight Shrimp-Steak restaurants to see if anything struck me as odd. For this I needed a computer. I thought I might also estimate the driving time between each location.

Budget cuts must have killed that idea. The library was closed Sundays, said the sign.

I drove to my office.

I booted up my system and logged on, then keyed in maps.google.com. While that loaded rather slowly – maybe the Masters' Golf tournament had turned on every television in the area – an item from the lemon sheet jumped back in view. "Ben plays poker every Wednesday evening. Started two years ago. Maybe closer to three. Game starts at seven-thirty. Never used to do the guys night out thing. I didn't know he played poker seriously. But then he was in the Army. All servicemen play poker, my bridge friends tell me. Spring better hope her high school graduation ceremony is not a Wednesday evening. Ben won't give that up. I tried for our anniversary last year. Nothin' doin'."

I had known guys who religiously guarded their poker nights and others who had the same penchant for their bowling nights, some for both. Except most of the poker players had been at it since the day they learned how to add up poker chips.

So why would a guy in his mid forties take up poker? He really wanted a divorce but didn't know how to ask? A cover for date night with the stringy blonde or someone else? A late night rendezvous with his money mover?

What time did he come home? I keyed in a note in the Z10 to ask Candice. Maybe Ben Franklin had two girlfriends? That could suck a business bone dry in a hurry!

I printed the area map I defined and saved the map as a JPEG, then e-mailed it to myself, storing it on the Z10. I pulled out a red felt microtip pen and a yellow highlighter. Fifteen minutes later, I had Benjamin Franklin's businesses laid out and color coded.

Only one thing struck me right off: Michelle's. It was a half-again longer drive from the nearest "family member" as any other. It was also the only one west of Interstate 45. Why had he bought it? When? I checked fluorescent lemon for a history of the restaurant group. None. I made another note in the Z10. Candice might grow to loathe my phone calls before the investigation was over.

Two of his restaurants called Webster home and were the two closest to each other – except one faced the I-45 feeder and the other was Charlie's on Hwy. 3, clearly tapping a different market. I thought the spacing of the locations looked perfectly logical, interspersed among the erratic residential configurations of the Clear Lake area. That would afford some travel economies in the managing of the restaurants. Even Michelle's in Friendswood seemed reasonable on the map. I probably had a case of the red ass for those folks.

What to do next? I surfed the web for a good fifteen minutes hoping for lightning to strike my gray matter. When I couldn't even generate a little static dragging my shoes on the carpet, I punted. Called the boss. Her cell gave me voice mail. Her house didn't answer.

Chapter 20

Sunday

The sun was almost down Sunday evening when I next spoke with Mrs. Candice Franklin. She returned my call around eight o'clock. I was just over the Kemah bridge on my way to Super Target, hoping it was still open.

"You need more information – on the restaurants?" she said.

"Yes, Mrs. Franklin. I'd like to know some data about each one." I figured resuming calling her "Mrs. Franklin" was the better part of discretion, given her slam-dunk departure earlier that afternoon.

"I see. Are they long questions?"

"They're specific. Would you like to write the questions down?"

I thought I heard a noisy drawer squeak open. "You think I'll need to?"

"Don't wish to be rude or rush you."

"You have a fax at home, too?"

"Yes ma'am."

"Type up what you want and fax it over."

She gave me the number, but sounded distracted while we chatted a bit further. I was about to say goodbye when she said, "You do e-mail, right? You have a smart phone?"

"Right, again, Mrs. Franklin. I have a Z10 – An Z10 operating system phone."

"E-mail me. Spring says I should use it more."

She must have gotten tired of brightly-colored, twenty-four pound paper. Her e-mail address wasn't on either of the sheets, so I got that and said I'd send her an e-mail in about an hour with a Word document attached. That way the gremlins of e-mail couldn't mess with the chart format I'd most likely use.

"Oh, one more thing, Mrs. Franklin – the poker games."

"What about them?"

"What time do they start? What time does Benjamin return? And where are they held?"

"Your answers are: seven thirty, I never know, and Fred Childress's mother-in-law cottage."

"Where?"

Sounding a bit put out, she said, "Small house in back and to the side of Fred's house."

"Childress?"

"Yes."

"Is he in the book?"

"Which one? I have four phone books just for Clear Lake."

She was right. In that many books you would often find conflicting or missing data or listings. My solution since I'd opened up the P.I. shop had been to use the Internet, starting with Google search. My Z10 handled it nicely.

"Mrs. Franklin, let me pull off into this parking lot," I said, just as I arrived at the expansive Target. I brought the Forester to a stop far from the store to save time and then said, "is that C-h-i-l-d-r-e-s-s?"

"Right; Raymond."

"What street they on?"

"Not sure. It's up in Clear Lake City."

"You have the phone number?"

She did and so I keyed in the ten digits using the parentheses around area code format, and hit ENTER.

The screen came back with two Fred Childresses – nothing new. There were four million folks in the Houston area. One listing was in Clear Lake and the other was nearly all the way over to Sugar Land.

"I've got him. I'm putting this in the Z10 and plan to watch the poker game unfold this week. You have anything to add?"

She didn't, said good night, and hung up.

When I returned home, I reviewed my notes and typed up the Word document inside one of their auto format tables. If Mrs. Franklin didn't know how to fill them in, maybe her daughter would show her.

After I sent off the e-mail, I keyed the poker game data first in my client case management software, then synched it with the Z10, all the time wondering if I had developed a rude streak or if Candice Franklin was the unreasonable unit.

The grunt work finished, I once again thanked whomever thought up the Internet as I typed another e-mail. This one would access one of the truly great resources for folks in my profession: a restricted group of chat / e-mail forums. I belonged to Golden Gumshoes. I paid for the membership but they didn't hold much on ceremony. The members seemed to like facilitating each other's success. All you did was e-mail in a question and presto, folks from all over the country tried to show how smart they were.

Ours was on Yahoo because it was about the first offered for free years ago, they told me. Once the membership got used to it, nobody wanted to do the work to move. And Yahoo was cheap. Free.

In pre-Internet days, it could take years to cultivate one or two friendly fellow professionals in other cities, folks you could ask trade-secret type questions without stepping on their local, neighborhood professional toes.

With the national loops, the competition problem was eliminated. The member size got so large that the "I'm the brightest one here" types surfaced quite quickly – and they really were well informed. It was truly amazing – and so was the fact that so many of them appeared to be evening shut-ins, like myself.

I sent the e-mail out describing what I figured the situation was with Mrs. Franklin, then checked back after I'd taken the trash out and visited the necessary room. There were five "quick guesses," four of which basically said to let her be her moody self but get cash up front, weekly. The other sounded like a psychologist. He had more questions than answers. Two repliers invited me to join them on Yahoo Messenger. I opened up windows to both. One was clearly just looking for someone to cheer up A Lonely Evening. The other had worked a similar case a couple years back. We did the hypothetic what-if thing for a good twenty-five minutes. At the end I typed I owed her a steak dinner at the next national convention. She said she'd save the transcript of our chat in an encrypted pdf file, just in case.

Chapter 21

Sunday

A bit later when I sat down at my picnic table beside the bayou to enjoy the sweet sounds of a spring night near the water, I shook my head and laughed in wonder: how did a nice kid (me) end up wading around in so much bullshit?

I enlisted in the Navy a ways out of high school. My hatred of classrooms had intensified. I was working two part-time jobs to have the money to attend classes I truly hated. The community college called them core requirements or something and wouldn't let me take what I wanted until I passed them.

A couple years after I opened up Trench Coat Investigations, sitting on that same bench by the bulkhead, I had an ah-hah moment: day one of my military career, I had created a different Nathan Edward Trench: Nate Trench, hard-ass. It must have been automatic. I didn't remember thinking about it ahead of time.

Why? I think it had something to do with watching too many World War II movies, the ones in black and white where the hero is absolutely bulletproof emotionally. You know the guy: he leads the charge up Normandy Beach; his hand is on top when they raised that flag on Iwo Jima; he's the pilot who could eject but steers his jet all the way to the ground to make sure it doesn't crash into a residential neighborhood.

How did those tough guys, those WWII hard-asses get the job done? I had no clue at age twenty. I'm not sure I know today. I do know how I handled it twenty-five years ago: I shut down emotionally. I lived in my head. Became a task-oriented workaholic. "It's all about the job," I used to tell my wife. I must have heard that in some old movie.

For me the United States Navy was also about steady work. Near the time I enlisted, Dad had been given an unceremonious ride down a chute into the slough that was the crash of the Texas oil patch in 1986. He went from riding high on the oil wave in the Permian Basin to begging short work at the Texas City refineries. At one point when he'd finally landed an oil rig stint, he agreed to stay out another six months in the Gulf of Mexico. He wasn't sure they'd be hiring when his down time was over. Mom hated him – and loved him for it at the same time.

I got the Oil Patch message loud and clear: regular money beats the hell out of "great money sometimes." I re-enlisted. And re-enlisted, and re-enlisted until I had my twenty.

By the time of the doings with Mrs. Franklin, I'd been a civilian for six years. And what did I have to show for my efforts: a client moodier than the oil business. Fortunately, Franklin did not show up in my first year or two. By the time she did, I had folks I could chat with online.

Lady Sleuth, the Yahoo Messenger screen name of a fellow Gumshoe, had seen a squirrelly couple two years prior. They were so devious, she typed on my computer screen, that some days she wasn't sure who the bad guy was – unless it was both of them.

L.S. and I went over standard and not-so-standard investigatory tactics that I might employ on the Franklins.

Nothing she suggested was really new to me. Still, a review helped to ground my thinking. And Lady Sleuth reminded me to keep track of my time – she said that Candice might waste a ton of it and then not want to pay me, citing lack of results. And, yes, she also repeated I needed to keep getting that five thousand dollars in advance, like the other three who'd e-mailed me directly.

Chapter 22

Monday

I woke Monday morning with something nagging at me. Something needed to be done. It hit me while I was shaving.

Eight-thirty found me in the office at the computer, fishing through my Z10 notes for the stringy blonde's license plate number. It turned out to be valid and was attached to the correct vehicle. Two certainties so early on a Monday morning. Amazing!

I was not, however, prepared for the owner data: Reginald Drew Kensington. How do you get a skinny blonde out of that? Her brother? She borrowed the car? All the time? Her husband's? The address mapped at maps.google.com showed an office building. Had to wake my boss up.

"Mrs. Franklin, I hope it's not too early to – "

"It's not. You have something for me?"

"Actually, another question," I said, hoping she wouldn't cut me off again. "The car the stringy blonde drives."

"The Buick?"

"Yes, you've seen her drive it, say more than once?"

"Oh, she had a Saturn before that. I think it was a Saturn."

"How long has she had the Buick?"

"Six months, at least."

I looked. The DMV listing showed it to be a 2013. "That works. Okay. Did you come up with an idea of the address where you followed her?"

"It's not on the lemon sheet, is it?"

"No, ma'am, it is not."

"I have to drive into Houston today. I remember where it is. I'll recognize the building. I'll drive by there and get you the address – or at least the name of the retail store."

I was chomping at the bit to find out the real story but decided I didn't want to get in her way so early on a Monday. "Great. And see if you can pinpoint where she parked the car. Like a garage, or where the driveway leaves the street."

"Yes. I'll look up at the building this time."

"Thank you. I have some… scenarios I want to check out as soon as possible."

"I expect I'll call you just before lunch."

She did. I was halfway downtown in anticipation of her call. Said the building was kinda tall and she was running late and sounded harried. She hung up after I repeated the address back to her. I dictated it into my phone voice memo software before I could forget.

I was psyched. That Reginald guy thing made the whole case so much more interesting.

< >   < >

I'd plotted the business address from the vehicle registration on my office computer using Google maps and then the Z10 map program. The directions Mrs. Franklin gave me put it right around the corner – must be a parking garage.

When I arrived it didn't take but a look at the corner from a block away: the retail store was the ground floor of a multiuse building, a growing fashion among developers in the Houston area. I went down the side street and found the ramp to the garage. Once parked, I downloaded the building's marketing material with the Z10's browser. The first floor was retail. The second was a restaurant. The third through fifth were the parking garage. The sixth through ninth were offices. Above that, six stories of condominiums. The suite number on the registration told me Mr. Kensington was just above me. Perhaps his secretary or office manager used the Buick on a regular basis. A company-owned vehicle? Of course. That explained it. Only an accountant would think of a perk like that for a *staff member*? Except for one thing: the registration was in Reginald's name, not a corporation or L.L.C. or such.

If you were a very slender, stringy blonde with a liking for hot midnight blue dresses who worked for an accounting firm, would you be: (a) the receptionist, (b) the office manager, (c) a degreed accountant, (d) a CPA, or (e) a partner? The correct answer to this question might indicate whether you went to lunch early or late. It was the noon hour. I should snoop around while many employees were at lunch. The office might not be as well protected.

The accounting firm in my office building staggered lunches, about half the staff going at eleven-thirty and the balance at twelve-thirty. My watch indicated twelve-thirty. I decided to wait ten minutes, then get a look at the first shift. If the stringy blonde was not in evidence, I'd go eat, make some calls, then return to see who all comprised the second shift as they returned. Maybe I'd get two different receptionists? Ask the same questions. Compare answers.

Chapter 23

Monday

I took the stairs up to the sixth floor. Wanted to get a feel for the bowels of the building. I also needed to know if the doors on each floor were unlocked or only opened for exiting. A directory and map were beside the elevator. At the southeast corner of the interior perimeter corridor, I found Suite 629, Bramblett-Dawson-Kensington Associates, CPA, LLC. Theirs was the brightest presence on the floor, twenty running feet of floor-to-ceiling glass, reinforced with chrome ribs in a herringbone pattern. Classy. Expensive. They wouldn't be doing my tax return, even if the silvery stuff turned out to be more protective reinforcement than decoration. Maybe it was break-in retardant glass.

My love of glass didn't last but a few nanoseconds. An interior partition, also of the floor to ceiling variety, blocked my view of all but the reception desk, a couch and side chairs for waiting, and a passageway cut in the far corner beside the desk. The girl behind the counter was blonde and her hair was up. It didn't look stringy. Women can do things with their hair, though. I wondered... then thought of a way to get more data.

I entered, feigned disorientation, and asked her to point me in the right direction. She stood – and answered my question. Even in the pumps I couldn't see but was certain she was wearing, the little darling didn't stand over five-three. Stringy had to be five-six, minimum. Benjamin, if my memory served me correctly and the lunar blue data were accurate, was past six feet. Stringy had challenged him next to the Charger. I remember that to this day.

Had I entered during the watch of the regular receptionist? Up close she was around five years too young or had never been in the sun. I had some luck with me, though. She got a phone call just as I was about to go totally stupid. As she talked and consulted a rolling tub file behind her, I managed to slide over and glance down the protected passageway.

Cubicle city. Carpeted modular partitions. Looked like Berber done in a tweed. Damn depressing.

And no blondes walking around looking for files and such. No one.

I excused myself out the heavy glass door, reminded of the firm's name by the two-inch letters etched in the glass just above the vertical chrome tug bar. Definitely out of my budget. Were they corporate auditors? Tax accountants? Financial planners? I had to find a resource. Z10 to the rescue.

I accessed a service that does business the way CompuServe flowed cash in the nineties: priced by the minute, rates higher for "sophisticated" services. In DataMine's mobile entry screen, I carefully keyed B-D-K's corporate name exactly as it was on the business card I'd lifted off the reception counter, then activated buttons beside Tier 1 and Tier 2, and clicked START.

Before I found the men's room, I had the shareholder partners names and photos, plus smaller pics of the non-owner managers, and a business/financial summary that Dunn and Bradstreet would be proud of.

Mr. Kensington appeared to be losing the battle of the receding hairline at a but was probably a good deal younger than forty. Dawson was female, but much older and brunette, although I was leaning heavily toward dyed, and shall I say *robust* in her appearance. She had to be nearing sixty. Bramblett I figured to be the son of the founding partner. He didn't look a day over twenty-eight.

No matter the real-time ages of the partners or mangers, Tiers 1 and 2 were devoid of blonde hair. The report did list a "total full-time employees" number of twenty-three, so my quarry could be one of the sixteen or so grunts whose photos weren't online – except for one thing... the car was titled in Kingston's full name. Not the firm's.

Wait. How dumb was I that afternoon? If not dumb, darn slow. How did I miss that earlier?

Surely Reginald wasn't lending the Buick out to some staffer to go get a piece on Saturday morning. If this case were unfolding in the Silicon Valley, I could wrap my mind around it but giving the employee of the week use of a company Buick for the weekend seemed way outside of GAAP (generally accepted accounting principles) for southeast Texas coming out of a three-fold recession.

Then I thought again. Was there some tax dodge where a professional corporation and a shareholder could dodge taxes by having the shareholder purchase a vehicle and lease it to the firm? If only Henry Block could have heard me then. Even with the tax dodge, wouldn't it screw up their business auto insurance, general and umbrella liability coverages – like I was some kid of licensed property and liability insurance agent.

Sure. Me and those farm insurance folks from Illinois had a long-standing agreement. I send them money. They do with it as they please.

On the stairs I decided my mind was mush. I went to lunch.

Chapter 24

Monday

I managed to spin my wheels for almost an hour before trekking back up to Bramblett-Dawson-Kensington. The deli a block away had a very slow line and downtown Houston prices, but the flavors were fresh, the texture of the Russian rye exquisite. I was fully recharged when I again approached B-D-K's office, this time from the opposite direction, hoping to avoid the short blonde, should she still be on the front desk.

I craned my neck around the corner wall. A redhead. A very tall one – was it a wig? She looked a bit heavier than stringy but maybe it was the bright yellow dress. Stringy had been in that midnight blue micro dress. Wait. What accounting type with access to a car wears a micro dress in public on Saturday? Then, again, if it's her day off – as long as Benjamin Franklin's not a client, what's B-D-K got to say?

Plenty. That's what. I'd bet they had big buck image goals. Toeing the line kept you employed at those higher salaries.

I entered, this time accessing a ruse I learned from Jim Rockford reruns, a bogus business card in hand.

"Hi. Trent Blankenship's my name. I understand this is a fine firm. Wondered if my concern, my personal issue, my small business, might be too small. You all do a lot of audit work, I bet. I need more of a tax planner."

After a three-second response gap, the redhead said, "The principals prefer that you speak to a partner or at least a manager. May I get you a soda or coffee while I check on the availability of Mr. Kensington. He's in. Or perhaps Ms. White."

"Coffee... yes, I'll have a cup. Black. Just a small one."

"Please have a seat. We'll be right with you." Her steps to the gate to the passageway were cut off by the ringing of the console telephone. She appeared to lose a shoe in her haste to pivot and answer it. I sat down slowly, a smile on my face. Tall leggy young ladies were the spice of life and I'd had one more question answered. The way she lurched, her red hair flipped forward on top of itself. If that'd been a wig, I would have viewed the binding and her natural hair. Sure, it was darker underneath, but it was bold in its redness. Rich and bold. Perhaps my blonde question mark lurked within.

< >   < >

"Mr. Blankenship," said a woman, confident of stride in her tailored business suit, smile honed to perfection by a million introductions. "Welcome to B-D-K! I'm Jennifer White."

I stood, returned her smile, shook her hand with energy, but inside I wasn't happy. I had hoped to shake Reginald Kensington's hand. Did he go by "Reggie"?

"Please come into our conference room," she said. "Tell me about your business." Ms. White and I chatted as professionals of all ages and both sexes passed by, heads lowered in deep thought, I presumed. No blondes. My nose and forearms developed itches. The air was very dry, something to do with records they kept on site? The small conference room's exterior wall of glass looked out on a residential neighborhood.

I used my best and brightest behavior to deliver circumspect answers to her questions. The one interrogatory I muddled was the inevitable *Who referred you to our firm?* which I sloughed off with a smile. "She said I couldn't tell because then her husband would think we were having an affair."

Ms. White was twenty minutes into the virtues of the firm when her cell phone pulled her out of our meeting, a look of concern severely creasing her marketer's smile. I had failed to come up with an offhand way of asking the firm's blonde census figures. It was time for me to go.

With as slow and quiet a gait as a former high school outside linebacker could muster, I made my way to the front desk. Not a soul passed me by, not one word was spoken in my direction, and Ms. Redhead was not at her station. I negotiated the large glass front door and turned left to disappear from view as quickly as possible. I had worn no horn rim glasses or fake mustache or derby hat so I was recognizable for the foreseeable future. Poor planning on my part. I needed to populate a wardrobe box in the rear of the Forester.

I deemed the mid-day outing a failure, felt bad about billing Mrs. Franklin for my time. I had waged nuclear war with that billing insecurity halfway through my third year in practice. It still raised its ugly head from time to time.

I made the proper notes in the Z10 while stuck in traffic, attempting to feel professional.

On the way back I contrived ways to view Reginald sooner than later. None sounded executable. I headed back to the office.

Chapter 25

Monday

It would be almost impossible to do a stakeout on Reginald Drew Kensington, CPA. There was no street to park on and watch his office. It was very difficult to park a body in an office building's corridor without attracting questions or uniformed personnel.

What about his residence? If he lived upstairs – dummy. I hadn't checked that. I pulled off I-45 at the Hobby Airport exit and parked in a hotel lot to put the Z10 and my research subscriptions to work.

I found that Reginald did in fact live upstairs, although not in the penthouse. His was a relatively modest abode, number 1103, two bedrooms in twelve-hundred square feet. With an office five floors down an elevator, I guessed that was all the space a single bean counter would need. Probably had an air conditioned mini warehouse outside the loop where the rates weren't so exorbitant.

My house in Seabrook held seventeen hundred square feet on two floors above a tidal garage, with a decent-sized yard in back. I'd always figured three thousand square feet would accommodate the preferred *necessities*, a large room for a pool table where your cue stick wouldn't run into the wall behind you, a master bath with a large Jacuzzi suitable for two, and a shuttered and screened-in porch with a hot tub for four to six. I sunburned too easily so I didn't care about a swimming pool. The sobering thought in all that daydreaming was that I'd need several ongoing accounts like Mrs. Franklin's to work on for a couple years before I could entertain such a large property tax bill. That's Texas for you: no income tax but watch out for the governmental property tithes.

Was Reginald single? I checked that next. No legal spouse. No prior marriage in Texas. Was he a native Texan? Another lookup. Yes. Born in Bastrop. Further Internet searching didn't list anyone else getting their mail there or having contracted for utilities.

Maybe I could hire some criminal justice majors to hang around the parking garage and watch the Buick, keep a log of his comings and goings and with whom. College students worked cheap.

Wait! I could do that. Would a guy like Mr. Kensington venture outside his office on a Monday afternoon? I headed back into town. If I couldn't catch him today, I'd get a couple kids to hang out in the garage, one during an extended lunch block and another early evenings.

< >   < >

Reginald must have heard me coming and left the building, at least the dull Buick was nowhere in the three-story garage. Then again, I hadn't looked for it when I arrived. Dumb.

A call to his office from the only pay phone for miles around confirmed this. Time to punt. I drove over to Upper Kirby to get some bulk cereals and nuts at Whole Foods, all the while mulling over Messrs. Franklin and Kensington. Who did Ben Franklin's accounting and tax work, anyway? I didn't recall that info being on the fluorescent yellow or lunar blue pages. Z10 took another note.

I wasn't one of those A.D.D. jumping beans who can't follow a train without being tied to it. But I did seem to get tired of thinking in one watering trough very quickly back then. I had found over the years in the Navy that answers came to mind while I was busy trying to do something else. Driving, for instance. Shopping for another.

Right in front of the deluxe cheeses bar at Whole Foods, I saw some light. That same cheap, abundant labor source that would help keep tabs on Reginald could also log Benjamin's comings and goings. Might take eight students. They wouldn't come cheap as a group but, what the hay, I was getting five G's a week *plus expenses*. College students had to be a bargain. They'd be contract labor and I'd have to mail them the IRS form 1099 at the end of the year. No big deal. Candice should be grateful. All college kids had cell phones and their own cars, so she wouldn't have to spend money on a walkie-talkie system.

Chapter 26

Monday

I searched my database when I returned to my office. Found the name and phone number of a woman I'd met at a business-to-business networking meeting a year back.

Teresa Royals toiled for the University of Houston at Clear Lake, a junior-senior-graduate school campus of the big U of H, located right in the middle of Clear Lake City, adjacent to the gorgeous Armand Bayou nature preserve. I never did understand the job title on her business card but remembered her job was to find her students jobs, both while they attended her college and after they graduated. I called her.

She said she could round me up several who'd already passed some kind of screening process that indicated they'd be suitable for my purposes without my going through *all that trouble*. Amen to that. My main concern was that the students have their own transportation and cell phones.

I said I might need at least ten for a couple of weeks. Teresa mentioned that some would probably have class attendance or other conflicts with what I had in mind, on different days, so the more the merrier. We somehow arrived at fourteen as ideal. She knew one kid, a real hard worker named Mo Saddiqi, who would be a great scheduler for me. Seemed he already had a job she found for him but his car had broken down and he needed some bucks to fix it. It was too good to be true.

I called Mrs. Franklin to break the bad news to her.

She answered the phone in a truly cordial manner, "You have something for me?" No "hello." Not even, "What's up?"

"I know who owns the Buick and I know where he works."

"He?"

"My reaction, too. I'm checking more on that and that's part of why I called. Do you have a moment?"

"Go on."

"We're going to need to blanket Benjamin for a week or two to get a better idea of his movements. The only place I know where to find him for sure is on Wednesday evenings. Even so, I'm going to have to arrive there at seven-thirty and sit tight until he moves on. That'll be costing you eighty an hour. Figure four hours, maybe more if he makes a couple stops after the card game."

"Your point?"

"The rest of the surveillance: I want you to foot the bill for college students who will get paid twenty *a day* to check four to five times a day to see if he's at their assigned restaurant. We'll also need a scheduler. Pay him ten an hour to keep track of the lookouts and generate reports. Math goes like this: eight times twenty is one-sixty plus another thirty or forty for the scheduler, so, round numbers, two hundred a day. After the first seven days, we may need them only three or four days the following week, depending on what we've learned."

Mrs. Franklin didn't respond immediately. No anger, no rude questions. No "What a great plan" either. The connection was so free of cellular static, I feared I'd actually been disconnected, so after what seemed like a very long minute, I said, "Mrs. Franklin?"

"I'm here. I guess I owe you an apology of sorts."

I was dumbfounded. Did she mean the ice cream slam dunk?

"Mr. Trench, forgive me. I had checked with Pinkerton and other large firms before I retained your services. I guess I should have told you that."

"Your job. Consumerism. Shop around. No problem here, Mrs. Franklin."

"Thank you. The large firms wanted way past a thousand a day to keep tabs on Ben unless I agreed to an illegal transmitter, off the record, of course."

"Now, in their defense, they would be posting professional investigators at each restaurant. I'm using college students on a drop-by and look basis."

"Rent-a-cops, Mr. Trench. Not their regular personnel."

I didn't know that. A rent-a-cop can still cost over ten an hour. Even if you scheduled things really tight, a thousand a day would be easy to run through. Nothing more I could add to the conversation so I waited for her.

"Mr. Trench, are you there?"

"Yes, ma'am. I am waiting for your questions."

"And I'm saying you've figured out a way to save me over eighty percent. Go ahead, please. Let's get this investigation into a pro-active stance."

"You mean high gear?"

"You men – yes; full speed ahead."

That was more my lingo. "Bombs away, it is. I'll get right on it. Could you arrange for two thousand in expense funds to get to me in the next day or two?"

"I'll be in your office... tomorrow, yes tomorrow. Probably after lunch."

I told her to call first, hung up and put my feet up on the desk. With any luck she would also bring the information I'd requested on the restaurants. I was starting to feel like real investigator for the first time in a year.

Easy does it, I told myself. That woman could change gears faster than a Gulf breeze. No sense getting the mainsail blown full only to have her cut the canvas with a knife.

Chapter 27

Monday

I went home for a light supper, decided I needed to visit some more of Ben's restaurants, and an hour later headed over to the Benjamin Franklin establishment in my neighborhood.

I hadn't realized North Shore Steaks and Seafood resided in the same strip center as Arlan's Market, at the entrance to Taylor Lake Village. It was another easy parking lot to check for a red Dodge. He'd most likely be in front parking lot. The parking in back was for cars with solid rubber tires only.

I found just one red vehicle, a GMC Tahoe, so I headed west on NASA to Space Center, up to Bay Area Blvd where the Bayou Grill fought with a night club named Sherlock's for after-dark parking spaces.

Parked at the curb in front of the restaurant, I figured Bayou Grill's short name and less-than-ostentations frontage owed to its location. Just couple blocks down the street sat U of H Clear Lake. The college probably knocked the prices down a few notches. The Bayou Grill's hours of operation weren't on either the lunar blue or the fluorescent lemon pages, and I'd look silly taking out my binoculars to read the polite little sign glued to the door thanks to Mr. MasterCard.

It was still early for Monday Night Football, so I shut the engine and walked up. Bayou Grill was not open on Mondays, open for lunch and dinner the rest of the week, closing at ten except for Friday and Saturday when the evening shift had to tough it out until one.

Back in the Forester, I started a new page in my steno notebook, posting hours for the eight restaurants. Since I'd come about this investigation business through the back door of people searches facilitated by computers and the Internet, I had learned that often all good research took was posting a matrix of all the variables and seeing what looked odd. Dumb stuff like variances in restaurant hours of operation could tip someone's hand if they didn't think anyone was looking over their back fence.

I had just keyed the Forester's ignition when it hit me: it was Monday. Ben was on his one true day off. Duh. All of his restaurants were closed except for Hurricane Alley. No wonder the windows of North Shore Steaks looked so dark. Dummy me thought it was the solar film on the south-facing glass.

If I wanted to find Ben Franklin, all I had to do was drive to their house. No wonder Mrs. Franklin had sounded so strange on the phone. The husband in her life who was never there must have been during at least one of my phone calls.

Should I call Mrs. Franklin on her cell, see if he was there, and if she expected he'd be leaving – or was he at Hurricane Alley on his *day off*? His sports bar on the I-45 feeder in Webster would be featuring *what* in early April? The NBA? Not on a Monday, even during the playoffs. Soccer? Clear Lake didn't have many soccer fans from what I could tell. Baseball? The Astros had to be it. The season was a week old.

I called my employer.

"You have something for me?" She sounded tight and distant again.

"Is Mr. Franklin home this evening?"

"He was."

"You know where he went? When did he leave?"

"I dunno. Half hour ago, maybe."

"Does he ever drop by Hurricane Alley on Mondays?"

"Mr. Trench, honestly, you seem to be a smart man – except when you're not listening."

I decided to listen and remained silent.

"You're scared of me now?" She laughed.

I was thinking of a cute reply when she continued, "Mr. Ben Franklin does not confide in me very often. He rarely announces his destinations and almost never gives a return time. He could be in Louisiana on a riverboat for all I know."

"That'd take longer than a half-hour drive."

She didn't laugh.

"Not if he's using the money he's skimming to lease a plane or helicopter."

"*What?*"

"Ben has always been jealous of those big business guys, like Fertitta."

"Who?"

"Little guy who owns Landry's Seafood and half of Kemah – guys like him who fly in on a corporate jet or rent a helicopter at company expense. That's what Ben envisioned when he started."

"So I should add 'helicopter' to our tentative list of motivations for skimming."

"Might as well. My husband is a strange duck."

I said goodnight, thinking that the work Mrs. Franklin had brought to my office was far from shooting ducks on a pond. If that tax attorney she'd spent some major bucks on couldn't find enough irregularities in all those tax returns and financial statements to generate a report that put Mr. Benjamin Franklin on the defensive, I wondered how the hell could I tackle the slippery goose that rendezvoused with a hot chick who drove a very dull car?

Chapter 28

Monday

I hit pay dirt on I-45 but couldn't cash the check. Red Charger with correct plate rested there but the damn parking lot was too well lit – and too poorly populated. No place I could park, sit and watch. I hate it when that happens. Benjamin had seen me at Charlie's on Saturday so I needed a very low profile.

On my wish list of further technology to purchase for Trench Coat Investigations was a car that could cloak itself like on Star Trek or morph into something else like a Transformer. Okay, I've read too many science fiction novels and seen too many movies. Wait, couldn't Herby the Love Bug do that? Never mind.

On my third pass by Hurricane Alley, Benjamin's Charger still occupied the same spot. The fourth trip revealed an empty parking slot, no Charger of any color. I was pissed. I needed to start carrying some kind of disguise, some extra shirts, maybe a couple hats, one cowboy and one Astros. I could hide the stuff under the Forester's privacy screen behind the back seat. Right then, all I could hide was my stupidity, although I did consider billing Mrs. Franklin for the time.

And then Mrs. Franklin threw me a curve on the way home.

"Trench Coat Investigations at your service."

"I don't mean to tell you how to do your job."

It was too late to worry what was coming next. "Okay, Mrs. Franklin. Go ahead. You're writing the checks."

"I'm paying cash. You have a terrible memory."

"I'm sorry. Figure of speech. Go ahead."

"Why do we need the boy scouts?"

No mention had ever been made of the young men in tan. I guessed correctly for once, "The college students?"

A pause, then, "Yes, of course. I was thinking – since you're not stuffy Pinkerton or Loomis or whomever – that it might be even less expensive to just go ahead and plant one of those transmitters on Ben's car."

I thought I'd given her a couple of "I do things by the book" examples in prior discussions. I wondered if she listened even more poorly than I did sometimes. "Ma'am, I just like my license too much."

A longer pause. "How much do they cost?"

"Well, you need some other equipment, not just the transmitter."

"How much does it all cost?"

"Mrs. Franklin, I'm not going to do anything that clearly illegal."

"What if I do it?"

"I'd still get hung."

"Why, if it's my idea? If I do it?"

I searched for some logic. She was a fairly bright woman. I roamed my mind for something to say that would keep the client active on my billing system and me not looking at life through ugly metal bars.

"Mr. Trench?"

"I'm here."

"Well?"

"I'm thinking."

"You *don't* have a good reason!"

It hit me. "Mrs. Franklin, if Benjamin is stealing, you want the money back and you want him in jail and you want the business, right?"

"I'd sell all eight of them. Take the cash and leave town. I have a sister in Atlanta."

"But you'd want things to work so you'd have a criminal case against him?"

"Well, of course."

"Then we can't use the transmitter."

"I don't see why not."

"His lawyer would say all the information we obtained came about because of the transmitter. Motion to the judge to throw it all out. The judge would agree."

"Maybe just getting arrested would straighten him out?"

There went those mixed messages again. I was getting tired. It was near my weeknight bedtime. I repeated myself. "It is my professional understanding that using the transmitter would cost you not only the case but could get you and me both arrested."

"You said they'd arrest you."

"Co-conspirator."

Silence. Lots of it mixed in with heavy static. My Bluetooth headset's battery had to be running low.

"You won't tell me how much it all would cost?"

"I don't actually know."

Another dose of static, then, "I do want him locked away for what he's done."

"They you have to be the saint."

"You go find out what he's done. You make sure he gets locked up, you hear me?" Loud and clear can be too loud sometimes.

Chapter 29

Monday

As I pulled in my driveway, I got a better idea than Mrs. Franklin's illegal transmitter. I'd play to my strength, inside my own home. For two hours beginning at nine-thirty, I searched for Mr. Benjamin Ivan Franklin all over the globe, courtesy of a little of Reliant Energy's electricity, the Internet, and my snooping subscriptions.

Why didn't I do that right off? I don't know. I should have.

My guess, remembering now how I'd cussed myself out as I sat in my computer chair and tapped keys, was that I'd been so enamored by the money and the physical elusiveness of the alleged villain that I saw the Franklin case as my big chance to quit spending so much time behind my office desk.

Beginning with the first entry I made that evening in one of those little white Internet search boxes, I thanked his parents for that special middle name. Otherwise the search could have gone on for days.

No graduations or degrees noted. One site listed a deferment from the Vietnam era draft. Nowhere could I find a criminal record or a bad credit report. Nor a single lawsuit. No judgments. No tax liens. No workers compensation disputes. Just a couple unemployment claim tiffs. Did see confusion over his birthplace. Five cities claimed him.

It did seem his Achilles was his kitchens. I found at least five citations each by Houston, Webster, and Pasadena health authorities. None in League City or Friendswood, usually the two pickiest jurisdictions. Go figure.

Towards the end of my Internet journey, cyberspace coughed up a doozie: Shrimp-Steak, Inc. was for sale. A well-know business brokerage firm, Richard Erskine Group, showed all eight restaurants going as a group. The listing was national. How'd I find it? I didn't. Two Gumshoes who live outside Texas found the listing. I didn't find it myself.

Erskine, I learned, had long been a sophisticated commercial real estate powerhouse, with local confidentiality the watchword and national connections to big money the corporate anchor.

It made sense from an ongoing business standpoint to keep the listing out of Texas. After much thought watching Headline News, I decided to leave Erskine out of my Tuesday morning report to Mrs. Franklin – just in case her hiring me was funded by the competition.

< >   < >

Back to being mad, angry: I wondered whether having a major bucks client was worth the stiff neck I had when I shut down my home PC. I'd been even-keeled since I retired, not near as tightly wound as I had been during the twenty-plus years on Uncle Sam's payroll.

I was missing my mellow temperament as I walked over to my recliner with a short detour to the refrigerator. The money was going to be great if I kept my patience with her. I wondered if the much-bigger money was worth it while stared at the Beck's Dark in my hand, my first beer in quite a while.

By the time the bottle was dry, I concluded I needed to view Mrs. Franklin and her case as additional training, like Chief's School or student teaching. If I wanted to get away from my office desk or at least quit looking at the monitor all day, I was going to have to learn more about dealing with people.

And people who could afford to hire me for large chunks of leg work were most likely not the sheepish ones on the planet.

Wasn't that why I'd located the office in Clear Lake? You bet it was. If I did good work for Mrs. Candice Franklin, she'd surely gloat all over the Bay Area of Houston. At least that was the plan.

Then again, if I botched the investigation, she'd put me on the same referral list as the tax accountant who'd cashed her check but provided zip in the way of results.

Chapter 30

Tuesday

By noon Tuesday I had misrepresented myself to a dozen commercial real estate agents. I told whomever would listen that I was looking to do the restaurant thing, buy a few. Had financial partners and such; wanted to know what was available. Answers were very polite but as close to "no answer at all" as a nanometer can measure. Posture-du-jour was that of the Busiest Real Estate Broker on the Planet: "Love to meet, but today and tomorrow are definitely out." Pushing a bit further, I got a unanimous response of "the only good restaurants were the ones that aren't listed" and the agents simply weren't able to discuss *those* without more time. One very cranky older fellow wanted me to go get my financials, with a specific, signed cover letter from my CPA, and each of my investors, addressed to him, signature notarized. I decided it was his way of saying "hell no." I did manage four appointments, spread out over Thursday and Friday.

I was wondering whether to visit the Erskine Group when I punted and checked in with Mrs. Franklin.

"If you have some time, I have a couple more questions for you," I said before she could ask me what I had for her.

She answered after a good five seconds, "You're wanting me to fill up another color sheet with data, no doubt."

"Not so. I was doing some more research on Benjamin and can't nail down where he was born."

"Fort Myers? It's on a blue page."

"At least five other jurisdictions say otherwise. How many Benjamin Ivan Franklins can there be?"

"Fort Myers. It's in Florida, west coast. I've been there with him."

"That's not one of my hits. What's it near?"

"Well," she said, sounding a bit vague, "maybe the hospital was in Naples."

"Bingo," I said with the enthusiasm of a TV game show host.

"What else?" said Mrs. Franklin, not inspired by my performance.

"Where did Benjamin go to college?"

"Maybe west Texas."

"UTEP?"

"Gosh no. There's a small school down toward the Big Bend."

"You mean Big Bend National park – near the Mexican border?"

"An hour's drive north, I think Ben said. It's in a town whose name doesn't fit its location is what he said."

"Okay, I'll check on that." I turned a page, said, "Did he graduate?"

"No. He couldn't stand being so far away from civilization."

"So he went only a semester or what?"

"I think he went the full first year and then didn't go back after Thanksgiving the second. What does it matter?"

"Known associates."

"Where are you going with that?" She sounded very angry, like I was talking about her.

"You wouldn't believe the number of people who make lifelong friends in college and then either make a fortune working together or go on trial side by side."

"Ben didn't ever speak much about anyone from college. Remember, he doesn't have many friends. That's why the poker game was such a surprise. Workaholics don't have time to play and Ben has never had a partner. I told you that."

She had. "Including you, it sounds like. Okay, one more thing."

"Is that a promise or an enticement?"

How could I answer that? I waited five beats, then said, "Lawsuits."

"That's a plural."

"Mrs. Franklin –"

"Candice, please, *sir.*"

"Candice, have there been any lawsuits filed and settled or gone to trial against Shrimp-Steak, Inc., Benjamin, you, or the two of you together?"

"Never."

"Not even a threat?"

"Oh, I suppose so. Ben wouldn't tell me the ones about the business, though – except...."

I waited.

"Before they changed the laws ten years ago, he got hit with several workers' suits."

"How so?"

"Workers compensation claims – that was it."

"Well, if a lawyer was representing someone, that most likely would have been a lawsuit."

"I can't say. Ben always carried that kind of insurance. Just seemed ridiculous, the amounts they were asking for injuries to fry cooks and such."

"Okay, were any of those claims settled in such a way that your husband indicated that the other side was very angry?"

"No. He – I guess you could say he won all of them. Maybe the insurance settled. I just remember he always refused to give in because it would raise his insurance premiums."

"And there haven't been any more in the last ten years?"

"Not that I'm aware of. Again, I keep telling you, Ben doesn't tell me much."

"Right. Yes, but has he said why they stopped?"

"The law changed. I just mentioned that."

She had. I was thinking of what to say when she continued, "You must have been away in some foreign country, in the Navy then. The Texas legislature made it more difficult for lawyers to make a lot of money on workers compensation, so the suits slowed down a whole lot. Ben did tell me that much. He was glad. Gave some legislator a campaign contribution because of it."

"Another empty well."

"Excuse me," she said, her tone more like you'd expect from the Queen of England when her expectations have not been met.

"The angry employee is another one of the things we like to check on when stuff just doesn't look right. If there hasn't been any trouble, then that well is dry."

"And that was your *one last thing*?"

I told her thanks and was turning the Z10 over to punch END when I heard her voice. I returned the electronic marvel to my ear. "Mrs. Franklin?"

"My turn to ask a question."

"Sure."

"Any new developments?"

"Just that your husband has left a very small footprint in cyberspace."

"Oh...."

"I'll be checking out the college angle later today." I found END very quickly.

Chapter 31

Chapter 31 – Tuesday

I didn't find much more information on Ben Franklin that Tuesday afternoon. I did confirm Benjamin Ivan Franklin had attended Sul Ross State University in Alpine, Texas. The main campus was right where Mrs. Franklin had said it was, way west Texas at the southern end of the Davis Mountains, north of the Big Bend on the Rio Grande river. I guessed he'd been sent out west by parents who either wanted him away from big city trouble, or out of their hair.

I set about getting things organized with my U of H Clear Lake student patrol. Two hours of voice mail tag with Mo Siddiqi made it clear my spy network wasn't going to come together that Tuesday evening. With Wednesday being Franklin's poker night, I told Siddiqi to figure on getting a crew together for Thursday. He agreed to meet Thursday morning before his first class to map out the logistics.

Then I wondered where the promised restaurant data was from Mrs. Franklin.

I'd also asked if there had been any changes in restaurant locations under their ownership as well as her take on how long senior managers remained in his employ. She had promised all this "by Tuesday at the latest."

Time for a phone call.

"Mrs. Franklin, I hope my call didn't interrupt your supper."

"It's just me and a TV dinner."

I doubted that. Figured it had to be leftovers. "Ah, have you finished eating? I can call back."

"Dinner's over. Just watching the cable news. What do you have for me?"

"I am short some information, Mrs. Franklin."

"Oh, you couldn't get your posse together to follow Ben? It's early, though, for that. You want to do that in the dark, right?"

"That will first occur after sunset on Thursday. I was checking my e-mail today looking for that chart I sent you on the restaurants. I had hoped –"

"Oh, that. I still haven't opened your e-mail. Computer jammed. Spring said she'd help. Something about the message still being on a server?"

Detecting little or no sense of urgency, I said, "Would that help be forthcoming this evening?"

"Does it matter?"

"I asked for the information on Sunday, actually. You mentioned Tuesday."

"Noon, tomorrow. That will have to do."

It would. I thanked her as a dutiful employee would and went down to the channel bulkhead to listen to the evening. I found peace quick enough to realize I needed to be in front of the monitor, pounding on the keyboard. The more I had learned about Benjamin Franklin and Shrimp-Steak, Inc., the more I realized I didn't know.

I logged onto each of my overpriced information retrieval services and searched each restaurant in turn. Public tax records helped feed parts of the chart I had asked of Mrs. Franklin. I was able to identify prior ownership in four cases, then guessed that Mr. Franklin had built the other four restaurants from scratch. What I couldn't find was any P&L's. Dunn and Bradstreet was thin on the numbers end.

Then I went back to Benjamin I. Franklin: did he have any hobbies? Candice said his business was his hobby. Any special interests? Performing arts, rodeo, Shriners, Rotary? All turned up negative.

He had no criminal record. No civil suit record. No traffic violations – how can a man that drives around town in a hurry every day not have a couple speeding hickeys a year on his record? He didn't, not even in speed traps Webster and Friendswood.

But still, every man has a special interest, is a fanatic about some sport or passionate about some cause. I pounded the keys for another half hour and found nothing I didn't already have – which was not enough.

I went to bed resolved to find the chink in Ben Franklin's armor, regardless of the voracity of Candice's claims. The situation had become – well, professional. I had learned a lot working with the NSG and ONI to know stuff could always be found. Just had to look in the right place.

Heck, "The Bourne Ultimatum" had been out four years by then. Everyone I talked with said they didn't believe the government could tap a phone that quickly. I'd seen the first waves of the Patriot Act on my way out the retirement door – and yeah, they could. Judges issuing search warrants were going out of business – the government wasn't requesting them any more.

Chapter 32

Wednesday

Office administrative crap was the order of the day Wednesday morning: cleaned up some files and followed up on some skip traces that had gone stale. Yeah, it happens. I was processing a couple partial credit card refunds on electronic searches that didn't end up costing near what I had estimated when a light knock fell upon the door. I usually leave it open but with all the enhanced privacy laws, I had too much private stuff visiting my desk and monitor to risk it.

And, yes, I know you're supposed to get up and greet someone directly when they have the courtesy to visit your business but, hey, I was in the middle of sensitive stuff. I stayed in my chair, took a deep breath and projected my voice as I had been taught by my eighth grade choir teacher. "Nate Trench at your service. Come on in."

She did. With class.

Wow. What an outfit. Did I truly know the woman? Every time I'd seen her before, she'd worn a gray business suit, the kind that turn women into neuter corporate robots. The kind you'd expect from middle management. I had no problem with those suits. I visit banks to do business, maybe looking for a loan, not a date.

This time she looked definitely looked like a date.

"Hi, Mr. Net."

I worked on catching my breath and keeping from blushing. I'd had no idea she was so shapely.

"Hey there, Allison, grab a chair." She scooted one over a bit, sitting directly in the middle of my desk, and close. No prolonged visual of her shapely legs prominently displayed by her short lavender skirt. The desk overhang, dammit.

"You want some coffee?," I said. "We have a service up at the front desk." I thought about asking her how she managed to bypass Lynnette Schnable. Allison's midnight black sleeveless top had probably communicated something other than business and Lynnette was a romantic even at thirty-five.

"I'll pass on coffee for now. I'm not supposed to eat on the job."

Oh, how was I supposed to respond to that? At that moment, clueless would have been my first *and* middle names. I said nothing. God knows what my face was telling her.

"You don't think I'm at work, I bet."

"Or something like that," I said.

"Actually, I am."

I must have stared at her. Maybe with my mouth open.

Allison Wilson was lovely in neuter gray. But shapely, giving off hormones or whatever you call it? Not at the bank, at least not when I was in attendance. She could have been one hot number in the vault, I guessed. And my office – it had never smelled better. Her perfume spoke of heaven.

She smiled. "I see I have your attention."

"Uhh, yeah." Dumb thing to say, but that's how I remember it.

"I've changed banks."

Different dress code?

"An outside promotion – is that what you call it?"

"Bankers pretty much have to move to get promoted these days. The industry has seen a lot of consolidation at the bank officer level."

"I keep hearing that, seeing it in the Chronicle, but all I ever see is more and more banks. It's to where bank branch offices – if that's what you call them now – it's like they now outnumber gas stations."

She smiled. "Are you real busy?"

"I was finishing up. Gotta do's and such. Did you want to schedule a meeting sometime soon?"

"I was thinking of taking you to lunch."

I lost it, again. "On the bank? The bank – your new bank would pay for it?"

"Yes. Are you free?" Her smile *and* offer were irresistible.

Free? My face told her I was. You know it.

I wasn't in the marriage market but I still dated, enjoyed female company, and tried to get out at least twice a month. Most of the women my age in Clear Lake were married. All the nice ones. And unlike "Desperate Housewives" they seemed content enough not to even hint about fooling around.

I said, "Are you on a tight schedule?"

"It depends, Mr. Net. What are you thinking?"

She was the only one I let get away with calling me that.

"I have to credit these two charge cards with a partial. It'll just take a minute. Let me walk you to the reception area before the Feds show up and tell me I'm violating one of those privacy acts."

"Right; I understand. I promise I have viewed nothing on your desk."

"Of course you wouldn't, you're a – a banking professional."

I remember floating on air walking her to the overstuffed couch that was the executive suites waiting area. I tossed Lynnette a wink. She smiled and tossed a big, overdrawn cartoon character wink right back at me.

Chapter 33

Wednesday

Allison was so hot in that black over violet outfit, I drank two glasses of ice water before our lunch was served. I had offered to drive her but she insisted, said it wouldn't be professional and drove her company sedan.

After we had ordered, she admitted she had not dropped by on a personal whim. In her new job – she called herself a business development officer – she was required to spend her mornings outside the bank in front of business owners, working by appointment whenever possible, but in front of somebody. A scheduled visit to someone upstairs had gone awry. On her way out, reading the directory as she'd been taught, she saw my name.

And she was hot alright: hot for new deposits, touting her bank's cash management accounts – why did they ever do away with the good old checking account? Easy: they had found a way to charge me more to hold my hand and my money.

Computers. The banks had them first – well, maybe right after NSA, FBI, CIA...Germans, Russians....

And she wanted loans, too. She hustled me to move my tiny line of credit to her new bank. When I asked her about the rate, she took out her iPhone and scheduled me for the next Wednesday at three o'clock. Said she'd have a formal, custom proposal ready for me.

I'd then have to sit in the corner with my notebook computer while I figured it out.

Except you're not supposed to do that inside a bank. It makes you look cheap – worse yet, poor, low credit scored. You want the bank to think you've got more money than they've seen. Keep them thirsty, some radio financial advisor had said on the air one morning. Keep them digging.

An hour after lunch I finally twisted my head back on straight, managed to clean off my desk, and cleared my email inbox.

I needed to get myself into gumshoe mode. The man who followed Benjamin Franklin later that evening had better be fully prepared technologically, mentally, and physically.

I ultimately decided I needed a nap. I'm not sure if I was afraid I'd have to trail the elusive Mr. Franklin all night – Mrs. Franklin had not said anything about his not coming home all night ever.

Or was I exhausted from the emotional roller coaster that had been my fantasy lunch turned business meeting with Ms. Wilson. Someone that hot anywhere near my age didn't walk in my office very often. Like only one other time – more about that later.

The poker game startup time was seven-thirty according to Mrs. Franklin. My first question was whether to follow Ben from their home or pick up the tail earlier to watch the last hour or so of his "pre-game" activities. That became its own problem. Where was he?

I needed more information. I called Mrs. Franklin.

"I know you don't have the e-mail," she said in a tone I've heard parents use when a child won't drop a request for the latest-gadget-the-other-kids-have. "I'll get it to you. I am on my way out the door."

"Your cell phone works in your car, doesn't it?"

"How rude." She stopped talking but I could hear a wood door close and then, a few seconds later, a car door pop open. "Call me back in five minutes."

I did.

The background noise of a car on the road was almost as loud as she was, but the tight cat gut nature of her voice made it easy to pick out her words. "I want to review the poker game schedule."

"You weren't calling about the e-mail?"

"I still need the information," I said, not letting her off the hook. "The sooner I get it, the sooner I can solve your case, the lower your bill."

"What do you want to know about poker. It starts at seven-thirty. I told you."

"Yes, you did. What time does Mr. Franklin usually leave the house for poker?"

"I don't know."

I'd heard that entirely too often in the scant six days I'd known Candice Faith Pence Franklin. It was like she deemed it her get-out-of-jail-free card, or something. "Okay, let's take this one step at a time."

No response.

"Does he leave for the poker game from home?"

After maybe five seconds, she said, "Sometimes."

I felt resistance. "What has his tendency been lately?"

"I really haven't noticed."

I wanted to throttle her. Put her on the teacup ride at the Kemah Boardwalk and watch her spin around for a while, maybe an entire afternoon.

I was losing control of another part of the investigation. She was clearly more concerned about her next activity.

It was five o'clock. I needed to firm up my plan. "How about, let's limit this to the last three weeks. Can we do that?"

Chapter 34

Wednesday

Mrs. Franklin didn't answer right away. I thought my request for information on Benjamin's activities around the last three Wednesday poker games was reasonable.

Small bursts of cellular static told me our call was still connected, so I remained on the line determined to wait her out, to win a small war of the wills, client or no client.

After maybe forty-five seconds she said, "I will... try."

Ouch. I could see her lips right after she said "try," just as if I'd been sitting across a table at lunch. Ultra thin, stretched tight as cat gut on a violin.

"Good," I said, trying to take the positive route, you know, the *glass half full* thing. "What has Mr. Franklin's routine been the few hours before each of the last three poker games?"

"Last week ... he ... left from ... here. Yes, he ate supper with his daughter."

"Spring."

"Right. She's on the blue sheet. We adopted the kids."

Late on that Wednesday afternoon, I needed to get the woman to help me instead of assisting the placement of another steel-reinforced concrete traffic barrier right in front of my parade.

"Yes, Mrs. Franklin, I was getting things straight in my own mind. Okay, Spring – did she enjoy dinner last Wednesday with her adopted father?"

"I would hope so. It was her idea."

"She invited him to have dinner at home?"

"In a sense. The weekend before, she told Ben how he ought to take a break and let someone else treat him to a meal – a home-cooked one at that."

"Sounds great. What time span did dinner take up?"

"Maybe five to five-thirty."

Thirty minutes didn't sound like much of a *let's share some quality time together.* Maybe it wasn't supposed to be. Who knew? The Franklins were sounding more and more dysfunctional. Then I remembered I was trying to get Franklin's pre-game time line. "Kind of early, for a restaurant guy – and a high school student with activities? And the poker game was two hours later."

"You're right, of course. It had to have been six to six-thirty."

Was she just making the stuff up – and not putting much effort into it?

"And afterwards...?" I said.

"Ben left."

An hour ahead of the poker game start time seemed too early to leave for a ten-minute drive, including walking to and from the Charger. "Do you know if he went straight to the poker game last week?"

"How would I know that?"

"Just trying to get at some tendencies."

"Ben Franklin *tends* to be non-communicative bordering on the *secretive*. I trust you'll commit this to memory and not pound me any more for information I'm paying you to find out."

She'd told me off and that was that.

"One last question – may I?"

"One," came out of her mouth with an extra dose of anger. Her lips might get so tight and thin they'd split one day.

"Do you have any idea of his dinner plans this evening?"

The line disconnected. I decided if she really had some strong information on the subject that she wanted me to have, she'd certainly call back.

She didn't.

I paced around my house. That always helped me organize my thoughts.

Except that time.

I couldn't. Something gnawed at me, like the dry, cranky voice of one of those weathered prairie grandmothers in the old westerns. It kept saying it was important for me to know what Benjamin Franklin did before each weekly poker game. My thinkbrain acknowledged that point without question but that cranky voice was more like a parade of ants in my britches – biting my ass every thirty seconds.

Maddening. Truly maddening.

I got hold of Muhammad Siddiqi and twisted his arm – an extra twenty dollars will do that to a student – talked him into checking three of the restaurant locations out for me right then and there. I took three others, ignoring Friendswood and South Shore. He'd call me either way from his cell phone. That seemed to quiet the ants in my pants. For a while.

Chapter 35

Wednesday

We found Benjamin Franklin thirty minutes later, as he left Hurricane Alley and headed the red Charger first east out the back of the parking lot, then north on Kobayashi up to Bay Area Blvd. Actually Siddiqi found him – and I lost him. I had successfully paced myself to meet up with Mo and take over his tail of Franklin just west of Highway 3, but I hadn't been on Franklin's tail in the middle lane for more than a minute when my cell phone rang again. I fumbled for it on the passenger seat. I'd evidently missed the cup holder in all my excitement.

After four rings I took my eyes off the road and looked down at the seat to locate the slippery little devil. It had shifted to the outside edge, probably when I changed lanes or something. I looked back up, saw Franklin turning left, north across Bay Area into a subdivision nestled behind the strip center fronted by FedEx, McDonald's, and Starbucks. The development wasn't a gated community or anything, so there were a zillion places he could turn and turn again and exit.

Fearful that Franklin had turned off Bay Area Blvd. because he'd made my tail – and therefore would recognize the Forester if he saw it again in an hour – I rented a Chevrolet Malibu from Enterprise not far from where I'd lost him. Then drove to Fred Childress's house. That took maybe twelve minutes. I parked two houses further down on their side of the street, content to watch things in the side and rear view mirrors again, my face out of view in a plain vanilla family car.

Chapter 36

Wednesday

At ten after seven, a small commercial van, not a minivan, pulled up in front of Childress's. The driver, tallish, of average build in a white shirt and black slacks, got out and slinked to the door of the main house. I couldn't see a face because of the Astros baseball cap worn forward and down like a lot of outfielders do. I made the driver for a guy by the way he walked, but wasn't sure. In a few minutes the driver made his way back to the van with two middle-aged guys sporting major guts rumbling close behind. Soon cartons were hauled out the rear of the van and carried around the far side of Childress's house, out of my view, presumably to the mother-in-law cottage.

It had to be a catering job. And why not? A serious weekly group of players would seat eight around a dedicated poker table for at least three hours. Who'd want to feed that many men on a weekly basis? Not me. Maybe each poker pot was tithed a chip to foot the cost?

In fifteen minutes the Astros cap returned, hopped in the van and drove off, right past me. There was still enough light to see the silhouette inside the van but not enough to see the face.

The sign on the passenger side of the van raised another question: who owned Lake City Catering...
??

My gut told me the driver was Benjamin Franklin. My trained Navy head told me someone needed to sit and watch the house in case I was wrong. Since Mo's last words to me were "I hope I'm not late for class," I was fresh out of help. No wonder police detectives work in pairs.

I went for the chase anyway, managed to start the Malibu quickly enough to catch up in little over a block and get the license plate. At the time I wasn't sure what good that would do but at least I was doing *some*thing. Two blocks later I decided to err on the side of caution. I disdained instinct and impulse, broke off my tail of the van, and returned to the Childress house.

I parked up the street that time and was bored to tears as the minutes trudged on. By eight forty-five I had watched four cars pull up and park. Only one had a passenger, a man who appeared shorter than Franklin, significantly stockier than the man I'd seen on Saturday, with a limp on his right side so pronounced as to erase any question. None of the drivers seemed the right size either.

If Ben Franklin attended the poker game that evening, he'd arrived before I did or while I was shadowing the catering van (maybe five minutes).

I grew more and more pissed. I'd not managed a break in the case, had nothing to report to Mrs. Franklin, nothing new that would help me make sense of the situation.

All I had were more questions – the whole case seemed to have gone that way. It started off simple with a guy supposedly skimming business profits to his wife's dismay. I added the question of why skim money in the first place and brewed up a caldron full of questions.

As I turned the key in the ignition at eight forty-five, I decided Franklin had been the guy from the catering van. Giving me the slip at six-fifteen gave him plenty of time to change clothes, switch to the van, pick up the catered food, and arrive at seventen. The card game was close enough to at least two of his restaurants.

But if Franklin were truly playing poker every Wednesday, why didn't he stay and play some cards? Had his skimming been to feed the gambling addition and, if so, had his habit become so expensive that he was paying the guys off with "free" food and not sitting in on any more games? The cost of the food would be lost in the sheer volume of any of his restaurants.

On my drive back to Enterprise, I reconsidered Candice's suggestion to use an illegal transmitter on the Charger. After maybe thirty seconds of thought, I declined again, figuring my license was worth more than any one client, no matter what the potential in billed time with her could be.

Still, I wondered if there weren't some electronic surveillance angle I was overlooking. Jason Bourne had showed the moviegoing public how the CIA and the rest of the Alphabet Soups had made a fine art out of at-your-desk air-conditioned real-time surveillance: digital transmitter tracking. Surely some of that technology had finally filtered down from the highly classified signal intelligence to the gumshoe-affordable level.

Then again, the Feds had the Patriot Act. I didn't.

What I really needed was a good buddy at each of the cellular providers. Triangulate Franklin's cell phone to find out which restaurant he was at. Piece of cake. I didn't need a GPS fix accurate to five yards. I wondered if I might take on some associates at the technology providers. Probably have to change the name of the firm to Trench Coat and Associates? A moment later, I smiled but declined on that option as well.

Chapter 37

Wednesday

I wasn't home ten minutes when Candice pulled my chain with a ring on my cell phone.

"Trench Coat."

"Oh, stop it. You're about as inconspicuous as a tank."

"Good evening, Mrs. Franklin. How may I be of service." Okay, so I laid it on a little thick.

"What have you got for me?"

I plopped down in my overstuffed recliner, sighed. "Nothing that makes any sense in a court of law."

"Do we need it that clear and obvious?"

If I had nothing. Certainly zero was clear and obvious. I played along with her silly little game. "What does your divorce lawyer have to say on the matter."

"She says the clearer the evidence, the better the chance I have of taking the whole pie."

So she did have a divorce lawyer already *and* she was after the whole pie. I had figured her for maybe seventy percent to make up for the years of skimming – but not the whole pie. Was

I about to have a philosophical clash with Mrs. Franklin? Could her view be that half of the assets plus fifty percent the remaining community property was the starting point of negotiations? If so we could soon arrive at the Tower Bridge for a battle royale. I hoped not. I wanted the cash flow. Then, again, I also wanted to keep my license.

"Nate, are you there?"

I knew that answer. "Yes."

"So you're real talkative when you want to pepper me with annoying repetitive queries. I put one simple one to you, you attach a sound bite and log off."

Where had she learned those terms? Well, everyone does know about sound bytes, since Bill Clinton and his focus groups, anyway. "I just got back from surveillance."

"I know. That's why I called."

How could she know that? But I knew. Of course. "You placed one of those mobile transmitters on my car instead?"

"More or less."

I thought I'd flatter her. "Tell me more."

"Know your place, Mr. Gumshoe. You do any real work today? I did."

I had mixed feelings about the advisability of asking her to elaborate on the real work she had done. Would it be taken as an opportunity for her to brag or would I be considered insolent for invading her privacy? Either way, I lost.

"Are you there?"

"Yes."

"Well, what did you find out?"

"That my client is into violating federal and state law."

"You watch your tongue."

"You placed a transmitter on the Charger, too?"

"No. I want you to do that."

She could probably walk on putting the beeper on mine. I was supposed to take the rap on her husband's Charger, though. Bum deal if there ever was one.

"Why me? You know when he's asleep. When he is, tell whoever put the digital wonder on my Forester to hurry up and do the deed."

A long silence, maybe thirty seconds, was followed by, "What did you find out with my money today?"

I counted to ten for dramatic effect – well, maybe to cool down my temper – then said, "Ben and poker – I don't think he's playing. More like he's catering."

She had no reply. Not a word. Not even a burst of cellular static.

Ten seconds... I went on. "Looks like he was driving the catering van but I can't prove it – yet."

"Oh," she said. "Now that is very interesting. Spring mentioned he asked her to fill in for the catering driver this week. She turned him down but he asked her again this afternoon – is that right, Spring... Spring?"

I heard some mumbling in the background.

"Yes, Mr. Trench, he asked her again today."

"So his driving the van doesn't surprise you."

"When you own your own business, who else are you going to call – Kelly Girl – Kelly Driver?"

"Does your husband have a ninth company called Lake City Catering?"

"Why?"

Because I was a court jester? "That's the name I saw on the side of the catering van this evening."

Silence.

"Mrs. Franklin?" I said after about fifteen seconds.

"I am not aware of it. Let me ask Spring."

This time she placed the phone against her blouse or skirt or something.

A few seconds later, Mrs. Franklin said, "Spring says the only time she saw the catering van, it was white without any sign. What else do you have for me?"

"Nothing. Not a clue."

A long session of telephone static, then, "Perhaps I have made a mistake... in hiring you."

"You decide that for yourself, Mrs. Franklin. I must tell you now I will remove the transmitter from my vehicle first thing in the morning and scan the Forester every day with equipment I have right here at the house."

"I doubt your technology is as cutting edge as the transceiver currently mounted on your Japanese vehicle."

I decided to shift gears. "May I speak with Spring?"

"Concerning...?"

"Driving a catering truck – err, van."

"I'll see."

It sounded like she'd placed the phone down on a hard surface. Some sounds and echoes but nothing intelligible for about three minutes. Then Mrs. Franklin's returned. "Hello? Spring said to call her in the morning – after eleven."

I didn't like that but it was better than a flat decline. "She have a cell?'

"Yes. I suppose you want me to give you that, too?"

"It would eliminate the middle man."

"I am still that," she said and the call terminated.

Chapter 38

Thursday

When I woke up Thursday morning to my alarm clock, I didn't care if Candice Franklin lived or died, fired me or kept handing me cash. What I decided to care about was me, again. She either took my services as a professional or she could go fly an iron kite.

Did she have a gumshoe trailing me trailing her husband? That was a crock. Oh, yeah, she could have been bluffing about the transmitter but how else could I explain her knowing I had just returned home?

Life was too short. That's why my initial focus when I'd opened my agency had been the computer search stuff. It was unhealthful to get out on the streets and mix things up with guys and gals who'd been doing the life-turns-on-every-dime-on-every-corner shuffle their whole lives.

After breakfast I located the transmitter in about thirty seconds. A cheap VHF/UHF/SHF scanner I'd bought at an army surplus store a year earlier did the trick. The spy module was near top-of-the-line and generated my next new questions: from where and whom? I would need those answered before I did any more work. Speaking of work, it occurred to me that I could schedule my Thursdays as many in the medical professions do, on the golf course. I'd played a bit on base when I was stationed in Rota, Spain (shore duty as always). I had a set of graphite shaft clubs in my garage – somewhere. I could head out to a driving range that very afternoon, get back in the swing.

< > < >

When I arrived at the office around nine, the first thing I did was key a request for the owner of the license plate I'd seen on the Lake City Catering truck. As I fiddled with the request interface, I wondered what my golf handicap was when I played in Rota. I did manage to enter the plate's seven letters/numbers correctly on the third try.

Golf and other such trivialities were sent out the back door when I heard the troubled voice on the other end of the cell phone.

"You've got to see me, Mr. Trench."

The caller ID only gave the phone number, not the caller. The voice was very young so I figured *teenage girl calling from cell phone*. I had a yellow pages ad and feared calls like this late at night after I'd settled in for the evening. "And you would be... whom?"

"Who – me? I'm me."

"Me – who?"

"Spring. Spring Elizabeth Franklin. You tried to talk to me yesterday evening, I think."

I about lost it in my skivvies . "Uhh – yes. Yes, I did. Your mother seemed reluctant for us to speak."

"I didn't know about you wanting to talk to me until this morning – after – after – after things got – got really shitty."

What did I say to that?

First I had to catch my breath. I was supposed to begin chasing her down at eleven. I wondered if she was like her mother. I decided to shut up and see if she answered her own questions.

"Mr. Trench, I'm serious. I need to talk to you."

"If your situation is so very grave, you should take it to the Houston police department. There's a constables' offices not far your home. I'm not a miracle worker. Just a worker."

No answer came.

I said, "Why do you need to talk to me?"

No answer, just line static shifting through time like sand on a pie tin.

I said, "You want to meet me – what time?"

"After school."

"Will you mother be informed of our meeting?"

"Only if she checks the family cell phone billing page on the internet."

"Fair enough," I said, not sure why I said it. I wondered what the law was. Could Candice have my license if she had forbid me to speak with her daughter? Candice hadn't *said* that.

"We on? You're saying you will?"

I paused. What was I saying?

"Please Mr. Trench Coat. Talk with me today."

Did I have a little drama queen on my hands? That would so not be close to any recreational activity I was familiar with.

"Why me? I work for your mother. I'm assuming she's part of *your* situation?"

"Mom says you don't bow and genuflect like you should."

"This takes us to your point... which... is?"

"Trust me."

What's a guy to do. I said, "Coffee Oasis, NASA Pkwy. at Kirby, west end of Seabrook, say four?"

"I can do that. Thank you. I'll – "

"Wait, how will I recognize you?"

"My Space."

"I'm not in your space – am I? I can't be."

"The web site. Mom said you were a geek."

Then I remembered. My Space was the combination personal brag and photo album web site that was falling to pieces beneath the hooves of Facebook. I had often wondered why the folks on there didn't get a life, do something useful. The answer was obvious, though, wasn't it. My Space was their life.

"What's your ID on there?"

"Spring85."

"I'll see you this afternoon."

"Thanks" came over the line, followed by one of those disconnect chirps. Annoying little sounds, aren't they.

Spring in the Spring. Spring in the Spring. Those four words bounced around inside my head for a good while, like a song from the radio that you just can't put out of your mind.

I did get my two cents worth in the database called Mo Siddiqi's voice mail. That evening's surveillance needed to be lined up before I went to meet with Spring, but be flexible so we could refocus our efforts should Spring give us a true insight into the comings and goings of one Benjamin I. Franklin, adopted Dad.

Chapter 39

Thursday

"What do you mean, you can't coordinate the surveillance this evening?" Mo Siddiqi was about to blow my faith in the working college student.

"My car. Not well. Requires my assistance; electrical system. You know of these things?"

"I have a great mechanic. Yours any good? Want to check with mine."

"Mr. Trench. No disrespect. I am my own mechanic. It is less costly that way. Much."

"You're saying you can't be where you need to be to work your fellow students on the surveillance?"

"Yes. I cannot work the job the way we have constructed it without a vehicle. I am to cover for anyone who reports not present or must leave suddenly."

"You saying the way I have worked it out is not a good, smooth method?"

"No, The plan is good. In truth, I like the plan."

I needed him to coordinate the other students – heck, I wasn't sure I had half their phone numbers. It occurred to me that money wasn't a problem. "Suppose I get you a rental car?"

"No, sir. I cannot afford a rental car."

"I'll pay for the vehicle – even throw in the gas. Have it delivered to you – where are you?"

"This is most generous."

"Then you'll do it?"

"Yes, I must apologize to ask. You will also pay my hourly amount?"

Poor college student. He'd probably never ask such a question once he graduated and got that good job. "Yes, your fee will be the same we agreed on. Your workers, too."

"I am most appreciative, Mr. Trench."

"Great. Now tell me something."

"Of course, sir."

"Where are you – better, yet, where will you be just before you need to be working for me?"

He gave me his sister's address. Evidently he picked up some money each week giving her a Mother's Day Out – well, half of one, anyway. He'd be there waiting whenever I got there.

I called my favorite rental jockey, a crazed Ukrainian named Ronnie. He owned a Rent-A-Wreck franchise, officed over on El Camino Real, near mine. I would have used him the day before but he goes home at 6:00.

He came in real handy when I needed a series of daily rentals to do a long-term stakeout. Okay, so I hadn't done many. Anyway, with a different used car each day, the odds of getting spotted *just down the street* decrease dramatically. I might have to drive Ronnie or one of his staff back from the delivery but we'd sure as heck get Siddiqi another set of wheels without blowing Mrs. Franklin's budget.

Spring Franklin was another matter.

I arrived at Coffee Oasis ten minutes early for our four o'clock meeting. I finished listening to Siddiqi's first field report at four-thirty before I gave up the ghost, waved to the barista, another college kid, and headed out to the parking lot and my Forrester, half-finished latte in hand.

< >   < >

A brief shudder had pulsed through my body while I waited for Spring. Gave me chills. It haunted me on the drive to Clear Lake Shores: could evil powers beneath the surface of the Franklin Case see fit to erase her name from the chalk board of life? I had no concrete reason to create the thought but I was there; again.

Kara's very short life echoed through me as I turned south.

I didn't want to be responsible for shortening the life of someone else's daughter. Had I already got her in trouble?

I hoped Mrs. Franklin's daughter was a bit of a drama queen.

Just down the street from my assigned restaurant for that evening's reconnaissance, Magnum Steak, my cell phone entertained a signal from Mrs. Franklin.

Did I want to answer it? Had Spring's mother engaged in foul play to further her own ends?

Candice Franklin was probably no saint but I guessed her too lazy and fastidious to murder someone, even Benjamin. Then, again, all that money she'd come into would purchase a real pro....

I punched the green button. "Trench Coat. Good afternoon."

"Oh, stop it. You're about as inconspicuous as a tank." She'd said that before.

The woman could try the patience of the pope. "Yes, Mrs. Franklin."

"You have anything for me?"

"Surveillance agents are in place, all eight locations."

"Where is Ben?"

"The Charger was spotted on I-45 after leaving Hurricane Alley about eight minutes ago. I got a text."

"You know where the car is now?"

"No. Your watchdogs are remaining in place, as instructed, logging significant activities at each location, not just *Benjamin's* appearances. Knowing the drives times between locations, we should be able to read a log of his activities good enough to detect a pattern. Once we've done that, we can go to a dedicated tail."

"Was Ben *in* the Charger?"

"All the ops have a copy of the photo you gave me. His dimensions are printed on the back."

"But you don't know for sure?"

"I know that no four-foot-ten blonde girl got in the Charger and drove it over the freeway feeder curb. If the money hadn't been so good...."

"Men and their obsessions with the blonde."

Her tone said she hadn't thought it. Can you spell *a-c-i-d-i-c*?

Chapter 40

Thursday

I didn't want to ask Mrs. Candice Franklin why she had called. I felt like she might tell me I was stupid for not knowing I should have called already. Maybe I was angry and couldn't dump it in my customer's yard. She might hand me my head.

I did not respond to "blonde." Just waited. She was sure to tell me why she called soon enough to suit her purposes.

"Mr. Trench, what do you expect to get out of you chasing around today?"

"Data on your husband's movements."

"And that brings me... what for my money?"

"Data. Patterns. Timings. Things that if they change from day to day will give us points of focus for further investigation."

"You sound like a politician."

"Never tried that."

"I want to know what he's doing – all the time. You go get a good mobile transmitter – maybe the one I had on your car – and you make sure it's securely fastened to the Charger. I want reports on the hour."

I waited to reply, hoping a terse, discussion-ending remark would come to mind. None did.

I was thinking some more when she blew my ear off the phone with, "Mr. Trench, get a tail on my husband!"

I counted to three, then, "Suppose he drives the catering truck?"

"Track that, too."

"You check your documents to see if y'all own Lake City Catering yet?"

Silence, except for cell phone static.

"Mrs. Franklin?"

Nothing.

She had dodged the question the day before. I smelled a rat. "I'm getting an annoying crick in my neck on this catering van," I said. "You're not telling me something."

Still nothing.

"What is it, Mrs. Franklin?"

"I have to go. Bunco night. Perhaps we'll chat in the morning."

"Mrs. Franklin, don't you also owe me some information via e-mail?"

"I sent you that."

"You may recall that I considered the information incomplete."

"Perhaps you did. Good evening, Mr. Trench."

She had hung up just as polite as you please, after having been as evasive as a businessman on "60 Minutes" in the seventies. I hoped we'd reached détente – a stalemate. If I was to do my job, she needed to stand clear and let me do it.

As I pointed the Forester to a decent parking space, a small degree of sympathy grew in my heart for Benjamin Franklin. I had a hard enough time following Candice Franklin's moods and translating her edicts. Being married to her could be a whole lot worse – and could explain why he was home so little.

< >   < >

The sentimentality left me later when I joined Siddiqi at Panera Bread to go over the reports.

He'd already assembled a table on his notebook computer.

"How'd it go?" I said.

"Very fine first run. Very nice."

"Anything unusual?"

"Out-of-sight durations close to measured driving times."

"So, really, we have nothing?"

"We have base data."

Don't you just love geeks? I do! I sat back, stretched a bit of the tired-too-early out of me. Nine in the evening is way too early to feel sleepy, for sure.

I said, "Is there enough to begin seeing a picture, a pattern, anything?"

"No. No conclusions to draw. We need run this again. At least twice more."

"Your gut is telling you twice more – or is that statistical standards?"

"Feelings are not involved. Simple arithmetic. He was only at three restaurants this evening. Therefore, we do not collect enough data for statistical sampling. Four paths between eateries, minimum. Variations in travel time need replication. Six more would be better."

Memories of high school science class came back, including my old fear of anything algebraic. That high school science teacher had made it out to be the basis of all probability, or something.

I smiled at my college whiz. "Okay, this is Thursday. What days can you and your crew work?"

"Must be Tuesday and Thursday. Most students are on Monday-Wednesday class schedule."

"You included? What about Saturday?"

"You will pay small fortunes for college students on Saturday evening. If they want to work. They already have better jobs."

I couldn't argue with that. "What am I going to do for the next poker game – next Wednesday?"

"You may follow more closely. Binoculars. Night vision like the movies. You have mobile audio transmitter?"

"You mean a *bug*?"

"More like a praying mantis. Doesn't just track. Live audio feed."

Great illegal gadgets were everywhere. "How much they run?"

He smiled. Didn't say anything.

"And speaking of Wednesday, I forgot to ask you if you made it on time to class yesterday?"

"Thank you for your courtesy. I did."

"That's great," I said, accepting the realities of going on the cheap. You got what you paid for. If you wanted excellent help, *on demand*, you had to pay a premium. If you just wanted someone to fill a chair, well the chair got a bit warmer for the minimum.

< >   < >

Mo waved to me, smiling, as I steered the Forester away from the curb in front of his sister's house. He was a nice guy. I wished good things for him.

Two right turns left me wondering what the hell to do. The college kids had all showed up for work. We had covered all the restaurants. There wasn't much to show for it. Just data. I had a client who didn't give a rat's ass for data. She wanted results, the bottom line on how her husband was skimming money, how she could hang him.

And so did I, never mind what the guys and gals on the Gumshoe network had said about this kind of case often taking months. It just seemed like a simple case. If I could find out a bit more, I might know which computer hard drive to mirror. Hell, I couldn't even find Benjamin Franklin's lover in the building where she parked.

I went to bed thinking the skinny blonde might be the place to be on Friday. Tail the lover for two days. Might lead right back to Helm Street.

Chapter 41

Friday

Me, the dumb ass, neglected to bring a novel to pass the time while I sat in a parking garage in central Houston, Texas, five slots down from the Buick that Benjamin Franklin's slender blonde drove. Dumb. Anyone knows an all-day stakeout can be exactly that: all day, a very slow day.

Maybe I needed to buy that iPad after all. Maybe Galaxy Note II.

By eleven I'd fiddled with my Z10 enough to run down the charge twenty percent so I plugged in the cigarette lighter charger.

It was getting darn near to the businessman's lunch hour when my cell phone popped up the name of the other woman who'd made my day on Thursday, Spring.

"Mr. Trench, this is Spring Franklin."

"Uh, huh."

"You must be mad at me."

"I have cause."

She didn't respond to that right away. Maybe I didn't need to grind pumice in her ear.

I was about to take a conciliatory tone when she whined like a four year old, "I still need to see you real bad." Her voice reminded me of the calls of the bats coming out at sunset from New Mexico's Carlsbad Caverns.

"Can't be all that bad," I said, going for the bored and tired sound. "It's waited a day, already. I might have some time Monday. Monday's soon enough."

"No. Please. Don't. Turn. Me. Down. I have. Real. Problems."

With parents like Benjamin and Candice, I had to give her that. "What do you want me to do?"

"Meet me."

"Been there; tried that."

"I'll show up."

"Where?" I was still being too nice.

"You pick it."

"What time?"

"Ahh, well, Ahhhhh... *now* would be good."

"You think I've been sitting on my butt at Coffee Oasis since yesterday afternoon, chatting with Rusty, working the crossword, just waiting for your call?" My Z10 cut in with its battery-low beep. "Oh, I'm a sympathetic guy, all right. My life's work is to rescue teenagers from the evils of the world – including parents."

"You do – you are?"

"Only the ones who level with me, show up when and where they say. We used to call that *dependable*."

Cellular static.

"Look, I'm about out of battery," I said. "Where, when?"

"I told you, *now!*"

She had. "Where?"

"Panera. Café Express. La Madeleine. On Bay Area."

I was oh so tired of franchise food and theme restaurants. "How about Franca's Italian?"

"I'm not hungry."

"*I* will be by the time *I* get there. I'm deep inside The Loop. Might be forty-five minutes."

"Okay, Franca's. It's down on NASA near El Camino?"

"Zip is 77058." I punched END before holding down the power key, not waiting for her response. Lithium batteries of that era would rebound a bit if you gave them a nap. I exchanged batteries anyway.

I twisted the key and the Chevy Cobalt from Rent-A-Wreck came to life, if with a bit of a wheeze at first. I looked left, then right. All-clear. Backed out, then twisted the wheel to the right to leave when, oh, what a sight: the blonde from the front desk of Bramblett-Dawson-Kensington opening the driver's door of the ugly Buick.

My disguise that morning was a Texans' baseball cap. I pulled it low and turned the wheel back left. This turned out to be a very bad idea. An H2, black as midnight except for the chrome appointments, came 'round the ramp as I returned to my vacated parking space. A glance back to the right showed the Buick backing right in front of the H2.

I hoped the black mass would take the Buick's slot. No luck. The Hummer was leaving, too. I joined the parade but the parade left me. The two vehicles in front of me were regular tenants. They went out the far right slot just as pretty as you please. I got to smile at the parking attendant's empty hand reaching out a window. You can figure it from there.

Chapter 42

Friday

I made it to Franca's at ten minutes after one, just in time for Spring to not be there, for a second time. I was royally steamed and soon not very hungry. My kind-hearted side said to give the girl a little slack so I hung near the greeter's station until one-thirty. No young girl Franklin-stein, no phone call, text, no email; no attempt at a good deed left unpunished.

I headed the Cobalt west on NASA Pkwy. to Coffee Oasis. The greeter at Franca's accepted a tip with my business card, so a very late Spring would know where to go. Why Coffee Oasis? Maybe Spring's terrified mind stuck on the prior location?

Lots of empty chairs at Coffee Oasis. The sandwich lunch crowd had cleared, leaving one rather rude looking woman assaulting an aged giant Toshiba laptop. No Spring nor any other season of the year.

I took the barista guy's face out of a mammoth college textbook – Rusty must have gone to the bank – long enough to get him to brew a mug of cappuccino for me. While he worked, I wandered around Coffee Oasis like a dog chasing his tail, searching for the precise spot to sit. I settled on the massive high-top table that held court from the east wall, not a wall, exactly: a floor-to-ceiling window serving as a wall. That gave me a perfect view of the parking lot and the front door – like that did me any good. At two-fifteen I decided Spring had turned to summer. I left Coffee Oasis for the house. On the way I came up with an internet search hunch I had to chase.

No, I wasn't after more useless data on Benjamin Franklin and his Sul Ross State Teachers College days. I wanted to see if Fry's carried a certain specialty wireless microphone.

I found it on their web site, then called the guys at the Fry's on the I-45 North feeder. What a zoo. They couldn't decide which department it was shelved under.

Wherever it was, their inventory system showed five in stock. I told the geek on the phone I'd be over there in twenty minutes to pick up one EaseDropper II – and how nice if he found it for me by then. I mentioned that I would charge them my regular hourly rate if I ended up helping them look for it. He said to go to the repair counter when I arrived.

< >   < >

At the far right wall as you enter the NASA Fry's is a counter just a bit further past the mammoth store's returns and repair counters. It's a little island with techs that help you find the right RAM and such for your computer. I told the very short geek behind it who I was. With one quick bend to touch his toes, he retrieved EaseDropper. He printed out an invoice ticket for me, smiling a bit too much, it seemed. That stopped when he saw my face as I read the total. He launched into a litany of upgrades built into the newly upgraded EaseDropper Model III cradled in his modest hands.

I needed it for Saturday. Candice would scream but being nice to her had not kept the cranky version at bay, so what the heck. With any luck I'd get to keep it after the job was finished.

"Just take the invoice with you to the cashiers, sir."

"Love your enthusiasm."

He placed E-D-III in my hand.

"Seriously," I said. "This is the best service I've had in... well, a couple months. Thanks."

I was still stunned when I left the mammoth building.

Chapter 43

Friday

I had just checked on the status of my request for the owner of the Lake City Catering van when Mrs. Franklin popped her clenched face inside my office door. Yup, it was just before five – again. Had she no respect for the Wall? Evidently not. I wanted to spit a wad of chaw on the floor, like in the old westerns. Two problems: no spittoon and no smokeless tobacco had ever touched my lips.

Two seconds and she had landed in a guest chair with a leg crossed over. "You have anything for me?"

"I just keep digging."

"Where are you planting your spade right now? Ben doesn't have a waitress in your office."

Now that was about as dumb-ass as I'd ever heard from a woman. It was time to extract the burr from under her saddle. "Why don't you tell me what the hell is the real problem?"

"Problem? I'm in charge here. I want today's developments."

I passed along the losing game of tag I had with the Buick but sidestepped no-show Spring.

"What have you been doing since lunch?"

"Working out a plan for tomorrow."

"Tomorrow?"

"Yes. I'm glad you stopped by. Did you ever develop a timeline on Benjamin and the Helm street house?"

"I told you, he's been at it for twelve months – that I know of."

Okay, maybe I used the wrong word. "At the risk of having you fly off the handle like you did on Wednesday evening, did you ever figure Benjamin had a routine he followed on Saturday morning, you know, visiting that house –"

"You bet I did."

Wow. She had some information. "What time does he get there?"

"He's gone usually by eight on Saturdays."

"So you would wait and then follow him up there?"

"Yes. Hid in friends' borrowed cars. He'd have his little tryst until maybe nine, nine-thirty."

"You ever catch him there on Friday evening?"

"Never tried."

I wasn't expecting that. "May I ask why?"

"Spring. She would run me full crazy on Fridays. Girl never has liked school."

Made sense to me.

"Mr. Trench, why are you pursuing this line of interrogation?"

"Mrs. Franklin, I'm looking for additional information. Trying to make sense of things."

She gave me one of those *no-way-I-believe-you-buster* looks like I'd used to see on my grandma's face when I'd not come up with a very good excuse.

"Mrs. Franklin, my gut, my instinct – you women call it intuition – keeps telling me there's something you're not telling me."

"Just one item – I'm holding back one vicious little secret – is that what you think?"

"Let's play twenty questions."

"Why?"

"My job is to ask questions," I said, wishing I didn't need the money.

"I hired you. I set the agenda. You agreed."

"I'm afraid I did not."

She sat bolt upright.

"Look," I said, "I have to poke and prod, ask questions of everyone even remotely connected to the case. The person who's hired me, on the other hand, is supposed to dump their heart and soul on my desk, provide me with any answer my heart desires."

Evidently, she wasn't expecting that. A frown morphed into raised eyebrows, into a couple of pink cheeks. "I know this is going to sound a bit off."

"Mrs. Franklin –"

"Candice."

Did I dare go there again?

"Look, I –"

"Mr. Trench, if I'm going to tell you this, you must call me Candice."

I nodded once, said, "Okay. For now...."

"Say it."

"Candice."

"Very well." She fidgeted a moment, then said, "The whole problem is sex."

Well. That stood to reason. Her husband was never home.

"Okay."

"It's not what you think."

"Try me. I'll hush until you tell me I can speak."

She declined to laugh or smile, instead stood and moved quietly to the window, stared out into the courtyard for a moment, then said, "The skinny blonde situation has always befuddled me. I never thought Benjamin really liked sex."

I wanted to ask why, but held my tongue, and waited for her to continue.

"Even at the beginning, we never had sex more than a couple times a week – oh, our wedding night and the first year or so *were* active, I suppose...."

"He could go at it all right. But he never craved sex – not like most men I've known. Ben's never came at me twice in the same day in all the years we've been married. You hear what I'm saying?"

I wasn't sure if that was a cue to speak or just agree, so I nodded three times, with strong eye contact.

"Ben is just different. I mean most guys wanted you to "play ball" with them a couple times while we were driving up to College Station for a football game."

Chapter 44

Friday

I about fell out of my chair when the snooty-to-the-point-of-stodgy Candice Franklin let go with that drive to College Station anecdote. I wanted to say something, worried about how to respond politely.

"So, you see, Mr. Trench, I was totally dumbfounded when I discovered the skinny blonde. It was one of the few times in my life where I couldn't put any rhyme or reason to a situation. An affair just didn't fit – so I tested him. For the first two months, I would go after him on Saturdays, first time I saw him *after* he had a chance to be with *her*."

I nodded again.

"And you know what? He never turned me down. Did just fine – for Benjamin Franklin, anyway."

I nodded yet again.

"I want you to find out if Ben has been skimming money out of our pockets but – you may think I'm being silly – I don't want to embarrass him. I'm mad at him about the money. Maybe I'm mad about him for not telling me the truth about something that's wrong. Maybe I'm mad because I spent all that money and the CPAs didn't give me a leg to stand on."

By then she was back at the window, talking to the birds or something. Eye contact was in short supply but I forgave her, given the private nature of her monologue.

"Could you probably see how I felt?" she said. "Like he wanted that grotesquely skinny thing instead of me, a woman who gets approached weekly at the country club by men of substantial means? She whimpered, maybe ten seconds or so. Then righted her shoulders with a sigh.

I waited.

Maybe a couple minutes later she turned from the window. "Mr. Trench, what makes a man do something like that?"

Was I supposed to start talking or was it, what you call it in high school, a rhetorical question?

"Go ahead, Mr. Trench. "You're the inquisitive, always thinking type. Do you have any idea?"

I motioned her back to the chair.

She shook her head slowly, declining.

"Okay, then, Mrs. Franklin – "

"Candice."

"Yes, Candice. I did twenty-plus in the Navy."

"Ben was never in the service."

"I'm single now. I'm not trained in psychology. I'm not trained to be a social worker. I don't know nothin'. I do have a new idea of how I can help you, especially with this blonde thing."

"Yes? Please. Tell me."

"I'm going to install a listening device with three remote wireless microphones on the house on Helm."

"Will you be recording what it listens to?"

"Yes. I can download what's been recorded by the controller with my cell."

"Splendid." She returned to the chair. "Let's see if their conversations give us an idea of their... what do they call it on *Law and Order*...?"

"Maybe you mean 'intent'?"

"That's it. That's it, exactly. I'll let you go."

With that, she pulled her purse off my desk, dug inside, pulled out a stack of Franklins in a wide rubber band which soon landed on my blotter with a gentle thud.

And she was gone.

Chapter 45

Friday

Being the consummate social mover and shaker that I was back then, I stayed home and tallied the week's accounts. A second count of Mrs. Franklin's stack gave the same results: fifty Mr. Franklins. I smiled but wondered if that stack was part of my ongoing retainer or payment towards expenses. I hadn't invoiced her.

As I made out the deposit slip, my overpriced license plate search engine came to mind. I'd filed a request for info on Lake City Catering's plate with them first thing Thursday morning. Two business days back. Shouldn't take more than a few minutes. How about a refund for this month's fee? Like that was ever going to happen.

I located my original query. No update. I opened the query field. The plate owner identification response field still did not list anything like "not on record" or "file not found." It was essentially blank, a long white rectangle, left center on a cerulean blue screen. The cursor blinked but that was all.

I e-mailed the system operator. Maybe he'd get back to me before Memorial Day.

I had other resources. First I took another shot at Benjamin's social security number. Nothing new came up on any of the free or pay-for-it services.

Next, his date of birth. A special search. Costly subscription service. Turns out majority of folks who hide behind an alias keep the same date of birth. Latest research was over seventy-five percent. Nothing new there either.

Then, his Texas Driver's License number. That one was usually lame. A big deal in the 1970's and 1980's, it had been surpassed by the Social Security Number nationwide by the time the century turned. He showed up right away, the same dummy who had once resided in Alpine, Texas. Nothing new.

Next, I tried the federal tax number for Shrimp-Steak, Inc. I'd copied it from Candice's follow-up data sheet, the fluorescent yellow. Had I tried that FTN before? I got a huge surprise in the negative. I would have remembered what I found. Damn. I verified through another service – took twice as long. Same answer: that FTN belonged to Lake City Catering, Inc., a corporation domiciled in Webster, Texas.

What did that mean? Had Benjamin Franklin disguised something with that FTN, maybe a reorganized Shrimp-Steak, Inc., as a subsidiary of Lake City; sold his/their business and not told his wife? He shouldn't be able do that. She said she was majority shareholder. Forging a signature would be fraud right out of the old detective movies. No one could be that lame after 9-11.

Unless she had lied to me....

I needed to not think so hard, let my mind figure things out by itself, work in the background while I did other tasks. Whenever I forced things, the answer usually came up *stupid* in the light of the next day or, worse yet, week.

I had a listening device to install and it was then well after dark.

Chapter 46

Friday

The fates were with me. Okay, so I used to dig Shakespeare. The evening cloud cover that usually hovers over Houston was missing, so the city lights didn't reflect back down. The moon was nowhere in the sight. That evening was about as dark as you could get in peaceful Clear Lake City.

I stole up Space Center – okay I piloted my Rent-A-Wreck du jour, a 2001 Ford Crown Victoria, up towards Helm Street. The sedan's powder blue paint job would be mistaken for white on such a dark night.

At El Dorado Blvd. I made a left and drove west past the first cross street before winding my way down to Helm in an indirect, try-and-figure-out-where-I'm-going fashion.

Helm looked peaceful. No parties. A few autos parked at the curb.

I had driven down Helm's length at least six times since the prior Saturday, logging a couple side trips in the Cobalt and Forester, as well as the Crown Vic to get a feel for which cars belonged where and which ones were visiting.

I parked on the side street on the west end of Helm and jogged toward Ben's hideaway like I was an old guy trying to get some exercise after work – okay, it was Friday but you get my ruse. On my second pass of the skinny blonde's place, I stopped to tie a shoe, decided all was clear – no car in the driveway. No lights on inside. No car across the street or next door on either side.

I first affixed two microphones around back. The plans I'd located showed I had miked the master bedroom and kitchen windows, and came with a disclaimer that the plans were only valid for when the house was first built. Any remodeling and I was S.O.L.

Those two finished, I worked my way back to the front in a low crouch and hid between the house and a wide oleander stand. It held court over the large living room window, a perfect location for the transmitter-receiver and third microphone.

Since sneaking around at night and illegal monitoring were not a practiced or often-used specialty of mine, a cat's sudden snarling in my ear sent me head first into the oleander. She claimed exclusive rights to the window sill and I bled slightly from my right temple.

I got the hell out of Dodge.

Back in the boulevard cruiser, I called up the Ease-Dropper III app on my Z10, then drove around the block and parked three houses down, facing my prey. I was good to go for whenever I wanted to pry into other peoples lives. The question of whether to make use of the ideal site and weather conditions by spending the night there played tennis in my brain for a good twenty minutes. Still undecided, the fates showed me the way by handing me another gift, a red Charger.

Okay it's difficult to discern auto colors in the dark, what with all the metallic and pearl coats adding luster to pigments. I'd had my binoculars and was able to pick up the plate as Benjamin approached the driveway very slowly. The State of Texas tag belonged to his red car – dummy, I never checked the registration, did I. Who held the title to the Charger?

Benjamin backed into the driveway as he had the Saturday before but didn't get out. I could see him but not hear him. That bugged me. I made a note on my scratch pad to transfer the sensitive directional microphone to my ready kit, a backpack more often seen on the floor of my small SUV than on any mountain trails. I'd rescued that sensitive piece of electronics from an Army surplus store.

Another car drove up to the house a few minutes later. I couldn't tell if it was the Buick or some other General Motors boat, the light was that bad, plus I was distracted by the opening of the garage door which began just before the boat turned into the driveway.

A large SUV occupied the garage alongside enough *stuff* to guarantee that not much more than a couple of bicycles could join it. The GM boat parked, stopping even with the Charger. Distracted by the garage door, I'd missed the license plate.

Whoever exited the GM boat – short, maybe five-six, dark pants or jeans, short dark hair – disappeared inside the garage. Benjamin remained in the driver's seat of the Charger – he hadn't even dropped down the driver's window to say hello, as far as I could tell.

Chapter 47

Friday

The EaseDropper III's app spat the thump of a closing door into my Bluetooth ear, then two distinct voices. Men? Sure. Sounded like it. I could make out most of what they said in real time. Later, back at my computer, the digital audio enhancing software cleaned up the background junk and confirmed the sex and the words I'd missed.

"Hey, Jeff, what's up with the schedule?" The first voice was a little thin and a little high, but figured to be a man's.

"What? What are you doing here?" The second voice was a baritone but cracking like under stress, its vocal cords strung too tight or its lungs about to witness a heart attack. Maybe a smoker.

"It's Friday. It's my house after sunset."

[*Jeff*] "Drew, you're pulling my leg."

[*Drew*] "Look at the window. Look at your watch."

[*Jeff*] "So it's late on Thursday. What are you doing here?"

[*Drew*] "It's Friday. Did you look at your watch."

[*Jeff*] "Oh, shit. Major trouble. I must have passed out."

[*Drew*] "For like twenty-four hours?"

[Jeff] "Dumb, huh. I shouldn't be surprised. Done it before, but long time ago."

[Drew] "You do the diabetic coma thing, maybe?"

[Jeff] "Hell if I know. You seen Thumper?"

[Drew] "I just walked in. Only one other unoccupied car on the premises is yours, in the garage."

[Jeff] "I don't have my glucometer, but like you've got to be shitting me – a cruel joke. It's not Friday." The baritone was shouting, voice cracking every other word. "I woke up about thirty minutes ago. Took a quick shower. Was sitting here, my head uneasy and hungry."

[Drew] "Well, I'm not joking. Neither is Ben. He's parked in the driveway. You know how skittish he is about being seen, *by anyone.*"

[Jeff] "Can you buy me some time, like maybe an hour? Let me get my stuff together and drive out while you guys are gone somewhere? You could go eat."

[Drew] "You don't think Ben can keep up with his meals? He's on a tight schedule, like always. I'll send him for a drive to I-45 and back, then help you get your stuff in the SUV."

[Jeff] "I am so tired. You've got to believe me. I didn't do this on purpose."

[Drew] "Fine. Let's get you out of here as quick as possible, on purpose."

[Jeff] "Yeah. Yeah, okay."

Drew's reply at that point was muffled and distant. I figured he had headed to the other side of the house. His voice got lost in a dead coverage spot between the kitchen and the master bedroom.

It didn't matter. I had more information that I could digest. Ben was meeting a guy? Maybe they were expecting two chicks in a little while. Or maybe they were both going to do the skinny blonde?

The EaseDropper worked like a charm – in the kitchen. I must have screwed up the setup of the master bedroom 'mitter. I never did get a peep out of that one. The next sounds I heard were exit timing instructions from Drew to Jeff.

A minute later, the driver of the sedan, who I now assumed to be Drew, was outside in the driveway and Benjamin had his window down. Without the directional microphone I could not hear what was said, but an automobile shuffle went down as I watched from down the street.

Maybe twenty-five minutes later, the SUV was gone, the Charger was back in the driveway, and Ben was walking into the open garage where Drew waited, his butt perched on the trunk of the sedan, feet on the bumper. I still didn't get a decent look at Drew's face, even with the help of exquisite binoculars. The garage door opener's light, an unshielded incandescent bulb in the motor housing, threw a glare on the lenses, contrasting the person in pants with deep, dark shadows. And I still could not get a good read on the sedan's license plate in the shadow of its bumper.

Drew hopped down and Ben followed. Drew was shorter than Ben by maybe four inches, but I was guessing. The angle was not good, one man in front of the other in semi-darkness. Even in a white or pale blue long sleeve shirt and probably dark gray slacks viewed through binoculars, one thing was clear: Drew was either undernourished or very slight in the frame department.

I gave EaseDropper III a pat, anxious for the next installment. None came. Three microphones, two silent. They either had some serious business or the evening had been a bust for both of them. The sounds transmitted from the kitchen mike held little information other than the use of the sink, refrigerator, and ice maker. I heard nothing from the master bedroom nor the live-in room. Maybe that mike was bad, too, even though it showed it logged on and synchronized on the software.

When Ben left ninety minutes later, exiting the front door, Drew stayed inside, foiling another face look. I followed the Charger. Ben drove to Seafood in the Oaks up on Clear Lake City Blvd., where he was inside for an hour, and then on home. He didn't enter or leave carrying anything other than maybe five 8.5X11 pages folded in half, lengthwise. No jacket; no briefcase. Those sheets could have been advertising flyers or sales reports or pick-em sheets for a pool on the NBA playoffs.

So what went on at the house on Helm? A meeting? Ninety minutes would work for that. Sex? Well, not unless Ben Franklin was bisexual. Of course, I could not say for sure that the stringy blonde was not inside. If she had been, well, then Drew might be their photographer, sex partner in *ménage a trois*, or manager – or boss. What the hell went on in that house?

< >   < >

As I drove home, I cussed myself out: how arrogant I had been to assume I could figure out if-how-and/or-why Benjamin Franklin was siphoning off money from the restaurants. The CPA auditor types had suspicions but did not document any specific red flags.

After a week's work, the only new information I had dug up was two guys, Jeff and Drew, and Jeff was evidently not affiliated with Ben. Without an accomplice, an inside man to spy for me, to feed the real skinny to my hungry ears, I was lost, powerless, ineffective. Given the nature of the help in the restaurant business, even the FBI would play hell planting someone believable and effective who wouldn't appear out of place, or screw up and blow their cover. What I needed was a transmitter around Ben's neck. Like that would happen.

I got back on the Gumshoe loop when I arrived at the house in Seabrook. Too many surprises and contradictions bounced around inside my cranial space. That hurt. Brain matter may be a bit too soft at times but the walls of their house are hard as bone, ricochets instantaneous.

I posted three different *calls for help*, with a two-sentence description of my confusion, over a twenty minute period. No takers. It was clear I was the only investigator on the planet who wasn't married and happy or out on the town on Friday night.

I settled for a bar – not your local tavern, but a dark, slender rectangle of 70% cocoa. Ate the whole thing.

Chapter 48

Saturday

When I woke up Saturday morning, I had one large headache of a decision to make. Did I tell Candice about the other guys on Helm street or did I sit on it until I had more information? By the time I'd finished breakfast, I had decided on more information, at least enough to be clear as to the other two guys' purpose. That would give her a deeper understanding that could cushion the strange news about the house being used by reservation only.

Halfway through my second cup of coffee, my cell rang.

"What do you have for me, Mr. Trench?"

"I'm. Not. Sure."

"You're the investigator. The detective. You're supposed to be great at analyzing data, information, and such. I'm paying you five thousand a week. It's been over a week. I've paid you for two. What have you got?"

While mustering up my courage to deal with Candice, in the middle of a very deep breath, I received a gift, an inspiration. "I had quite a surprise last night."

"A surprise?"

"Yes."

"What kind of surprise."

"Ahh, well... did you know other folks are using that house –"

Her gasp was so loud it interrupted me. She *didn't* know.

"At least two men," I said, feeling a bit of the power ebb my way across the balance beam. "Watched them coming and going last night."

She didn't reply.

"Candice, are you there?"

Another moment, then, "Yes – I was interrupted. Go on."

Like I believed her.

"Ma'am, you never saw anyone else there, just Ben and the stringy blonde?"

"Maybe a yard crew in the middle of one week...."

"Well, here's what I saw. Yesterday evening Ben was there for maybe two hours, and another man left just after Ben *arrived*. That man's car, an SUV, was inside the garage, door closed, when I arrived, Ben arriving shortly after me."

"Oh."

"Even more interesting... another gentleman showed up shortly after Ben's arrival. That guy was there the whole time Ben was and did not leave when Ben did."

"How was he dressed?" She sounded surprised, her tone replete with things vicious.

"Which one?"

"Both."

Women! Clothes are always the thing. "It was dark out. I was using binoculars from three houses down, across the street, so I can't tell you much about the quality. Colors are always off in weak incandescent lighting."

"Yes, yes. Go on."

"The one that left, he wore a suit coat and lugged a soft-sided duffel bag."

"Color?"

"The bag?" I thought to be mindful when accepting future clients as to whether they allowed me to finish a paragraph without interrupting.

She coughed, one of those polite ones they teach in finishing school. "His coat."

"Dark. Could have been a black, navy, dark green blazer. I don't know."

"So you don't really know."

"That *is* what I said, Candice."

"The other one?"

"No coat. Long sleeves, a dress shirt, maybe white. Could have been light blue or green. Slacks, not jeans or Dockers. Dress shoes." Did I really remember his shoes?

"Okay, what do you make of the two of them? You were going to install listening equipment?"

I knew only maybe a third of that answer. "I don't know exactly what to make of them yet. I'm going to go back over there in a little while and see what's cooking this morning."

"Cute. I pay you to be cute...?" She paused, then, "Tell me what you overheard."

One minute she'd be crass and pushy – arrogant. The next, sarcastic. Did she forget her medication?

My turn. "I didn't mean I was going to go over and see what everyone had for breakfast."

"Never mind that. Ben's in the restaurant business."

"But, he doesn't serve breakfast."

"Mr. Trench!"

"Okay, sorry. Let me get organized here so I can get back over there before ten. Maybe by Monday morning, after two or three more visits, I'll have a better idea of what's going on at the house on Helm Street." I half hoped no one would be there so I could check the EaseDropper wireless microphones, but that would have to be later.

"You need to have that idea by two tomorrow afternoon."

It had worked. She'd attacked my silliness and forgotten I hadn't told her what I'd heard. And I did not have to disclose the two mikes' not transmitting.

"I do?"

"Yes. We're going to have ice cream at Marble Slab again – and do it right."

I wanted to back her off the master-slave, queen-indentured servant thing but decided I wanted the Franklins.

"Right. Could we make it half past two?"

"Men!"

One of the nice things about cell phones is that the party on the other end of the call can't slam the receiver down in its cradle, can't send you an audible indication of their evaluation of your conversation.

Chapter 49

Saturday

After a quick shower, I located the high gain directional microphone, packed it and myself off to Rent-A-Wreck to exchange rides. I drove out turning the wheel of an old Plymouth Voyager with captains chairs. My hamstrings and back would be much happier at the end of that afternoon's surveillance.

I parked east and on the opposite side of the street from Ben's love nest, driver's window down, ready to bring up the microphone should the skinny blonde follow Ben out again. She could plant another goodbye kiss....

I'd also upped the ante another way: a wig of short mangled rusty locks, a flannel lumberjack shirt with the long sleeves cut off at the elbow, and painter's jeans. I had the microphone in my lap, my cell phone in one hand and a city map in the other, forearms resting on the steering wheel. Anybody strolling by should conclude I was a directionally-challenged journeyman.

The Charger drove past me and backed into the driveway about a quarter to ten. Ben entered through the front door, after knocking and waiting for maybe half a minute. It appeared he didn't have his own key. Strange or not?

Shortly after the front door closed, I kicked my ass. I didn't have my 12X zoom digicam. What good was daylight surveillance without a camera? Heck, the Franklin case could end up being a divorce nightmare or bankruptcy quagmire.

The digital video camera was technology's gift to the husband-tailing private investigator. No one could argue with the participants or dates. The folks in the video were known and locations were native to image. Dates and times displayed in real time. What more could a court ask for?

The audio. Did I need a sidekick?

Although Candice had not asked me to verify that her husband was cheating on her, it would make her lawyer's presentation to a judge or jury much more credible. My camera had that "no jiggle" feature which made it a lot less tiring to watch for long stretches.

I didn't hear anything for maybe an hour. One microphone working, two down, was costing me. Big time.

Then, footsteps, sounded like, and, "Yesterday, my damn manager in Friendswood threatened to walk across the street. Said Antonio Donatello offered him another grand a month."

It was Ben. I'd only heard him speak a few words at Charlie's the Saturday before, but his timber was there, unmistakable, even with the microphone using a window pane as a diaphragm. Whoever Ben was talking to had to be in another room. The replying speech was probably male but unintelligible.

As the rest of Ben's visit continued, he was the only one I heard. I didn't even know if that guy Drew was there. The garage door was closed.

Here's a transcript of what I heard Ben say:

"After all I've done for that guy, damn him. How many employers make an employee's bail?"

"No, I better get going. You leaving soon?"

"Okay, see ya."

The front door opened and Ben walked out... by himself. I felt cheated. With no sex life of my own, I had been rooting for Super Ben to get his goodbye kiss from the runway-model's-figure stringy blonde.

I followed the Charger, giving it lots of room. I wasn't afraid of losing him as I'd developed a real-time feel for the locations of Ben's restaurants – and the traffic routes to them through Webster, Clear Lake City, Seabrook, Clear Lake Shores, League City, and Friendswood. That may sound like a lot of territory and the area was home to maybe a quarter million folks back then. Houston had grown right through the small incorporated areas (some over a hundred years old) and had annexed Clear Lake City before the residential development in Harris County could organize an election on incorporation. Ben's restaurants' market area was less than a third the size of Lubbock, Texas, but without all that red dust. His had a small lake in the middle of it.

Ben first visited Bayou Grill, then worked lunch at Charlie's again. I perched down Highway 3 for almost ninety minutes, too far to use the directional microphone when Ben walked out to the Charger, cell in his ear. Since his stride was gentle, I figured the bald crazy guy had not dropped by for a visit.

Ben drove off west on NASA Pkwy., a route that would take him to Hurricane Alley, or Michelle's in Friendswood. I gave him lots of room.

I gave him too much.

Webster has lots of stop lights and slow speed limits.

Yes, I lost him.

The Charger wasn't visible at Hurricane Alley. By the time I arrived at Michelle's, the parking lot held nary a car. Lunch was way over.

< > < >

Fry's. Fry's. Fry's.

I needed two more wireless microphones.

They had three left. I bought them all after telling the staff about the problem. Guesses included a large mirror in the living room blocking/reflecting/absorbing the signals from the back..

I called it an afternoon and drove to Wally World.

Chapter 50

Saturday

Wally World is a strange place to get sentimental, but seeing all those little girls dresses across the main aisle as I rounded the corner from the coffee shelves gave me pause. I wanted to wander over and reminisce but didn't want to get arrested as some kind of weirdo. That Super Walmart was very new, had cameras everywhere. You could even watch yourself enter and exit on a monitor hanging way down from the high ceiling. As much as it cost to hang the thing, I figured the flat panel was there to intimidate, not as an information service. They must have a mean group of lawyers in Arkansas.

I mustered some courage and crossed the wide aisle, saw a dress in Kara's favorite color, lime green. She loved her dresses and ribbons and bows.

I was saved from busting into tears when a girl of about four said, "You seen my mommy, mister?"

I hadn't but her query encouraged me to use my investigator's expertise to help. "No, honey. Do you remember what she was wearing today?"

The little girl's hands were on her hips and she twisted them hard left and right like she was working a hula hoop or something, then said. "She has a hat on."

"Is it a pretty hat?" I said as I dropped down on my heels to meet her eyes.

"Mommy wears baseball hats," came punctuated with a firm, long up and down nod.

"What color is today's hat?"

"Need find Mommy."

"Yes, I will help you find your mommy."

"Now."

"Now? Why, darling?"

"Because potty." The hips' twisting took on new meaning.

"Let's find one of those red phones and call you some help, okay?"

"Red? Mine is yellow."

"Yes, honey. What's your name? I'm Mr. Trench."

"Mommy told me never to talk to strangers."

I had crossed some programmed protocol and was trying to think what to do to cross back to the other side when she literally flew up off the cement floor.

My eyes followed her up.

"Sorry! Brittany wanders."

The little doll of a girl swayed and wiggled inside the right arm of a tallish, late-twenties woman in a powder blue tank top, faded black jeans tighter than many leotards in all the right places, and an Astros baseball cap.

"No problem," I said as my knees creaked up out of the crouch. "I was, err – she wanted me to find her mommy... potty time."

"You look like I'm gonna call the police," she said. "She tell you she couldn't talk to strangers?"

I guess I had kind of a sheepish look on my face. "Yes – after she told me to find you and she needed go potty."

The woman laughed, took off her hat to reveal hair just a tad longer than Sinead O'Connor's when that wonderful singer made it big. She slapped the Astros across her thigh and laughed again. "You must be all right. Brittany doesn't usually talk to anyone."

A warmth blossomed in my cheeks. Kara was still with me.

< >   < >

Whatever happened to my fun, leisurely weekends?

Oh, yeah, Mrs. Candice Franklin happened.

Saturday evening I wanted to dump the Franklin case in favor of the NBA playoffs. The first round was just underway, ushering in two months of intense pro basketball.

And it's darn difficult to watch television while on stake out.

I needed a break from nine straight days of whatever was going on with the Franklins.

Chaos?

Mass deception?

And I needed to get out, go to Helm street and replace the two EaseDropper III's microphones that didn't work.

But maybe things were way too busy on Helm on Saturday nights – lots of parties and family visiting, car after car coming and going, watching my every move.

Getting caught would be a very bad idea.

I knew I'd lucked out with the installation – someone was in the house and didn't hear me. Could I be that lucky again?

Besides, it wasn't like a murder would take place if I didn't figure out what was up with the whole case by Sunday morning. Or could things escalate on short notice?

I really didn't know what was going on.

I really didn't know what was going on.

And I wished Benjamin Franklin's activities were more along the lines of my verifying he really was in the lab burning midnight oil inventing bifocal lenses and investigating lightning, not conducting clandestine rendezvous in a residential neighborhood.

The billable hours, the cash money were super. Yet there was something about Candice Franklin and her life that put upholstery staples in my coleslaw. Did I need a new staple gun?

Chapter 51

Saturday

I padded over to my coin change dish to fetch an executive decision maker to tell me what I should do next. Z10 had other ideas.

ID showed Spring's number. How angry was I with her?

What if her mother had confiscated her phone, found my number in Spring's call log.

What if it was Mrs. Franklin using Spring's phone to chew my ass raw?

I tapped SEND and held the phone away from my ear. "Trench Coat Investigations."

"Mr. Trench. Mr. Trench."

Not Mrs. Franklin.

"Mr. Trench!"

"You got it right all three times. So, Miss No Show, what 's up?"

"I have got to see you. Talk to you. Meet you."

"And the reason I should stop what I am doing on a Saturday evening to meet with an unreliable teenager is…?"

"I am totally sorry. Totally."

"Heard that before."

"But I have awesome reasons."

Awesome was the most overused word in the language back then.

"And I have awesome reasons – two precisely – for denying your request."

"Please. You gotta listen to me. You gotta. We gotta meet."

"Reasons. Reasons. Clear ones. Give me two *reasons*, Miss Spring."

She didn't respond immediately. Surprise – not.

"I, uhhh, have a story. Takes a while to tell. You will be my B.M.F.F. once I've told you."

"B.M.F.F.? Is that a company like AMF, the bowling folks?"

She laughed for just one beat, then said, "No, seriously. Best Male Friend Forever."

I didn't really want to deal with her. I had her mother and father standing in the way of the NBA playoffs. She could wipe out the whole playoffs.

Kara tickled my mind, told Great Guy Nate to give Spring one more try. "In half an hour. Where?"

"Oh, thank you. Thank you. Crazy cool."

"Where, Spring?"

< >   < >

Spring picked a place I never go in the evenings: Denny's. And she picked the location on I-45 beside Baybrook Mall. It needed a parking lot lighting makeover.

I was early. Got us a booth.

And she was on time. "Hello, Mr. Nate Trench, sir," she said, hand outstretched.

"Sit down, Spring. You better have lots to tell me."

"I do but can't stay long. Don't want to be seen with you."

A guy always wanted to hear that from a pretty girl.

"And why is that?" I said."

"My tribe would figure you for my dealer or a perv. I don't do either."

I didn't reply right away. I had no idea what I was dealing with.

Spring looked honest as the driven snow and wild at the same time. She lacked tear stains, but her eyes were bloodshot. Hadn't jumped right into her story, yet was telling me she couldn't stay long. Nervous or pure teenager?

"Okay, Spring, how long is 'can't stay long' – give me a number. Use minutes."

"Mom said you were a geek."

"What's your answer?"

"I dunno – well, I do but don't want to say."

"Start now. Maybe you'll like it here," I said, not sure where the words came from. I had no guess as to what she had to say – but I sure wanted to hear it.

< >   < >

Spring fidgeted with the menu for a minute, then excused herself to the bathroom. I ordered for us. I don't remember what I had, but Spring had a milk shake. Chocolate with extra cherries.

When she returned her energy seemed off, her posture not as sure.

I called her on it. "What's the matter? You the same Springy girl I saw head on over to the bathroom? You're not an android replacement are you?"

She smiled just a bit, said, "No. It's me. It's just… what I have to say, is, ahhh, not so loyal."

To whom?

"Okay, you're ratting on someone, is that it? Who?"

"A parent."

That I wasn't expecting – typical for The Franklins case.

"Okay, which one?"

She slid out of the booth, purse in hand, and scooted out the door.

Chapter 52

Sunday

I'd woke up Sunday thinking that the one person sure to pay an early visit to the morgue over the Franklin case was... me.

I padded around not doing much of anything. Arising at seven leaves a lot of hours to dread meeting a client for ice cream at two in the afternoon.

I did break the spell, though. I leapt over a fear. Well, I got up the heart to go shopping for a replacement for Trixter, the half terrier–half undetermined that had romped up and down the boat channel behind my house for three years. Poor fella contracted some mutant heart worm or something. Me and the vet had put him down just before Halloween the year before. Anybody that'll tell you there's no grieving period over the death of a pet is just plain cold.

One of the local Friends of Animals organizations had an orphan roundup at a pet supply store up on Bay Area, just a few doors down the strip center from Ben Franklin's Bayou Grill called home. I'd be able to kill one bird and open a heart.

After first my thinking was golden retriever. Then I remembered my friend Reggie had owned a golden that grew to weigh over ninety pounds. Any dog I got would have to fit through the doggie door I'd already installed, so I downsized to another terrier mix, another male, maybe six months old and showing hints of greyhound, with collie in his coat.

The teenager who had served Zip as foster parent during his screening period explained that he'd not lived up to his name. He had been so calm, so well behaved, her mother had allowed the spry lad inside. He did not disappoint.

That was good enough for me. I found out within the hour that the young fella was indeed well behaved. Zip hopped right up into the Forester, joining me for a stakeout of the Bayou Grill. No complaints, no whining, no hopping around. He did like the panoramic view from the Forester's front passenger seat.

While I was busy watching the front door, Zip spied something around the side of the strip center, getting my attention by tossing his snout in the direction of his suspicions.

I turned the Forester right out the driveway by Jack-in-the-Box and immediately turned right up the next driveway into the parking lot for two stores, yuppie bicycles and hardware.

We soon had a clear view of the side of the building down from Bayou Grill. A burly black motorcycle sat parked underneath a squarish small window. Zip and I watched a hand reach out over and over again, delivering one small package after another to a leather-jacketed guy's waiting hand. The packages, the size of a cream of wheat box, were then tossed into the biker's stout sidecar.

I keyed good old 911, then sat back to watch the fun with Zip, scratching behind his ears. What a welcome to the profession.

A Harris County Constable was there in two minutes. Slow day? An HPD unit with two officers came around from the back of the building. The biker quickly comprehended the jig was up.

Chapter 53

Sunday

Zip smelled Trixter, despite the new dog bed and such, sticking his nose under and behind things looking for *that other dog* the rest of the day. I'd had the carpet professionally shampooed since Trixter went to canine heaven, so I figured I had acquired a smart dog with a great nose, all for under a hundred dollars, American.

I had tossed or given away all Trixter's doggie paraphernalia, so making Zip right at home would require a trip to Sam's and a second trip to the pet store. They knew I'd be back, you bet. Why else give so much space to the Friends of Animals?

I got the little fella anchored to a back patio support with a length of chain short of the water. He wasn't too happy with the chain but I didn't want to trust him inside the house without my supervision just yet. I hated to leave all that intelligence and enthusiasm but the lady who owed me five thousand dollars a week wanted to see me at the ice cream parlor.

< > < >

Prompt as usual, I secured the rearmost table where we'd had so much fun the week before by placing my Day Runner on it. I wanted some blueberry cheesecake ice cream but they were out so I went for amaretto, in a small sugar cone. Those big cones come with two steep prices: money and calories.

I had eaten my way to almost the bottom of amarettoville when Candice made her entrance. She saw me but took her time getting to the rear of the store, feigning inspecting flavors and such.

"Good afternoon, Mr. Trench."

Taking my cue from some movie, figuring to model my behavior after that of an English gentleman at afternoon tea, I rose and said, "A pleasure as always, Mrs. Franklin."

"Oh, please, call me Candice."

She was back to that – again?

"What flavor have you decided on?" I said.

"I think I'll splurge with a banana split. I didn't see it on the menu but surely they have some bananas?"

They did.

We chatted briefly about nothing I can recall, then sat in silence as Candice consumed a thousand calories in a ladylike fashion.

I didn't care much for the wait. It gave too much time for me to entertain my fears, fears of what she might have up her sleeve – and, yes, she was wearing a long sleeve blouse with frilly cuffs that matched a frilly collar. Don't ask me about the skirt or shoes. I don't recall.

She finally sat back and dabbed her mouth with a napkin one last time, then said, "They know how to put robust flavors in their ice cream, don't you think?"

What could I do but agree. "Yes. I hope they stay open forever."

"Spring likes Marble Slab, too."

Her daughter! I said, "How exactly is Spring today?"

"I haven't seen her much in the last week or so. Not sure what she's got herself into – not sure what boy she's got into her, but, that age, you just can't put your foot down like you could when they were eight or nine."

I managed not to have a Kara moment. "She's what, eighteen?"

"Yes, just turned. A senior."

"She dating high school or college boys?"

"You do know a few things, I see. I have forbidden the college ones, but that doesn't mean they can't fool me with a young face."

"You meet each date before they go out?"

"Oh, I was wrong to compliment you. That sort of *screening* went out with the dark ages. My parents had that protocol but, Spring, well... she's got a strong will. She says she's going on a group date and leaves."

"Like her mother's will?"

"Is that flattery or angst, Mr. Trench?"

I wasn't sure. "You choose. It's a lovely day." I said that? I did. Chills like fingernails on a chalkboard coursed through my knees.

"That it is. And its probably time I told you why I wanted to meet, meet at all, and here in particular."

I nodded, smiled briefly, sat back, crossed my arms – then remembered that was body language for closing the gate, so I scooted my chair in a little and placed my forearms on the table, smiled again.

Chapter 54

Sunday

She said, "I think we should not worry so much about abiding by the letter of the law when I have such a strong intuition that something is rotten with my husband."

There. She'd said it. Again.

"Perhaps you have some particulars at this point?"

"You know, of course, my feelings about a wireless transmitter on a car."

"Yes – I have yours in the Forester. In the ash tray. You planning on having that same operative place one on the Charger?"

"I bought three. Perhaps you'll find a use for them?"

I wanted to respond but the English gentleman in me precluded such a dispersal of venom.

"Mr. Trench, those devices could almost replace you. My boyfrahn –" She stumbled on the word. Coughed. It came out sounding real close to "boyfriend." I was sure of it.

I sat still but elevated system readiness to high alert.

She coughed again – the one they teach in finishing school. "I understand they can be monitored from my cell phone." With that, she pulled out a Samsung Galaxy S3 or 4, I think, slim with a gorgeous display. A girl phone. Lots of toys. Features they called them. Definitely not a Z10.

"You've got a lot of power in your hand," I said, "way more than the Apollo had on the first trip to the moon."

That left her dumbfounded. For a split second her jaw remained fallen. Her recovery was soon pristine, however. "You... don't say?"

"Oh, I do say. Amazing what's inside there."

"Yes, I thought the opening logo quite fancy. If I have a transmitter on Ben's Charger like I had on your Forester, my mobile logs whatever location you stop at for more than a three or four minutes – I forget what I set it at."

Did the boyfriend who planted the transmitter on me have an important role, a mission in Candice's plan? Did he maybe want in on the kill for financial gain or was Candice using him like she might be doing with everyone?

And why did she make such a fuss out of my acting like a date the Sunday before, there at Marble Slab?

Each piece of new information in the Franklin case brought with it four or five new questions.

"Mr. Trench. Hello? You see what I mean?"

I hadn't responded.

"I know precisely what you mean," Candice. "No matter, government at several levels calls attaching that transmitter as invasion of privacy. The only ones who can place those at will on vehicles or in briefcases and backpacks and such are the local police and sheriffs – they need a warrant – and the Feds who don't. FBI. CIA. DHS. ATF. Not hardly ever since 9-11.

"The 2001 Patriot Act is alive and well – and still doesn't empower distraught wives."

"It should." She hadn't let a beat go by.

Where could I go with that? "Let's just say we agree to disagree."

Her turn to go mute.

I waited a good three minutes, then said, "Mrs. Franklin, even with the monitor, we don't have much. The overhead of those college kids won't come to much more than those devices, the good kind, anyway. What I am tracking him for and what those college kids can do is watch what he brings in and out of those restaurants and wherever else he stops. Banks. Bars. Houses. Mini warehouses. Stock brokerages. Whatever. Your gems of technology just beep the coordinates obtained from the GPS satellite. Nothing more."

Silence by Candice continued.

"The transmitter won't know if he just stopped to buy a newspaper, talk to someone in another parked car, or gone inside a business for just a moment or two."

"They say they can plot within a few yards."

"You're not listening."

She looked angered – then depressed, for just the briefest fraction of time, then jumped up out of her chair and thumped the small, short pedestal table with the heel of her hand. "I want this to get figured out now! Yesterday would be better. Do Y-O-U hear me, Mr. Trench?"

I stood, took a slow, deep breath before saying, "And, Candice, I too want this figured out yesterday. I most certainly do. And here's why: the quicker I figure this out, the better my reputation becomes, the deeper my future customer base. You're a businesswoman. You get this, I'm sure."

"Yes." She sat back down, the look on her face one I couldn't translate.

I sat back down, too, wondered what had happened to the snooty woman who had said she had enough money to pay me through August. A couple Fridays back, she hadn't sounded like someone who needed instant gratification. All business. All about the money.

Maybe she most wanted the answer to my search to agree with her opinion, or did she have a timeline she hadn't shared, one whose deadline was drawing near. I didn't know. And I didn't like not knowing.

What had changed? What had happened in nine days?

A moment of silence later, her countenance morphed into a new person. Was I in store for a third Mrs. Candice Franklin?

"Mr. Trench, I'm afraid I haven't been altogether truthful with you."

Bingo.

"Candice, I'm all ears."

Chapter 55

Sunday

"Ben is not the only one with a lover."

There it was.

I counted to three, said, "Given what I've learned so far, Mrs. Franklin –"

"Candice, please. Candice."

"Okay... Candice..." I stopped, dropped my head and shoulders just a notch, attempting a visual display of understanding and compassion, "given the stringy blonde, I get it. Go on."

"Thank you, Mr. Trench."

I gave her a moment, then said, " Thanks for telling me. So, Candice, where does all this leave us? "

"Are you going to want to speak with him? Do you need a data page on him, too?"

"Your boyfriend –"

"Lover."

"Right. Lover. I don't think I need to talk with him right now..., unless he has material information or some direct connection to the restaurants."

"Certainly not."

An escort service would be paid to not have any information...

"You can work up a sheet if you want to."

"No, he's fine just where he is. You see, last weekend..."

I waited a good two minutes, before she said, "Last weekend, I was saying, we'd had a fight, Saturday evening. I told him I had hired you. He didn't approve. That's why I was so... melancholy...."

"You told your boyfriend – lover – that you hired me."

"Yes."

"And that's why you were a bit 'off' here at Marble Slab."

"You understand....then."

"Yes, Candice. Yes I do."

"That's all I wanted to cover today. The transmitters and... my... apology."

"Thank you. We're fine."

She sat in sort of a fidgeted state, twisting in the chair, crossing and recrossing her legs. Seemed like this went on for several minutes.

I pulled out the Z10 and checked my e-mail. Maybe somebody from the Gumshoe loop had been having a rip-roaring Sunday afternoon and taken pity on me. There were three Gummy entries but the subject lines weren't mine. I looked back up at my client.

"You okay, Candice?"

"Yes. I think so. Do you have anything you want to bring up, Mr. Trench?"

"Yes." I presented my next advance billing and the first week's expenses as two separate invoices.

She nodded. Opened her purse, pulled out a small bundle of cash than last time but it was all Franklins. She turned toward the wall to hide what she was doing, then counted out ten faster than I could have imagined possible.

My stomach relaxed. Expenses reimbursed. I was in business for another week.

Chapter 56

Sunday

I walked out to the Forester wondering if Zip was already suffering doggie abandonment. Then there was the matter of the NBA playoffs. I realized I'd neglected to ask that nice teenager if Zip liked to watch sports. I would soon find out first hand.

Or would I? The Helm house needed two working wireless microphones.

The Forester was right where I left it and started right up, as always. And, as always, I couldn't resist checking my e-mail. The Z10 told me one of the Gumshoes had a couple of questions. I headed over to my office and got online. Smartphones are darn convenient but full-size keyboards are the only way to type.

I found the gentleman and moved our conversation off in a chat room. He let me update him on The Franklin Case before bopping me up side the head, cybernetically, of course. This transcript picks up where the chat got interesting:

islandgenius > you check the plate on that sedan, the one that stayed Friday evening at the house

Sometimes I (*lakesleuth*) am just so stupid!

islandgenius > you did copy it down?

lakesleuth > okay, I forgot to copy it from photos

islandgenius > did you ever sit your client down and grill her?

lakesleuth > she would never sit still for that

islandgenius > 'bout time you sit her down

lakesleuth > I hear you – you mean sit her down, not ....

islandgenius > you broke or something? need work at any cost?

lakesleuth > she paying $5k / wk plus $1k expenses / wk

islandgenius > sold your soul – at least you got a good price LOL

lakesleuth > first big out -of-the-office job – investigation

islandgenius > the hubby is having too much fun "outside"?

lakesleuth > maybe not – just found out the wife/client has boyfriend

islandgenius > great. And she's paying how?

lakesleuth > in cash

islandgenius > where's she getting cash – she stays at home, no?

The bills were not new. Not moldy. Gently used. Damn. I had no idea.

islandgenius > jealous, I am – you don't need my help; you hold seminar, tell rest of us how to pull that off, okay?

lakesleuth > get out!

islandgenius > get the plate; check back if surprised; e-mail to this screen name c/o the co-op. things slow in Hawaii – just way I like

He sure knew how to hurt a guy. And I deserved it. I didn't follow my own protocols. I didn't do the detail shit work like I learned in the NSG. He bit my ass. I had it coming – for the second time on the Franklin case. When was I going to learn? Don't let the client manage the investigation.

I couldn't decide if I should punish myself by *not* watching the NBA playoffs or by cleaning out my boat. I'd let Zip decide.

He did. One day maybe he'd take a liking to resting beside my chair while I watched the games. That afternoon, though, Zip came off that chain with more energy than an howitzer.

Just as I was finishing up swabbing out Sailor's Skiff, Jimmy J.R.B. came over from next door and introduced himself to Zip. Their instant friendship was aided by the ham bone Jimmy had brought with him. Zip endured the full measure of a big man's teasing ways before earning the bone with three successive full-body rollovers on the grass.

Chapter 57

Sunday

Early Sunday evening found me working with my notebook computer out at the picnic table while Zip sniffed everything including me from stem to stern. In between happy moments with my new dog, I searched the web for any activity, any commercial information on Shrimp-Steak, Inc. How was business last year? The year before? Was it for sale? Did it owe anyone?

Nothing I didn't already know.

How about Lake City Catering, Inc.? Only the Texas Attorney General acknowledged the living existence of that corporation.

I had yet to run S-S by Mrs. Candice Franklin, never mind Lake City Catering. Dumb and dumber. Maybe I wasn't cut out for long-term projects. Just the hit 'em and dump it jobs on the internet for the skip trace market.

You'd think I could handle such a situation. I'd sure done a lot of managing in the Navy, especially the last five years. That's what Chief Petty Officers do. I retired a Senior Chief Petty Officer. I'd seen what NSA and NSG could have fun with. I wanted a piece of all that computer accessible knowledge fun for myself.

The problem turned out to be that my adopted "retirement" home was the largest, water-connected United States city without a U. S. Navy installation. Coast Guard, yes. Navy – the guys with big guns and big boats – only ship around is the retired Battleship Texas, on display in a wet dock just up the road in La Porte.

I went looking for the report on the license plate of the Lake City Catering van. I was sure I had sent my request in... Friday. Yes, there it was. And days and nights and it was Sunday evening. It ought to be in. It... wasn't. No message from the sysop. No "record not available." Nothing.

I thought about taking Zip out in the boat. It was too dark to try that on a new dog, I decided. Not that he would drown or anything. He'd just be real hard to chase if he hopped out of the boat. Instead, I took him inside and we watched a bit of basketball, playoff style. A Dwight Howard swat of a hopeful jump shot, the NBA's version of "you're not allowed in here," woke me up to an explanation on the lack of reply on the plate of the Lake City Catering van: the information had to be blocked by the feds.

Had I stumbled into something bigger than my Texas Investigator's license envisioned? Was the catering van a cover for a covert sting on guys with too much money and no good reason for it? Was Candice a Person of Interest to the alphabet soups in Washington?

Or maybe I was a late addition, Candice having started her campaign against Benjamin by calling in a political favor with her congressman say a year earlier? Maybe the favor was promised but the feds had taken their sweet time checking it out, just now appearing on the scene in the form of Lake City Catering?

Wait. That didn't explain LCC owning the Federal Tax Number that Candice says belongs to Shrimp-Steak, Inc. And wait some more. What if Benjamin Franklin had gone and got sideways with the IRS?

After another couple of minutes, I realized that there was no way that tax seizure stuff could happen without it showing up on my search engines or Candice being served as well – unless she lied about being the president of Shrimp-Steak, Inc. Then, again, S-S was listed for sale outside of Houston. Plus, despite her magnificent performance that afternoon, my guess had it that Candice was still holding back information of one sort or another. I'd bet on it.

Or – the exhausteds hit me right then. Call it brain overload if you want, a simple case morphed my mind to zombie status –

Ben Franklin's activities were turning out to be a goofy mess: nobody had been shot or fired at, no attempted hit and runs, no midnight phone calls, no poison pen letters, not even flaming e-mails.

That I had received or been made aware of.

I showed Zip to his patch of rug on the back porch and was on my way to bed when I remembered the wireless microphones.

Chapter 58

Sunday

I was tired. Darn tired. I was also a Private Investigator with two-thirds of his best chance at new information not in working order.

It was Sunday night. Who does trespassing for a living on Sunday night?

It was Sunday night. Maybe an off-night for stay-overs at the house on Helm Street.

Someone was paying me the big bucks to get the job done.

I parked the Plymouth Voyager two houses down before eleven. No lights on in front nor the side I was looking at. No moon and a shortage of curbed vehicles nearby told me "all systems go." Had to give it a shot.

I put the rest of my blackout gear on, the gloves, the ski mask, the long sleeve black t-shirt.

One foot out of the minivan, the vibrations in my pocket told me my cell was ringing.

I pulled the other foot out and waited for the vibrations to stop. Didn't want the Z10's screen lighting up the neighborhood. Got back in and shielded the phone to check who'd called.

Spring.

What the hell?

I slid the phone back in my pocket. Wished I had a piece of gum.

Why would she call so late on Sunday? She'd ran out on me twenty-four hours earlier. Had to be one unstable teenager – but weren't they all?

A short vibration and I knew she'd left a message.

Should I play it? Should I wait until after my clandestine chore was finished? Should I wait until I got home? I figured she'd trash my nerves no matter what she had to say, so I voted for "either b or c," and exited the Voyager.

< >   < >

I followed the same route around the house, managed to get to the kitchen window without drama. Worthless microphone number one was still there. A quiet single edge razor blade and it was back in my hand. A few seconds to activate and affix its replacement... done. The kitchen window's mike was the only one that had worked, so I snuck back around the side to the oleander bush in front like before, remembering that time I was about to invade the territory of a not-so-shy cat.

My pulse was way too rapid as I got behind the bush. What the hell was bothering me? I'd done the gig before. Maybe it was Spring?

I was about to reach up for the other bad microphone when I heard voices inside. Well, I thought they were inside.

Funny thing. After maybe fifteen unintelligible seconds, the voices stopped.

I waited. I waited some more. I had placed my analog wrist watch in the Focus's console and didn't dare pull my cell out to check the time.

I'd wait a bit longer.

I waited. I worried. I figured the longer I stayed the more likely I'd be discovered – some late-night jogger or woman walking her cat. I also figured I had frozen in place, might not even be able to get up.

I waited. Still no sounds.

I eased up out of my crouch. Creaked would be the better description.

I looked in the window. No luck. And luck. The drapes were drawn. Microphone wouldn't do much good if they stayed that way. Blinds can conduct sound. Heavy drapes with lining, not so much.

Dare I creep over to the front bedroom window and place the little electronic jewel there?

I lowered myself down.

I waited.

I waited.

Some more waiting, then my cell vibrated.

< >   < >

The cell had scared the shit out of me but it also did me a favor: it kicked my ass in gear. If it took ninety seconds longer, how much worse could my chances of getting caught be, late on Sunday evening?

What the hell.

I'd picked up that third wireless microphone at Fry's as a backup. But the creepy-crawlies on my skin told me I'd never be back, for any reason, at least not at night dressed like a ninja warrior.

I had the living room window mike changed out in record time, then checked the base unit. Its LEDs blinked like they were supposed to when I pushed each of the three test buttons.

I then crouched lower and duck walked over the nearly dry grass to the front bedroom window. No wonder I did the living room the first time. I had hell placing the new third mike. It, too, had to be out of direct view. I sure don't know what kind of bush I fought but it had thorns. By the time I got done, it had fewer.

I made it. Even the dull, rattle-trap Voyager seemed warm and cozy as I drove back to Seabrook wondering... had I really heard voices? A conversation?

Maybe their next door neighbor had turned on their television, not realizing how loud their kids had left the volume.

Like I said, I made it out of there and on home to Seabrook, Texas. Life was better. And, yes, I forgot to download data from the base.

< >   < >

I forgot something else. Someone, actually: Spring.

I pulled into Arlan's parking lot, parked under the brightest light, and checked my phone.

Spring had been the second caller as well. Left only the first voice mail:

"I know I'm a little shit. Yeah, I walked last night. A shit. Yeah, I'm sorry. And, yeah, I know, everybody talks that shit. I mean it. I am sorry. Okay, I have issues. I'm a good shit. I am. A damn good shit. You'll see."

Her voice mail didn't indicate she wanted me to call her back, so that was strange. But if she didn't want a call back, why did she call again?

Was she with someone – boyfriend – that wouldn't approve? Or was she under house arrest – Candice keeping close watch on daughter Spring?

I decided to let it ride around in my mind until I got home – if I could still see straight.

Chapter 59

Sunday

No sooner had I let Zip in the house than a knock at my front door scared the shit out of me.

11:45 PM

I decided I was so tired, I had to be hallucinating. Zip agreed. He hadn't barked.

Another knock. No louder. No longer. That time Zip gave a short bark.

Hmmm, maybe I wasn't hallucinating.

I needed to use the bathroom, so I headed toward the hall.

The knock had other ideas. Triple rap. Louder with each. Good rhythm.

I've never had rhythm so I couldn't have managed it. Zip didn't think so either. He gave it three short barks.

I walked to the door, tried the peephole. Those are only good if the outside party has both thumbs twiddling. That one didn't.

If I turned on the porch light, well, that would be admitting I had heard the knock. All the knocker knew was I had a ferocious dog with a high voice.

"Mr. Trench! Mr. Trench!"

"You got to be kidding me," I muttered in a tired yet resigned tone.

I knew immediately why Spring had: (a) said she was a good shit – she had located my residence which was no small feat – and (b) not left a voicemail.

I tried to put on an angry face but was so tired, the muscles just wouldn't cooperate.

With both terror and a sizable physical effort, I opened the door.

Spring rushed right past me saying, "Shut it. Quick. I need to use the bathroom."

Luckily, I had two.

"Hallway to your right; first door on left."

I shut the door, as instructed, then moseyed on over to the left and the master bathroom.

< > < >

"Glad you're up," said Spring, looking up at me from a slightly ducked head. "I didn't want to wake you."

"That's easy to fix," I said, standing at the crossroads of my home, the refrigerator. It stood a few feet from the hallway entrance. "Call any day Monday through Friday during working hours for a daytime appointment – and show up."

"I know. I know. I know."

I said nothing, figuring silence slapped her around worse than almost anything.

"Okay, I'm sorry. I'm three times sorry. You have to believe me."

I wanted to inform her that I didn't *have* to do much of anything in my life at that point – except sleep. I didn't say it or anything else.

"You're not going to let it go?"

I had no idea what "it" was so I continued my impression of a mime, without the hand gestures.

"What did my mother tell you about me?"

I laughed. A short burst, but still a laugh which screwed up everything. Deep inside where Marshmallow Nate lived, I really liked the kid and wanted to help her. I had a conflict, though. I'd spent over twenty in the Nav and I was used to rank having some respect. And my grandpa had been big on "respect your elders." When would be my time?

< >   < >

It took maybe fifteen minutes of silly talk, sports and stuff, before Spring agreed to talk serious.

"So what do you think is up with your folks?" I said, a large glass of ice water in my hand, the cold helping to keep me awake.

"I dunno."

"Then why are you here?"

She went back inside her shell.

I wanted her out of it. "You said something at Denny's – about being disloyal to a parent. That's when you boogied."

"I did what?"

"Left in a hurry."

She didn't answer.

"Disloyal, to whom?" I said, not wanting to let her off the hook. "How?"

"I'm eighteen, finally, but part of me is still a kid. You know?"

I could go there. I said, "Sure. Adults call it 'conflicted.'"

"Okay, good word. They teach us in school or church or wherever to respect parents – unless they're abusive, like that."

"Right. Sure. What about it?"

"Well, what do you do if a parent person is doing illegal stuff."

"Selling crack – smoking weed?"

"You kidder. Everybody tokes the weed."

"Okay, so tell me, what, exactly?"

"Maybe not exactly illegal, but weird."

What other word in the dictionary could have so many hazy connotations? "Pick another word. Some people think I'm weird cause of my buzz cut. Others would think you're weird just 'cause your eighteen – no other reason. Weird is a weird word. We need one that is clearly understood."

She still seemed conflicted.

"Okay, how about, which parent?"

"See, now I feel like I'm not loyal. Like I couldn't possibly love her or –"

Out of the mouth of babes.

"Look, Spring, I was hired by your mom. You know that."

"I think so."

"Do you know what I'm supposed to do?"

"I figured she was looking for money. She values money. But see, she's my real parent. Makes me major disloyal to talk about her like this – that."

"Real parent...?"

"I'm adopted. Well, we're adopted."

"Your mother was married before. Your dad adopted you and your brother."

"No. Dad was a widow-er. First wife died in a car wreck. Young. Way too young."

"Okay, I'm confused. Tell me."

"Dad adopted me and mom adopted Drake. Dad's kid."

I had never heard of such a thing.

"This is really hard for you, then, Spring. I get that right away. And I've got what might be an even tougher question for you, I think."

"Beans are all over the floor. What you wanna know?"

"Do you love them?" I said immediately, hoping for a gut response.

"Both. Sure."

"One more than the other?"

She quit breathing. It was like she became a stone statue for a good minute. Then, "That's where I first got all confused."

I let her talk.

"Mr. Trench, I was like legally adopted before I knew – remember anything. Three years old, plus some months. My *biological* dad cut a deal with Mom where, if he disappeared from our lives, gave up all rights, Mom would let him off the hook for child support and stuff."

"Why did she do that."

"Mom had money, I just figured out just a couple years ago – from an Aunt. Not rich, but we would do mostly okay without his money and he was a real asshole – well, that's her telling it."

"So you might want to meet and talk with him someday."

"Not sure. But maybe, yes."

"Okay, so we went off on this tangent about your biological father when I asked you if you loved one of your parents, Candice and Banjamin, more than the other. What are you saying?"

"Well, it's like, my Mother is my natural Mother but I'm more like her possession daughter."

"She's not good with the motherly warm fuzzies?"

"It's like she could read about what to do in a book, but it never happens for her emotionally. Like she's a Borg or Android robot or something. Like her programming's lacking."

"Okay, so have you told her this is how you feel?"

"I'm sure she knows how I feel but I don't think she *feels* how I feel."

What a mess, huh.

"Okay, Spring, back on track. This is still supposed to be about if you love either Candice or Benjamin Franklin more than the other."

"You are a pain. I don't want to go there."

"I can tell – but we have to. Until you clear this, you're gonna keep running out of Denny's."

And she did.

Chapter 60

Monday

On Monday morning Jim from Rent-A-Wreck stopped by the house to pick up the Plymouth Voyager. Said customer got in town a day early, would e-mail me the bill for the past week. Hell, he had a valid credit card number on file he could tap anytime he wanted to. Nice to work with people like Jim; even nicer to know they're not a dead breed.

I revved up the Forester – loved that turbo – and headed to the downtown office of the Harris County Tax Assessor-Collector's to check their internal records on the LCC van. In Texas, the Tax A-C is the guy who gets the money every year when you renew your license plate, never mind that your license plate's father is the State of Texas Department of Motor Vehicles. Oh, sure, there's a Tax A-C annex in Clear Lake, but those gals knew me. I didn't want to appear totally out of my mind. It also gave me another chance to drop by a certain multi-use building and sneak a look at Reginald Kensington, CPA.

The trip into town on I-45 was uneventful – a not-often treat. Unfortunately, so was my visit to that particular parking garage.

Reginald Kensington, CPA, had not bothered to park the Buick sedan that morning. I gave him a full forty minutes of my time, but he chose to be elsewhere. Web browsing on any smart phone can try one's patience after a while.

The Tax Assessor-Collector's office had been a bust as well – no record available – so I drug my sorry ass back to Clear Lake where I finally settled in my office on El Camino Real at one-thirty, having spent the lunch hour semi-parked on the Gulf Freeway South. They were widening it again, still, and more. Freeway construction never ceases in Houston. Never.

< >   < >

Back in the office, my main computer's flat screen stared back at me, unread. The ghostly presence of the National Security Agency, the spookiest of the Feds, floated about the ether playing with the insecurities in my mind. Hard to fight an adversary you can't see or touch. Damn hard.

The NSA creature was born over half a century back, in the aftermath of World War II and the onset of the Cold War, from the womb of the Black Chamber. It rode the first waves of cyber world, catapulted to prominence by cutting edge electronic and computer engineering. NSA basks in the sun of the Patriot Act, executive orders, and secrecy in the name of National Defense. She goes anywhere and everywhere, enters the most remote of silicon wafers, and extracts whatever she will.

The question: had someone – or any one of the alphabet soup federal agencies, not just NSA – done a cyber morph on Shrimp-Steak, Inc. and/or Lake City Catering, Inc.?

Without attributing the missing data on LCC to an NSA ghost thing, I had no logical concept to explain what the hell was going on, if anything, with Benjamin Franklin. Nor Candice. I'd done a little knocking around looking for interesting info on her – would normally do so before even taking a case – and needed to do more. She had ghostly morphings of her personality, for sure.

I prided myself in solving puzzles quickly. And I liked answers. So much for pride.

Online I checked the LCC van plate again. My request was not even active on their system!

I needed a live Gumshoe to settle my mind.

< >   < >

"Mr. Peterson, you got a minute?", I said through my Bluetooth Headset.

"You got a debit card?" said William Peterson, PhD, MS, MBA.

He and his Half-life Investigations had a national reputation for cyber sleuthing. If you were a fellow investigator, his expertise came with a price. Sometimes it was money, sometimes it was courtesy with several dollops of gratitude, sometimes it was gumshoe leather, and sometimes it was patience. Every once in a while he would jet off on a tangent and *forever* would become defined.

After one investigators' association national conference luncheon, he took off on "American Corporate Security" like a fire-and-brimstone preacher. Twenty minutes later, I was glad I did mostly skip traces.

All his bluster was tempered with true genius.

"I believe you have my card on file," I said.

"Nope," said William. "Destroyed the database. Didn't want the liability."

Also a conservative and a bit data paranoid.

"Okay, I have it right here."

"Keep it warm. I'm not on a jet and I'm not testifying this week. What's up?"

I summarized the Franklin Case to him, keeping names out of it, heading William toward the questionable and incomplete records of the two corporations.

"So, big guy," I said, "what do you figure might explain these missing registrations and such?"

"Little guy, it can only be two things: sneaky lawyer or mob sequestration."

"The mob?"

"Just yankin' your chain."

"Who then?"

"Mexican Mafia."

My prior communications with Peterson had been pretty much black and white. Oh, sure, there had been some iffy conjecture here and there but nothing so crazy.

I said, "Now you're really messin' with me."

"No. I'm trying to help a greenhorn."

"Great. Thanks," I said, meaning the opposite. "How about straight English?"

The connection was almost static free as I awaited his response.

Finally, "You've got an over-active imagination, my young fellow. Seen too many Bourne movies or read Ludlum many late nights."

"Naw. His books are too long. Let's say I'm a retired Navy dumbass. Spell it out."

"What do you think it is?"

Why the hell was he asking me? "Feds."

"Ludlum's on your brain."

"Which more likely?"

"Which?"

I felt like hanging up but you have to coddle the gods from time to time.

"Attorney or Mexicans?"

"Attorney or Mafia."

"What the hell?"

"Both."

"Both?"

"Sure. You asked me, basically, two questions – two situations. One could be a screw-up and the other payola. Dig more. There's got to be a footprint. Look under more rocks. It's impossible to hide all traces of electronic transactions or transfers or large chunks of money. There's a server somewhere that has at least two: the one that conveyed the data – and the one that erased that transaction. You already know all this. Get back to work."

I thanked him for his time, but didn't feel any more settled or confident. There was one positive: he hadn't asked for the sixteen digit number.

< >   < >

Twenty minutes later Lynnette's knock caught me standing at the window staring up at the clouds. I had been visualizing the locations of unturned rocks.

I turned, woke up my smile and said, "You... rang?"

"Did I catch you deep in thought?"

"Oh, I don't get too deep. Not tall enough."

"Are you busy?"

"No. Come in."

She was a bit young and way shy for me – not that I was de facto against dating younger women, but I needed the mental aspects of a relationship. Lynnette and I had never had a fact-finding conversation in the two years she'd been at the front desk. Never been to lunch. Only chatted a couple of time when the power went out.

She had a face I was sure photographers loved and a body that was still A+. I had learned from the building manager that she was a widow with no kids whose first job ever was the one down the hall. She was always on time in the morning and after lunch, even though she had that tendency to leave early, like when Candice snuck in.

"You, ahh... have a good weekend?" she said.

"Maybe. So, now you're interested in my social life?"

"May I sit down?" she said, sheepish as all get out.

Now that was a new request.

Chapter 61

Monday

"Sure," I said as I left the window and resumed my throne, the high back overstuffed leather executive chair, the present from an old girlfriend who said I needed to have a more successful appearance to the walk-in customers.

Lynnette fussed with getting comfortable in the left visitor's chair – scooted it over a little closer to mid desk.

I said, "You need help?"

She gave me a quick smile, tentative, unsure of itself. "You know that woman that came by last week, the sorta pushy one."

"In the really nice clothes, *dressed to the nines*, you women call it, I think."

"Yes."

"She's a banker."

"Oh, is that what she does? I thought she was a real estate agent."

"Both selling something, money or land. What's up?"

"She was *only* business, then?"

It didn't sound like Lynnette was about to ask for help finding her sister's skipped-town ex husband. We had never had a conversation that even mentioned the word "girlfriend" in the two years she'd been at the front desk.

"I have no idea. On her part, I'm not sure. Might be nice. She does want me to change banks to her new one. She's a looker, huh?"

Lynnette looked like she was about to bust out laughing.

I said, "T.M.I.?"

She let loose a full-gut laugh, blushed just the slightest amount of pink on forehead and cheeks, then readjusted herself in the chair and said, "You... surprised the girls in this building."

"I what?"

"Today at lunch?"

"You all had a group lunch?"

"Not on purpose."

"What then?"

"Mr. Trench, well, you don't exactly look like a nice guy. I mean the buzz cut and the – you're not exactly into clothes and six-pack abs."

"If you had my hair, you'd chop it off. Nothing but ragweed."

She laughed but we were interrupted by the goofy chime of her telephone console as it echoed down the hall.

"Sorry," she said and lit out my door with more grace and speed than most cats.

Would Lynnette be back? No telling. I figured sixty-forty she would.

Before I could know if I was right, my cell phone brought me back to technology.

Private number call. I was in business so I answered those back then.

"Trench Coat Investigations."

"You Nathan Trench?" The near-male voice was loud, sounding like it had been run through an early Moog Synthesizer.

"Today, yes, I'm certain I'm Nate Trench. You would be...?"

"Not important."

"I'll decide that."

"No you don't." The connection terminated.

I don't know about the average guy, but rude anonymous hang-ups have always bothered me. What with all the telemarketers and wrong-number collection agents, one should develop a tough skin toward such harassment, but I never did.

That "never mind" and the synthesized tone stuck in my craw for most of the afternoon. NSA haunting? Digitally remixed voice?

I chased around cyberspace upturning rocks everywhere I could think of. Unless you were an online one main street merchant, Ben and Candice Franklin were ghosts in their own right. Debit and credit card transactions showed they were far from imminent bankruptcy. Drake's costs to attend U T Austin began with tuition much higher than I thought it would be. The bookstore apparently sold gilt-edged books as well. Spring had two credit card accounts – no debit in her name – with ten-grand limits. The activity on the Visa was nil. The MasterCard was strange. A couple grand one month, nothing the next two, then paid off the third. Repeat. Nobody had a criminal record, moving traffic violation, or summons.

Lynnette never came back down to finish our conversation and I left the office at five-thirty to meet with Mo Siddiqi, too late to chat her up on the way out.

Yeah, the afternoon had been a bust.

Maybe Siddiqi would cheer me up.

Chapter 62

Monday

A delicious and overstuffed Neptune Sub was supper Monday evening, a practical meal while I camped out at Hurricane Alley. I was determined to discover something unusual in Benjamin Franklin's activities, my tank refilled with motivation by my meeting with unusually-organized-for-his-age Mo Siddiqi. His work ethic knew solely of task completion, a gloriously refreshing attribute. He had commandeered a full crew on both Tuesday and Thursday, two standbys in reserve both evenings.

I'd popped inside Hurricane when I arrived, downed a quick draft while checking out the players, the ones most folks would call the *regulars*. When it comes to a place that's a bar trying to look like a restaurant, the regulars are players in an ongoing soap opera, a gossip gin, a little theater group. Oh, Hurricane Alley had the NBA playoffs live off a satellite feed, so the crowd was early and the take would be more than decent that Monday evening, although the players on their bar stools weren't too happy about having their private little world awash with interlopers.

Benjamin and the red Charger arrived a half hour later, after I'd settled into the Forester just after seven. While I waited for him to come back outside, my mind wandered through the myriad of contradictions endemic to the Franklin case. Finding no clear path, I moved onto lighter subjects while he remained inside, like "Does Benjamin like basketball?"

Benjamin, it turned out, liked to surprise me. He succeeded just before nine when he exited the front passenger door of a nondescript four-door sedan. Had he told Scottie to beam him up?

I'd have missed the event had I not decided some in-car stretching was in order. I had twisted far to the right to stretch my left obliques, I about shit my pants when he got out of that car.

Benjamin walked directly back inside Hurricane Alley and reappeared outside in about half an hour, long enough for me to torture myself. How had I missed seeing both Benjamin and the nondescript sedan? Damn.

Benjamin got in the Charger and I followed at five car lengths most of the time, happy to finally tail him more than five blocks, anxious to learn where he was going. He made over ten different turns inside Clear Lake City subdivisions but never stopped for more than a traffic signal on the way to his ultimate destination, his home.

Did he make all those turns to verify he'd made my tail? I had no clue but wished for a remote audio transmitter behind the dash of his Charger. He had been quite animated when he touched his left ear while stopped at a signal on El Dorado. Animated like, say, a real estate salesman in conversation with a prospective buyer, arms flapping, head bobbing and all that. Maybe Ben had a sweetheart on Mondays but she had called to turn him down that evening?

I'd seen the wireless headset on his left ear when he'd departed Hurricane Alley. Maybe what I really needed was a

Bluetooth interceptor. *If* the sender cell phone hadn't been restricted, interception was a no brainer, provided you could get close enough to receive the signal. Most Blue devices had a woefully short effective transmission distance, though, and car bodies soaked up a good share of signals.

I left Ben in Candice's supervision after texting her to let me know if he left the house again. Next stop was Helm. Time to download some incriminating conversations. The case was going to be clear as Plexiglas by the end of the evening.

As I sat in the Forrester happy to see that all four wireless microphones were in service, I realized I'd made a tactical error: I was in the Forrester. I had not rented another chase vehicle. That was the Forrester's fourth or fifth visit to Helm. Not good. Not good at all.

I activated the download. In five minutes it was completed and I got the heck out of there.

Chapter 63

Monday

When I arrived at the house, I took a shot at the Gumshoe loop again, hoping it wasn't the rare evening when William Peterson would be online. I didn't want him to feel insulted that I was asking the same questions I'd put to him earlier.

When I logged on, the social mover and shaker in Hawaii was pounding away at the keys in an open chat room, his posts nearly half of those during the prior two hours from what I could tell. At that rate, I didn't think I had much chance of getting his attention. The fates came to my aid again, thank goodness.

islandgenius > so, where you been?
lakesleuth > chasing a ghost – want to hear the latest?
islandgenius > that strange restaurant guy and his wife?
lakesleuth > them be the ones
islandgenius > you ever get that plate?
lakesleuth > ...no.

I brought him up to speed on LCC and Shrimp-Steak, Inc., then dropped Benjamin's Monday evening activity into the mix.

islandgenius > you check with Half-life?

lakesleuth > how'd you guess?
islandgenius > Just seein' if you got good sense
lakesleuth > I have / I did
islandgenius > ...and he said...?
lakesleuth > sneaky lawyer or something else
islandgenius > what's the something else?
lakesleuth > that's mine to figure out
islandgenius > he's making you work
I thought I heard a laugh.
lakesleuth > I do work. Lots of extra hours on this case
islandgenius > so what' your best guess now?
lakesleuth > feds
islandgenius > why feds?
lakesleuth > dunno. just popped onto the screen
islandgenius > well, I need to pop off the screen. work to do here on the island
lakesleuth > I know: somebody's gotta do it
islandgenius > what I really need is a cash cow like your Mrs. Client
lakesleuth > she'd drive you nuts; moody; demanding

He argued with me, saying I was an ungrateful sleuth, that more of us needed to do the hard work, be real Gumshoes, not just rely on electronics – otherwise we were nothing more than Internet Database Access Data Entry Clerks. I acquiesced, logged off and cabled the Z10 to my P.C. to download/backup the EaseDropper III files.

Amazing: twelve files. Maybe thirteen. One file seemed corrupt or of the wrong format. I couldn't tell right away as the file extension was not visible in the monitoring application listing on the Z10.

It hit me that I could listen with my cell headset. Outside was still very nice, so Zip and I walked down to the bulkhead.

While he begged me for attention, I played the oldest recording, one from the back bedroom.

Since the system was programmed with an audible auto start switch, I was surprised to find over a minute of hissing before I heard anyone speak. It wasn't a clear recording but the voice sounded like a woman's. The longer I listened, the more it sounded like a middle-aged couple arguing.

At last I could make out a name. His was Archie. Accent like back east. New York? Another minute and it sounded like her name was Edith. Still a verbal fight, an argument. I listened for another five minutes (twelve total).

This is where I love computers. I stopped file number one at that point (it had another thirteen minutes to run) and played file number two. No rewinding. No removing cassette box and inserting another.

The second file didn't start with hissing. I did have another couple fighting. Her voice a bit lower pitched and stronger, his slurred by a foreign language, maybe Spanish.

I stopped that one after three minutes.

I skipped a few. The seventh, front living room, had no hiss. After listening for four minutes, my guess was that a mother was arguing with her two daughters. Enough.

File number nine, front living room, also no hiss. First, a guy talking for a while. Then a female, young voice, answers. After a couple of minutes, many voices, both sexes, like a party. Maybe three or four girls talking and just as many guys. The voices were very loud but the recording was more clear, perhaps owing to the much larger window, again acting as a microphone diaphragm.

I played file number twelve (front bedroom). No hiss. No audio. Ended after thirty seconds, the default shutoff point after the last sound is detected. Crap.

Zip started jumping up and down beside me, tongue out, smiling. I guessed he was out of food, so I turned off the app and headed back up to the house.

Sure enough, the bowl was short on dog food – like empty. Water low, too.

While I opened the forty-pound bag I'd stored in the utility closet, I tried to drop anchor on the thought that had been trying to contact me. I knew it had something to do with the recordings. And I knew it was driving me nuts.

I filled Zip's bowl, closed the bag, and shut the door to the shed.

I filled Zip's water bowl with the garden hose.

I stood straight up – the anchor landed on my foot.

Those conversations from the house on Helm Street were not people *in* the Helm house. They were TV sitcoms, the first, All in the Family. The second was probably I Love Lucy. The third was familiar but I didn't recall the name. The fourth – no idea. Somebody either had a fetish for old TV shows or they wanted to give my wireless microphones something to work on so I would not hear the actual conversations going on inside the house.

One thing was sure, my investigation had gone from almost solved to sewer mud. Thick, black sewer mud.

To be a pro, perform like a pro, I needed to play, summarize, and catalog the other eight or nine files regardless of how obvious it was I'd been had.

I was tired. I'd do it in the morning.

I was also depressed.

But, I had to do something to feel useful. I did twenty-five minutes of pounding keys which got me nowhere. No real corporate information came popping up out of the ground.

Finally, *islandgenius* got back to me. His check of the Shrimp-Steak commercial real estate for-sale status still showed an open listing with the Erskine Group, nationwide outside of Texas, including in Hawaii.

I was still tired, and yet I had to do more, so I spent the rest of the evening researching other listening equipment. The most effective worked well for the feds who could commandeer an office or residence in which to install a laser microphone. You couldn't glue one to a window and you couldn't sit in your car all day aiming the device at the house across the street – you had to "shoot" perpendicularly to the target window. Umm, how would I *not* be noticed?

I left the alcohol alone and let the anger and its brother depression chase me to sleep around 11:30.

Chapter 64

Tuesday

I looked in my bathroom mirror. Managed a smile. Hurray. It was Tuesday. Mo Siddiqi and friends would take another shot at the wandering Benjamin Franklin. Hopefully Candice wouldn't take another shot at me afterwards, although I couldn't really argue with her attitude.

She was fronting good money. She had a right to expect something for it. She probably figured her money meant she didn't have to listen to my cautions. The Friday she crossed the Wall, I'd explained to her that cases like hers often drag on for four or five months. I had repeated my cautionary at least twice, I think. She did hear me. Whether she listened or not was known only to her. She did say she had enough money to last to August.

It occurred to me as I guided a razor past my nose that I should have made her sign a form – except, she could use a different investigator. I was on a week-to-week deal. Rich but insecure.

And I still had that problem over at the Helm house: the EaseDropper III was not worth the sales tax I paid for it.

I started the workday with that. I logged on to the internet to call islandgenius.

Except I didn't. My memory woke up. Honolulu was five hours behind Houston. Seven minus five equals one angry genius.

I left for the office early. The morning was much ado about nothing. Missing people who turned out to be in Louisiana holding down regular jobs – after searching only two cyber sources. I called *islandgenius* at noon.

He listened for five minutes while I told him about how I'd come to acquire my new sitcom collection, then tore me another new ass for fifteen very long minutes.

I never have related the details to anyone and that will not happen here.

He did threaten to have my membership in the Golden Gumshoes – the society – "cancelled for cause." The *cause*? He offered several. Said pick one: laziness; stupidity; naïveté; incompetence; complete disregard from standard procedures. I had to show marked improvement within twenty-one days or be relegated to computer data entry for the skip trace market. Said he'd pay to have a real gumshoe check me out – I wouldn't even know whom or when.

If I didn't pass muster, not only would I be tossed by the Gumshoes, I'd stand a good chance of losing access to several special cloud sources of information. He had friends. Lots of them. Everyone owed him favors.

I listened to it all, mute and defenseless. Probably the most unsettling part was his simple question asked me at the end, just before hanging up: "Where do you want to spend your jail time?"

< >   < >

The afternoon wasn't much better, but when I called Mo Siddiqi after supper for an update, he was prepared and as calm and matter-of-fact as ever. I wished him good fortune, then headed over to Helm with an additional piece of hardware, a signal scope. If those little Fed devils were transmitting with any wattage whatsoever, the ugly gray metal can on the passenger seat of the latest Rent-a-Wreck, a four door Nissan Altima, would pick it up.

The flaw in my plan splashed in front of me as I turned onto Helm: being the third week of April in the subtropics, Daylight Savings Time in force, it wasn't anywhere near dark enough for me to slink around without being detected.

I got the heck out of Dodge. Well, not exactly. I parked six houses down, on the same side of the street. That viewing angle and distance made casual discovery of the Altima unlikely.

A check of the control box showed a medium-strength signal with all four wireless microphones online. I retrieved the BB pistol from the backpack in the trunk, one less detail to remember when it got dark.

About twenty minutes into telling the sun to go away and inviting the stars to displace the hazy overcast, the fates from another galaxy smiled kindly on the start of my week.

A car pulled up in the driveway of the Helm house.

Not just any car: a Buick Sedan. Reginald Kensington's vehicle. Was he driving? The garage door raised and lowered, Buick inside.

I put the ED-III's headset on to check for situation comedies. All four mikes were quiet.

About five minutes later, though, a low-register baritone became audible. I didn't recognize it. Sounded like he must have lost his keys. I listened to his side of three telephone conversations in search of them, none of which left him a happy camper. Not the fare I'd hoped to feast on. It was all so comedic, it had to be another TV sitcom rerun.

The Buick of Reginald Kensington departed the Helm Street house a short while later. The garage door opened, the driver already behind the steering wheel. Couldn't see anyone inside, even through the telephoto camera lens. I did manage to confirm the Buick's license plates. At least I wasn't crazy on that count.

The semi-smile on my face didn't last long. My phone chimed with another of those private number calls.

"You Nathan Trench?" said the early Moog Synthesizer voice in an encore performance.

"So far. You would be – a machine?"

"Not important."

"I decide that."

"Sure, you do," said Mr. Synthesized, his accompanying laughter reminiscent of a low-budget sixties horror movie. After about fifteen seconds of mechanical laughter, the call terminated.

Chapter 65

Tuesday

A quick gulp of air came naturally but did little to calm my anxiety over the elusiveness of Benjamin Ivan Franklin. "Mo – we lost him, again?"

"Mr. Franklin executed a left turn across multiples lanes. At least two. Javier could not follow. Because of car beside him."

And I thought I'd imagined such a move by Mr. Ben Franklin the week before. "This on Bay Area, Starbucks and MacDonald's?"

"Perhaps. I will check."

"Who's Javier?"

"The accounting major who was in pursuit."

"Do that. Everybody else is at their assigned restaurant?"

"Yes. I directed Javier to return."

Everyone was supposed to sit tight, record data, and call with anything unusual. "Why did he follow?"

"He said Mr. Franklin carried a silver briefcase. Like Apple notebook computer."

That started me thinking. "Maybe it was a computer and not a briefcase?"

"I would not be offended – perhaps better you speak with –"
"Great idea, Mo. Call Javier and have him wait there for me."
"Very well. I make call now."
I reached for the red end key – froze. Then, "Mo, you still there."
"I am, sir."
"Which restaurant – which one's Javier at?"
"Charlie's Steak, Seafood –"
"Got it."

It was time to do a serious, government type debriefing of young Javier. Fifteen minutes tops to get there. I couldn't wait to get back into live action.

The first thing I did was get Javier to move his car off the lot. If Benjamin had made him on Bay Area, it wouldn't take but a phone call to the night manager at Charlie's to make things more difficult.

A smallish Puerto Rican, maybe, with gnarly black hair and a pencil thin moustache, Javier bounced and squirmed in the Altima's passenger seat as if it would eject him at any moment without notice. The muscles in his arms and shoulders were tight as cat gut on a violin, protruding in knots, poised to protect their owner. Maybe he was afraid he'd screwed up and had forfeited the twenty-five bucks we were paying him. I tried to assure him otherwise.

Javier answered all my questions with a darn good recall and eye for detail. I told him so and encouraged him to think about working for the FBI. Those three letters seemed to send him back to hypertension, so I spent some time talking about working signal intelligence in the Navy. I'm not sure if I gained his interest or he just ran out of energy to gyrate so.

One thing we couldn't nail down was the brushed aluminum hardware. Javier said it wasn't an Apple notebook because it did not have the trademark on either side. I pressed him as to whether he had actually seen both sides. He was reluctant to back off from his assertion. After fifteen minutes or so of debriefing, I let him go.

I thought it would be a break in the case if Benjamin were transporting a computer to different locations. I called Mo and told him to ask each operative specifically if they had seen anything remotely resembling Javier's briefcase and make that part of the exit report for the evening.

< >   < >

And that was the evening. The guys were signed on until ten and it was nearly past that. I sent Javier on to Siddiqi's rendezvous point while I strolled into Charlie's to see if anything seemed unusual.

The unusual part was me. I ordered the wrong beer it seemed, my mind reading "you are stupid" on the bartender's face. What's not to like about a draft beer? I managed to stretch out the draft for half an hour watching the game. Never saw Ben, which was probably a good thing. He'd probably wonder where he'd seen me and I was not gifted in the verbal lie. Didn't strike up a conversation with anyone. Did pay cash with half-again tip, though.

I headed over to IHOP on NASA Blvd near El Camino Real, and had a late supper of bacon and eggs while I waited for Mo. It was past eleven when he arrived. I apologized for once again keeping him up so late on a school night.

He was his usual overly polite self. "We must do work well."

"And you work to make it so. I appreciate that. Now, Mo, did you see anything unusual on your first time through the reports?"

"I did not. More tomorrow when all data is loaded and graphed."

"You have made me a copy?"

"Yes."

He handed me photocopies of the handwritten logs, thanked me and said I would have the electronic stuff by four the next afternoon. "We will do better even on Thursday. Practice in observation is critical element."

"And now we can alert everyone to a shiny aluminum case," I said, knowing I had something to drop in Candice's lap before she jumped my ass.

She didn't call.

I didn't call. I was in no mood to joust with her.

Chapter 66

Tuesday

I chased Benjamin and Candice Franklin around the Internet while I sipped a cold Fat Tire. I headed off to bed around midnight. It had been a decent day – Candice had not called.

So what else could improve that Tuesday? How about being woken up by the ringing of my cell after I had successfully checked out to the sandman?

The timing of the call made perfect sense. It was ten til one. The young lady caller never said hello, never identified herself, just started carrying on in a tear-laden, choking tone, speaking so fast she might as well have been using Mandarin.

Did I recognize who it was? Well, who'd it have to be?

After maybe a minute I said "STOP!" so loudly Spring actually stopped talking; stopped gurgling, too.

In maybe five seconds, she said, "Mr. Trench, it's you, umm right?"

"Yes," I said, going for harsh. "What the hell is up?"

No response.

"You woke me up, Spring. You got five seconds."

It took her four and a half to say, in the same six-year-old's whine as Friday, "Mr. Trench. I need your help real bad.".

"Real bad? We've been here. Twice I've agreed to meet you. You follow up two no-shows by appearing at my house. No call. No advance notice. No text."

"I'm... calling... now..." she said between sobs.

"So what? Why should I see you? You ran out of my house ten minutes after you got here."

"I'm sorry. I'm sorry. I'm sorry."

I waited to see what she said next.

"Mr. Trench?"

"You know what? I'll tell you what. I used to date an alcoholic. She said 'I'm sorry' all the time. Never changed her behavior. So, I'm thinking H.P.D. needs to search your car. You gotta be on something."

"You wouldn't!"

Did I have her attention? Okay, it was a trick. I was mean, but somebody *had* to do a reality check on that teenager.

I said, "Couple guys in uniform owe me favors. Big favors." It was true. I had chips at HPD and Harris County sheriff.

"It's not fair; it's just not fair. Not fair."

"What's not fair? You think you know about what's fair?"

Spring's crying magnified to near convulsive.

"Okay, okay," I said. "In five words or less, what isn't fair?"

"Someone's... tailing my Dad."

From out of nowhere, new information.

I couldn't let on. "Tailing?"

"Following his car – like in the movies."

"He call you?"

Another dose of empty cellular static.

I wondered where her attention went. "*Miss* Franklin?"

"Don't – stop it." Loud. Frustrated.

"What?" I said, trying to sound more angry than I was.

"Not you. My... my... *friend.*"

Boyfriend?

I considered saying that word out loud but held myself in check. "Tell me about the tailing."

"That's what he said."

"What about it?"

"Mentioned it."

"When was this?"

"When he wanted me to drive the delivery van. My Mom told you that, I think."

So, Candice knew. Very interesting.

"Your mom told me your dad wanted you to drive the van Wednesday evening, last week," I said. "That's what she told me. Was that the only time he mentioned a tail to you?"

"Today."

"Did he say more? More about it?"

"Can I just come see you?"

"So there *is* more?"

"There's always more."

"Okay, I'll turn the porch light on for you."

Chapter 67

Tuesday Night

I was Spring's mom's handsomely compensated investigator. That's where my loyalty had to lay. Still, I hated for parents to war around their children. It kills children, their spirits anyway, gives kids ulcers as they try to balance loyalties between two gods, father and mother. When I was a kid, I'd witnessed all too much War Between the Joneses, the family next door. The parents got high blood pressure, the kids got boils.

Could Spring's whole drama queen bit be a ruse, a suggestion of her dad, or was it her standard operating procedure, her personality, her coping mechanism?

Or could Spring be her father's best foot soldier?

And could her dad actually be in a serious trouble, the tail he actually saw was not Mo's or mine?

Sure. Why not?

But I doubted it. He had turned hard left across lanes on Bay Area twice.

Plus there was something just plain not right at the house on Helm street.

And what if Candice Franklin wasn't entirely weird, nothing better at her core than a devious, calculating, manipulating selfish bitch with a fictional story: chunks of money bypassing the books of Shrimp-Steak, Inc.?

Was Candice the grand façade in all this?

And what was her goal? What did she really want? The company in a divorce settlement?

And where, exactly, was Candice getting the Franklins?

And why did I not have a copy of that CPA's report? No way I was going to let *islandgenius* know about that. Totally dumb. Totally.

< >   < >

"Give it a rest," I said, loud as I could, as I finished washing my hands. Spring had managed to synchronize her arrival – and subsequent repeated doorbell thumbing – with my visit to the bathroom.

I dried my hands and walked to the front door but should have checked the peephole. I would have made more room for the two charging teenagers that entered.

The girl who followed Spring had to be at least six-two, a good half-foot taller then Miss Franklin.

"Who is this, your bodyguard?" I said, only half joking.

"Funny. Ha ha," said Spring, turning around. "This is Jocelyn and she wouldn't let me go out alone."

"She was at my house. Came over late," said Jocelyn. The giant had a smile worth a king's ransom. Did she know it?

"Oh," I said, "so you were the one she told to stop doing something while we were on the phone."

"Stop it. I've got a real problem," said Spring. "Both of you."

"Sit down," I said, not exactly in a cordial tone. I was on the edge of pissed with Spring's commanding attitude and the arrival of the second teenager.

"Over there," I said, waving my hand. "Dining table."

"Sorry it's late. I can tell you hate surprises," said Spring.

"Sorry, my ass. You don't have any credibility, Miss Franklin. You've made sure of that."

"Sorry."

"Stop with the sorry. Doesn't mean anything."

"Yes, sir."

Had I actually heard that?

"Want to change your status?"

Spring stopped pulling a chair back and nodded.

"Then start talking. Details. Be coherent.

"You," I said, nodding to Jocelyn, "make like you lost your voice."

"Where do I start?" said Spring.

I thought a moment. "How's your loyalty problem coming along?"

"How about whoever is tailing my Dad?"

"You asked where to start and I –"

"I've changed my mind. Can you believe someone is tailing my dad?" she said, screaming out one word at a time. Drama queen on steroids. "Who would be so rude?"

"You want me to find out, Spring?"

"Yes."

"So you're here to get me to find out who's tailing your dad?"

"Yes. Mostly."

I wondered what the remainder of her agenda looked like.

"Your mother hired me for other reasons. She's not paying me to help you."

"It's the same family. Helping Dad should help Mom."

"You were supposed to contact me, return my call – messaged through your mother – to set up a time so I could interview y-o-u about the van and other things – for your mom."

"I don't know who else could help – or would – find out who's tailing Dad. The police won't help."

I knew that. No verifiable crime committed.

"Okay," I said, "you'll be happy to know I can do that rather quickly. How about my question?"

"You can? How fast is quick?"

"Very. First we have to tackle your parent versus parent problem."

"The loyalty thing?"

"Yes."

"Second choice?"

"Spring, dammit."

"Heya, there, Trench," said Jocelyn, "you can find out quickly – who's doing the tail?"

"Mr. Trench to you, Ms. Jocelyn. Stay out of this," I said. "Spring, I get the loyalty problem. What I don't get is why you have contacted me what, four times now. How do you need *help real bad*?"

Spring pushed the chair back, stood up. I was on the verge of telling her to sit back down when she pulled something out of her soft and smallish cordovan leather purse and slid it across the table. "Mom bought this."

Sorta looked like an old phone pager but was much heavier, had what looked like a magnet on the back, its full width and length. I had a small metal rack on the table for salt and pepper shakers. It clamped right to it.

"I'm guessing, maybe a transmitter?"

"Yup. Mom had me put it on Dad's car. Up underneath."

"So, basically, your Mom's the one tailing your dad."

"No, she's *tracking* him. GPS and all that."

I'd told her the truth, indirectly, and she'd gone right past it.

"Why didn't she install the transmitter herself? Might take five minutes, a change of clothes at worst."

"Mom doesn't get dirty. A bit sweaty watching tennis on a sunny day – maybe. Never dirty. She's also a minus five on the mechanical aptitude chart."

No surprise.

"When did you first put this on?" I said.

"This isn't the first one."

"What?"

"He found the first two."

Chapter 68

Tuesday night

"So your dad's into tech?"

"No. That's another weird thing. He's not. Not at all."

Weird and The Franklins continued to be synonymous.

"So how do you know he found them?" I said. "He bring them home and show them to your mother?"

"No. They would just quit working. Mom had me retrieve them. Both times, gone."

"Did you place them underneath on a–"

"I *am* tech, Mr. T."

"You bet she is," said Jocelyn. "Won awards at science fairs and such. Captain of the Lego League team."

I gave the giant a deep frown, then looked to Spring and said, "Sit down. You're not leaving until I tell you, anyway."

At that, Jocelyn jumped up, her chair crashing behind her.

"It's alright," said Spring, doing the palm down calming motion to Jocelyn. "I'm going to the max with this guy."

"Thanks for the vote of confidence, Spring – I think," I said. "You are very much confusing"

"It's my job. I'm a girl."

"Grrrr," said Jocelyn.

"Cute," I said. "Okay, go back to why your Mom wanted the transmitter on the Charger."

Spring spent a good ten minutes talking about her Mom not trusting her dad for the prior twelve to fourteen months. Spring wasn't sure exactly why, but the lack of trust was severe. She could feel it.

Candice had Spring place the first transmitter on the Charger back in February. That lasted maybe a week, she thought. One evening the cell phone app reported no data.

Spring put the second one under the car in March. It was out of commission and gone in four or five days.

After I'd refused to attach one, Candice had Spring install the third, the one in my hand. That she did yesterday morning and was following her dad for the fun of it when what turned out to be Mo's car cut in front of her. So she was following both of them. That explained why her worry factor ramped up and she took the transmitter off after her dad came home.

Spring had then gone over to Jocelyn's for support. The bodyguard wasn't keen on her calling me, thus the fidgeting and lack of continuity in her phone call.

"That's about it," said Spring. "Maybe I should go."

"Jocelyn, if she moves, sit on her," I said. Then, turning back to Spring, "We need *all* of this out on the table so you're not leaving, like I said."

"You watch me."

"Knock it off. You say you got problems. Face 'em."

Spring said nothing, gave me a familiar glare that would do Candice proud.

"Alright. Let's get after it. What is your loyalty problem – exactly?"

Spring looked over to her bodyguard who didn't move a muscle, then back to me and said, "I don't want to talk about it."

"I know that. Sure, except you kept telling me you really needed my help. Nothing over at The Franklins seems very far out of the ordinary at this point. And so I don't get what your problem is, really. "

Spring stared me down for a good bit, then looked over to the bodyguard, said, "What you think?"

Jocelyn shook her head. "I don't get any sicko pervert vibes from him."

Spring looked back to me with a lighter tone on her face and said, "Me neither."

"Talk, then."

"You have beer? Two?"

I was surprised.

"I have beer. Good beer. *You* will not. Bodyguard neither."

"Mom lets me have a couple every once in a while."

"Not gin martinis?" I said, still on the pissed side.

"Her mother does the vodka ones," said Jocelyn.

"What's your problem with a couple beers, *Mister* Trench?" said Spring.

"I could get arrested for contributing to *your* delinquency and lose my license. Besides that, I'm against it on general principles – and you've been a pain in the ass from the –."

"Sprite, just get down with it," said Jocelyn, using what I later learned was her nickname for Spring. "If he gets too rude, I'll slam dunk him with this chair."

"Thanks for your support, Ms. Jocelyn," I said. "Now, please do as I asked and hush."

Sensing no argument from the bodyguard, I turned to her sidekick. "Spring, you've got the floor. What's the loyalty problem?"

"Aww, man. You are rude."

"Don't care. I'm tired. You're a pain in the ass, a brat."

"Like you're not the ugliest old fart in Clear Lake."

I wanted to laugh. Seriously. Didn't even care about the "old" part . It was just funny coming out of her mouth.

I worked up a frown, said, "This is Seabrook. Out with it."

Spring pushed her chair back.

I stood, glared my best, my ugliest.

Spring looked to Jocelyn who promptly threw her the finger.

"Awww, man. You both suck."

"On the table, now! What's the deal?" I said, slamming the table.

"Okay. Okay. Okay," Spring said.

I waited. Jocelyn kept her mouth shut.

The pressure of silence is severe on impulsive people. Spring didn't look one bit comfortable. I enjoyed the moment.

Finally Spring said, "Okay. My Mom's the one who needs following."

I had to sell Spring on the idea that she'd surprised me.

I popped eyes wide, then sat down, said in a calm tone, "How do you know?"

"I just know."

Giant said, "You got –"

"Jocelyn, stay out of this – for now."

She spanked the table herself, mocking my move, probably, but then sat back, hands behind her head.

"Okay, Spring, why? How do you know?"

"I just know."

"That's crap"

"Oh, stuff it."

We were going to work on my terms or not at all.

"Get out," I said.

"Get out!" she said, laughing.

"Wrong 'get out,' Brat. Leave. I'm done. Going to sleep."

Chapter 69

Tuesday night

"Sorry. Sorry. Sorry," said Spring, holding up both hands, palms out and open wide.

The take-away had worked.

"Sorry, bull crap," I said. "What's the real story?"

Spring turned a little pink, then dropped her head a notch and said, "She's got a lover."

Made sense.

"Boy or girl?"

"Man you are most rude. That's my Mom, your boss, you're —"

"You seen this lover?"

"Ahhh, no."

"So you know, how?"

"I know."

"You say that too often. Details, Brat. Details. Now would be good."

Spring shuffled her feet, no small chore in running shoes. "Awww, man."

"You watch them holding hands, maybe."

"Not exactly."

"What, exactly? You seen this lover?"

"No. I told you. Just strange fidgeting by Mom, leaving suddenly on vague errands at nine in the evening. Coming back at eleven thirty."

"You sneak texts off her phone, get hold of her emails?"

"No."

"If you could, would you really know her lover's sex from reading the text?"

"Oh shut up."

"No, you tell me how you know. You want me on a wild goose chase? I don't."

I waited. Stared.

"What?" said Spring.

"Maybe she's got a lover who is otherwise engaged – like with a wife *or partner* – who doesn't control his or her time. Means they have to get together when the opportunity arises. So, Candice gets excited but doesn't want you to see. She tries to hide it, but that makes her tighten up, fidget. She sputters in misdirections as she hurries to get ready to head out the door. Makes sense to me."

"Asshole."

"Am I wrong?"

"Yeah, like that."

"Like what? You agree with the possibilities I just listed? Is that what you're saying?"

"Yeah, like that."

"Jocelyn, think a minute but don't answer out loud. Would *you* put up with this kind of b.s. from Spring?"

The giant put on a wicked grin, then reached her very long arms straight out and turned thumbs down.

"Thank you, Jocelyn," I said. "Now, how about I give Spring one more chance. If she craps out on us again, then you get to pounce on her."

Jocelyn slapped the table with both palms, said "Yes!"

"Assholes."

Jocelyn stood ever so slowly.

Spring looked over to her friend, then to me, back to Jocelyn, then cratered. "Okay. Okay. Okay. I heard Mom talking on her cell, in the master bedroom, door closed. Sounded like, you know, something from the movies."

"You put your ear on her bedroom door?" said Jocelyn. "You dweeb."

"And that makes it a guy?" I said. "What she say?"

"Sprite is what you call clueless, Trench. She doesn't get it that *the action* runs hot both ways these days. Why, you say. We look the same age, huh. See it's that Sprite never played sports or nothing, never was around girls messing with each other in the locker room. Like that."

Spring needed grounding and Jocelyn was just what the doctor ordered.

I had to stop and think, though. I had never considered the sex of the lover, either.

"Okay, Jocelyn, thank you. Now, Spring," I said, "there is something that you need to talk about. Shall we get to it?"

She fidgeted some more, squirmed in her chair. "You mean the loyalty stuff?"

"Ex-actly."

"Asshole."

"I'm listening for just one more minute," I said, sitting back, crossing my arms.

In about half a minute, Jocelyn said, "Mr. T., you want me to take her outside for a whippin'?"

"She's got another fifteen seconds. Let's see."

"Assholes." Spring kicked the table leg.

"Feel better now?" I said.

"Okay. Okay. Okay. I like Dad better."

I was not exactly expecting that.

"Why?"

"Mom's not as, you would say, warm as Dad."

"You talking about affection," I said, "or stuff like encouragement and pep talks and patience and just listening to you sometimes, and being there for you when times get bad?"

"You know so much, why did you ask?"

"I didn't know, Spring. I'm just familiar with the behaviors."

"Yeah, sure."

"Are you a Daddy's Girl?" I said.

"She nobody's girl," said Jocelyn, "she –"

"Shut up, bitch," said Spring. "Mr. T., Mom's my natural parent. I get tugged her way because she *is* my Mom. She not good at mom stuff, like being supportive – that's it. That's the adult word."

"World revolves around your mom," I said, "in her view. Is that what you're saying, Spring?"

"You know too much."

"So, when she wanted you to attach a tracking device to the Charger, you felt like you were being disloyal to him, even though he's not your real dad – but feel you have to help out your mom, 'cause she's your *mother*, or you'd be disloyal to her."

"Shut up. He *is* my dad. But like that. What you said."

"So, you're conflicted."

"That. Yeah, that. A good adult word. For sure."

I let the moment settle gently on the table while I debated whether to push her one more time.

Chapter 70

Tuesday night

I pushed.

"So, Spring. You say you need my help. You call me. You sound desperate, about to crash. You come here and won't talk. We have to drag it out of you.

I don't get it. Your situation, your feelings and your parents, it all sounds typical of a lot of American families, their internal conflicts and stuff. Goes on all the time."

"You just don't get it."

"I just said that. What's to get?"

"My Mom's cheating on my Dad."

"I'm not a marriage counselor."

"But you have some power."

"Power?" said Jocelyn.

"Bitch! You know my Mom can't stand most men. But she's shelling out cash money for Trench Coat, here."

"You know this how," said Jocelyn.

"Mr. Trench, I have seen the green she's paying you. I've seen the wads."

"Wads?" I said.

"Hundreds, in a stack made a lump in her purse. Thought it was kind of funny. I mean, our last names are Franklin. Ben's on the hundred."

"So, you think she drops them by my front door?"

"Yeah."

I couldn't let her know the truth.

"Those wads could be for someone else – like her divorce attorney; for her lover's divorce attorney."

"Don't say that."

"Why not? She pays cash, your dad doesn't know where the money went."

"Don't say that."

"Why not? If she's got a lover, could mean a divorce is on its way."

"Don't say that."

"Get over it. What you want from me?"

"You got some pull, Mr. T. Use it. Get her to stop."

"Stop what?"

"Stop the lover."

What could I do with that kid? Eighteen going on thirty going on twelve. Damn. No way I could tail them both even if my bank accounts saw Franklins from Candice and Benjamin.

"I'm not a registered arbiter either," I said, "and don't want to be. I snoop. I snoop electronically. Sometimes I snoop physically, like now."

"You've got to help, Mr. T. Please?"

That would get us nowhere so I switched the focus.

"Where's she getting the money?"

"How would I know?"

"You're nosey, you're a teenager."

That seemed to get Spring to stop and think for a second.

And gave Jocelyn an open door.

"You been holding out on me, Sprite. What's up with that?"

"Now, hey, don't get bent, bitch. I'm the one with the conflict."

"You're going to have one with me, you don't come straight."

"That's it. I'm leaving," said Spring.

She stood. Jocelyn stood. I sat back. Crossed my legs. Smiled.

No need for me to intervene. The odds were clearly in my favor.

"You're about to get your act together, Sprite," said Jocelyn, clamping a large hand on Spring's head.

"It ain't fair. It ain't fair. It ain't fair."

"Excuse us," said Jocelyn. She winked at me, took Spring by the wrist and walked her on back to the bathroom. Girl to girl, friend to friend – could be a help.

< >   < >

One problem I was facing: I figured if they left me alone too long, I'd fall asleep where I sat, maybe roll right out of the chair, I was so tired. Even though the discussion with the two of them had got my adrenaline goin', I immediately felt it falling off heading me to a fall off the energy cliff. It was after 1:00 AM. It had been an exasperating Tuesday.

The other problem – maybe "question" is a better word: how does Candice come up with lumps of cash for me? Where's she getting it? I figured a bank. Nobody else kept that much cash on hand, especially in one denomination – well, except dope dealers. She wouldn't go there – wait, she'd paid me in circulated bills, not crisp new ones.

There had to be a secret fund of some sort or Ben might question it. Same for the bucks that went to the CPA audit bill. Must have been another five or ten grand. I doubted the CPAs would have taken cash – but you never knew.

< >   < >

The girls came out of the bathroom before I fell asleep with kind of a giggle about them.

I said, "What's up?"

They glanced to each other as they sat down, before Jocelyn said, "Spring's got an idea."

"Can't wait," I said.

"Truth, she doesn't sit still and wait very well. I'm her B.F.F. and I know. So, go ahead, Spring."

I turned to look at Candice's daughter.

"I'm thinking I want to help."

"Get out – not your version. Both of you. I'll call later today or on Thursday – after I've had some sleep."

Chapter 71

Wednesday

It didn't take Candice long on Wednesday morning to reassert her position as boss.

I was a half hour late getting to the office, arriving right before nine, and made it just in time to be sitting down when her call came through.

"Well, what is he up to, Mr. Trench?'

"Don't know. Do know he's made our tail."

"He made a tail – told a tale?"

"He figured out he's being followed."

"That won't do," she said, her tone just this side of angry.

"I know. He took another left turn across two lanes on Bay Area near Starbucks-McDonalds, like he did with me last week."

"Was the same car following him?"

"No. No I wasn't – it wasn't."

"Well... how do you know he knows?"

I kept Spring's secret.

"Had a tail on the tail. And Ben turned at almost the same spot. Area has too many through streets, escape routes. He has to know that. Remember, from last week when I chased him in there?"

"Well, at least I'll save that expense. What are you going to do? How's the secret microphones?"

"Umm, I'd like to keep the surveillance on the restaurants another evening, tomorrow. He may be wise to a tail but he may not be to a stakeout, especially since we are using different cars at every restaurant each time."

"I don't know."

"Well, I would actually like to add four students that one evening, tomorrow evening. That should give us enough to cover the usual transit routes. Then, if Ben leaves one, a call is made to Mo who then alerts the route lookouts. We just log when he left, where he was spotted in between and where, and when and where he shows up next. The times will tell us if he made a stop in between or took an indirect route." I didn't tell her that if we discovered a point-to-point time of travel disparity, we would need to do it all over again next Tuesday.

On the way to the office that morning – up late and goin' crazy – the idea to change the way we worked the dragnet popped in my head, said, Hey Stupid. If that idea worked, I could grill Candice on what was near the route that could cause Ben to "take too long."

"One more evening," she said. "I'll think about it. What about the recordings?"

She had me.

"In a word, Candice: worthless. Three have recordings of old sitcoms. The fourth has started up only once but recorded nothing but silence."

"What, the people in that house watch basic cable all day?"

"No. The recordings don't have any commercials."

Dead air, then, "They could have DVDs."

"Well, then there were DVD players in three different rooms playing different sitcoms at the same time."

"That is possible, isn't it? Could have programmed each player. Programming is the right term, is it not? Start and stop when you want?"

"Sure. But we are looking for people in general and Benjamin in particular. Best I can tell, nobody was home. At most one person is there on any regular basis. There were three once but only for about two minutes. The videos are a sham carried out to laugh at us – or a method of masking conversations."

"So... there is something illegal going on inside there."

"That would be my bet. Or something government. Mr. Franklin could conceivably be working with the Feds."

"Oh, you men so stick together, don't you. Whatever could he be doing working with the federal government? He's got a lover in there. You saw her."

"What I saw was certainly flirtatious. Outside."

"Evidence. You will testify, won't you."

"Happened only once during my many visits," I said. "He wasn't there every time. I have logged three instances where he was there. The blonde was not there for two of them."

"Your job is to get me evidence of his infidelity. I am paying you rather well. We need to settle this very soon."

"Mrs. Franklin, I –"

She disconnected before I got any further. What happened to finding how Ben was siphoning off money from Shrimp-Steak, Inc.?

Things continued weird with the Franklins. I wondered if her hourly rate for an infidelity investigator was also eighty an hour?

I settled back in my chair and gazed out the window – then remembered Mo. I knew he'd be in class and left him a detailed voicemail of my plans.

< >   < >

My cell rang mid morning, a few minutes after a divorcée left my office much happier than when she arrived. I'd found her no-child-support-paying ex in five minutes, printed it all out and handed it to her. Then I noticed she had a flash drive on her key chain, so I also scanned the printouts to a pdf file and copied it to her drive as well.

The number on the caller ID was familiar so I said, "Burger King. We don't open until eleven."

"Mr. Trench! I'm at school. Can't talk long. I have some ideas."

Of course, Spring was a teenager.

"Mr. Trench, when can I see you today?"

"How did you know I'm not seeing someone already."

I had been so cold to her a few hours earlier, in front of her best friend, that I had made up my mind to be warm and funny.

"Mr. Trench!"

"Sorry. Not really into that. No time. Lots of work. Maybe in June."

"Mr. Trench, I'm serious. I've go to get to my next class."

"Call after you finish for the day. I'll know what the rest of the day holds for you by then."

"Promise."

"Do *you* promise?"

"Okay, *fine*," said Spring and disconnected.

With Jocelyn's help I had managed to get Spring out of my house before she wanted to leave. Said I needed sleep, which was true. I hadn't promised to let her help. And I hadn't said "no." Yes, I was a chicken.

Spring had found my house – owned not in my name but by a special legal entity I had paid good money to have formed to protect my largest asset in case of a wild lawsuit – so that was something. She could probably run my electronic services without much training, assuming she was computer literate which most kids were by then.

Working the streets was a whole 'nother country – just like Texas.

Chapter 72

Wednesday

I sat in a Honda Fit on Helm and waited for the download from the microphones' base unit to finish. I didn't fit well in the small economy car but business had been booming at Rent-a-Wreck. They promised me a no-charge trade up if I came back after one.

On the drive over, I heard from Mo. He liked my idea and promised to find us four more soldiers that afternoon. He'd meet with them that evening so they would be better use to us the next evening.

The download seemed to be taking longer than usual and I was getting antsy when a knock on my car window scared me half to death.

What the hell?

I twisted away from the window, looked up, cell in hand, and forced a smile.

An elderly gentleman, perhaps in his early eighties, made the old cranking sign for rolling down your window and I obliged – with the little electric lever.

"Good day, sir," he said.

"Yes. Yes it is. April is always great in Houston."

"Ah, yes, when it's not raining."

"You got me there. How can I help you?"

"Saw you just sitting here and, if you don't mind...."

He trailed off and I knew again why I did not like field work.

"Go... ahead... sir?"

"This car. You are much larger than me. I was thinking of buying one. Consumer Reports is high on them. May I ask you... do you like it? My wife is skeptical of Japanese cars."

Never would I have anticipated such a question. I figured he was going to ask me who I planned to visit in the neighborhood.

"Must be straight, sir. It's a ... loaner. Mine's in... the shop. Just stopped here to... download something to my phone. Car seems nice enough, though. Peppy."

"Oh, so you don't own it?"

"No, no I don't."

"Makes sense. I had wondered about the Renta decal. Sorry to bother you." He did a military about face and was up and over the curb and onto the sidewalk in no time. I had worked in sequestered workspaces as one of Uncle Sam's geeks for so long, I didn't do people surprises well. Not well at all.

I looked down at my cell but had trouble reading it because my hand was shaking so much. I grabbed my right wrist with left hand and placed it against the steering wheel.

Okay, download had finished. So was I, doubting if I would ever retrieve the components of the remote wireless eavesdropping system. Whoever controlled that house was most likely videotaping all sides of the building, 24/7.

As I drove off, I thought about Spring. Maybe she could be a big help. But her deep fears and worries, her excitable personality and dramatic tendencies... did they extend past her immediate family to life at large?

      < >   < >

I played the first of the downloads on the way back to Rent-a-Wreck. It was another sitcom, The Jeffersons, I think. I stopped it at five minutes and keyed the second – there were only five – while I sat in their office and waited for a Saturn sedan of some sort. The recording sounded like a broadcast of Sixty Minutes. And old. I let it go ten minutes before keying in the third. That was an episode of Rockford Files. I knew Garner's attitude and voice anywhere.

I was listening to Jim Rockford when they brought out the Saturn keys. The Saturn small SUV was big enough for me but I received consecutive calls on the way back to the office before I figured out where all the switches were. I was sure I had seen fog lights on the front end.

Just when it looked like I might have caught up with the data requests generated by the two phone calls, Spring burst into my office. That was around three-thirty. No knock. No phone call. No text. No email. And she left the door open.

Had I really expected her to follow instructions? Unfortunately, yes.

"Hey Mr. T."

"Hey yourself."

"Can I like sit down. Do you have any water?"

"Not a restaurant. At the front of these suites, go left. Water fountain's outside the bathrooms."

"Oh, that's okay," she said, landing her jean shorts in a chair. "I'm not that thirsty."

"What are you then?"

"Ready to help!"

I was afraid of that.

"Where's Jocelyn?"

"At Sonic. Working."

"Really?"

"She graduated early. Hops cars."

"I didn't know they had car hops any more. She seems smart enough to work inside."

"She's too tall. Hits her head. It's crowded in Sonic kitchens."

I had not considered that, either. Not one of my better thinking days, evidently. Of course, by "inside" I had meant in an office.

"So, Spring, you still conflicted?"

"Of course. Dad and Mom. Mom and Dad. I wanna help."

"Won't helping out here constantly challenge your loyalties, slap your sensitivities around like helium-filled balloons?"

"What are you saying?"

"Your mom is paying me to investigate your dad. Didn't your mom have you help her before she hired me?"

"Sometimes. Yeah."

"And since then you've followed your mom and figured out she has a lover which makes you sympathetic toward your dad, right?"

"Yes. He's not screwing around."

"Okay, then why help investigate him? You should be tailing your mom with an infrared camera and getting photos of her and her lover."

"How 'bout I know my Dad is innocent. So, if I help you, he'll be cleared sooner?"

"Sooner is a good thing. Gotta be more in that head of yours."

"Mom is getting bitchier every day. There might still be a chance to get her to recognize a big Ah-Hah moment if we can get him cleared soon. Three more weeks. That's all I give her. She'll lose it by then."

"And what about telling him what you know?"

She shot up from the chair and raced out of my office. I was used to the behavior. And wasn't worried.

Her loudly-decorated clutch purse lay on my desk. Maybe she decided she was thirsty, after all.

Chapter 73

Wednesday

"What did you figure on doing to help out with the investigation?" I said after Spring had slunk back in my open office door and walked to the window.

She turned, a stupefied look on her face. "I umm liked tailing Dad, actually. Tailing Mom, too."

"Second choice?"

"Have you been inside that house?"

I had figured her mother had told her about Helm, but in general terms.

"Which house? Why?"

"The one in the older part of Clear Lake City, not far from the old golf course. Where Dad goes sometimes."

"Have you?"

"No. I wanted to. Jocelyn wouldn't be my lookout."

"How do you know where it is?"

"Mom would head over there now and then. I followed once. After that I'd swing by sometimes just to see what was in the driveway. Eventually the Charger showed. Kinda hard to miss. And sometimes I followed Dad."

"I had a regular excitement junkie on my hands."

"Well, Spring, there is room for a car in the garage. He could have been there many times."

"Dad's Charger's always outside."

"Unless it was already parked in the garage and door closed."

"You're saying, what...?"

Why give her the advantage?

"Come sit down," I said. "That window makes for lazy minds."

"Adults," she said, shaking her head, but complied.

I waited until she was settled, then changed the subject, sorta. "Your Mom know you followed her?"

"No. I've never been caught tailing anyone."

"A sport of yours?"

"Naw. Just something I do. Am good at. Find interesting."

The look on her face seemed like a melding of joy and fascination.

"I'm not going to ask you if you tail boyfriends, okay?"

"You know it."

T.M.I., huh.

Had she tailed me? Was that how she knew where my house was? Damn.

I settled down, returned to my point. "How'd your mother not notice you at least once in all those times?"

"I'd ride with Jocelyn in her mother's car. Park way down the street. Used binocs. Dad's."

"Okay, so you're resourceful. What else?"

"I love a good mystery."

I'm sure I moaned. That was so lame.

"So," I said, "you have a good thirst for reading books and watching movies. That would never hack it. Investigating is tedious. That's spelled b-o-r-i-n-g, bor-ing."

"I watch CSI."

"I'm not surprised."

"All of them – shows like that."

"Hear this: those programs have no foundation in the real world."

"I specialize in thinking outside the box."

"Good for you. First you have to find the box."

"I might be better than you – you could be afraid of that."

A true gumshoe has to have a lot of nerve....

"No, Spring. I don't have access to Star Trek's Enterprise's labs just yet, and I can't afford to allow you to explore outside the box on your own."

"Why not? You can trust me." She was smiling.

"Right. Look, I've got it that you like a good mystery *story*. Any investigative skills?" I said, my fingers making quotes in the air.

Chapter 74

Wednesday

"I like puzzles," she said with a wink. "Did a pretty jigsaw every week when I was a kid."

I couldn't resist saying, "And what are you now?"

"Spring Elizabeth Franklin, graduating senior. Old enough to vote. Wise beyond my years."

I had to give her a smile. "Modest, too."

She sat up straighter, nodded. Smiled back.

"What else?" I said.

"I have nerves of steel. Guile. Endless curiosity. Red belt in karate."

She would not be denied.

"Okay," I said, "I'm pinning a nickname on you. Precocious. Get used to it."

"Does this mean I can help?"

"I may be able to use you for very narrow tasks posing little or no physical risk."

"Oh, I don't do that."

"Oh, you don't?"

She stood, leaned against my desk. "No."

"Spring, this is my agency. Your mother is my client. I'm worse than a parent."

"Hah! You just want me to think that."

"Try this on for size," I said, wondering if I could direct her talents while protecting us both from her inexperience. "I have this license. I have insurance for my screw-ups. Not sure if you'd be covered. Need to find out."

"You haven't checked already?"

I had, actually – she'd be covered for short intervals – but I didn't want her working any leverage.

"I have a question, Ms. Spring."

"And that would be?"

"Who died and left you in charge?"

Spring had no answer for that. I stole it from Dad. He had used it all too often.

< >   < >

It was four in the afternoon at that point.

"How about you go do homework and I text you when I get something in your skill set?"

"Homework? You serious?"

"Damn serious."

"Just messin' with ya. It's done. Did most in class; the rest at lunch, instead of hanging out. I came here prepared to work late."

"And I'm not prepared to send you anywhere."

"Like tailing my Dad?"

"Not gonna happen. Go home."

She stood, stared at me for a moment, then sat right back down.

"Now what?" I said.

"Time I asked you a question."

Nothing in that sentence could result in good things. I knew it. I felt it. I tried to sit still and wait her out.

"Now who's a clam?" She stood, walked around her chair to the window.

In maybe thirty seconds, Spring turned to me, said, "Why do we follow my Dad?"

Whose investigating firm was that?

"We?"

"Okay, why did my Mom hire you?"

"Asked and answered – already."

"Prove he was fooling around."

"That's... been the focus, lately."

Spring turned back to the window, looked up toward the clouds, pretty much a permanent fixture in Houston. The rain Houston clouds dropped was mostly warm, often came down in torrents but not for long, so I didn't mind the clouds or the rain. Best weather I ever met.

Still looking out but not up so much, she said, "That word 'lately.' What's it mean?"

"Currently. Now."

"So maybe you were supposed to do something else before?"

Red handed, she had me. Caught red handed, I was.

< >   < >

I took Spring on a long verbal journey down ethics road, around safety bend, and up the hill to mother's plateau where the drive-in theater was playing shorts about her mother being her mother – *and* my client. Spring grabbed at the wheel over and over again with a guile not often found in middle-aged folks, never mind girls of eighteen. That was maybe ten minutes.

Towards the end, it did seem like Spring tired a bit. Maybe she thought of our "discussion" as a game. I never did know. At the time I guessed she relented ultimately to my stubbornness, or maybe boredom with a game she was not winning.

I did promise her I would call later.

She left for parts unknown.

Chapter 75

Wednesday

I got home sometime before six, freshened Zip's outside food and water, cleaned up the kitchen a bit, then took my little pal for his first boat ride, just a short and easy one in the skiff.

I wanted him to get used to riding in a boat and *staying* in it, so I kept us in the canals, staying out of the shallow lake to avoid the choppy waves that could get whipped up without much notice. If Zip had the urge to chase something, he'd not be far from a bulkhead and land.

Zip, his tongue hanging out in wonder, wagged his tail the whole time. My new buddy!

< >   < >

Around eight-thirty my cell chimed. I looked at the screen. I was about to be reminded that I hadn't kept a promise. Heck, it wasn't nine yet.

"Trench Coat Investigations."

"I know you know who's calling."

"Hi, Spring."

"What's my assignment?"

"Maybe special scouting tomorrow evening."

"Wrong answer."

She knew that I knew what she meant. I chose to ignore what I knew.

"Wrong answer," said Spring. "I'm used to guys doing what I want."

That was too chauvinistic to let pass.

"Guys? I don't think so. Maybe boys."

"Okay. Okay. Okay. Jocelyn dared me to say it."

"She does have quite a bit of physical leverage at her disposal."

"Oh shut up."

I didn't say anything.

I heard a second voice, not as loud say, "Give me that phone."

I waited for Jocelyn.

"Heya, Nate."

Yup, Jocelyn.

"Yes, Bodyguard."

"Sprite's got this need to physically engage the events around her."

I didn't recall Jocelyn being erudite the night before.

"Bodyguard, you saying Spring's antsy, driving you nuts, wants to do *some*thing. And that *some*thing *is* to be involved in her parents shell game."

"Pretty much."

"Okay. Give her the phone back."

"No."

"What the hell?"

"Yanking your chain, Mr. Nate. Hold on. You're about to go on speaker."

"I always wanted to give speeches."

I heard a duet of groans, then what sounded like scratching.

"Hey Mr. T." It was Spring.

"So you want more drama in your life," I said.

"No she don't," said Jocelyn. "What she needs is to be in on the action."

"And," I said, "the difference would be... what?"

"Action is, ummm, action," said Spring.

"Exactly," said Jocelyn.

"Mr. T.," said Spring, "you have an assignment for me this evening?"

"No. I told you maybe tomorrow."

I heard some scratching and fluffy air sounds, then, "Sprite has a plan."

"Not on my watch. Not today – tonight."

"Mr. T., I need to. I need to. I need to."

"Needs are everywhere. You're eighteen. You're still in high school. Your mother is my client. No, dammit. No."

"Sprite's going to do something," said Jocelyn. "Back at you later."

The connection terminated and so did my patience.

"Dammit!"

Zip lived up to his namesake, yipped and disappeared down the hall into the spare bedroom I used as a home office.

Spring Franklin was not my daughter. She had come to me as a niece might approach an uncle. She wanted help. She probably didn't know exactly which kind.

Finding help of the tough love, cautious parent variety not to her liking, she was taking matters into her own hands.

Calling Candice would result in – chaos. She probably didn't know where her daughter was. Spring probably wouldn't answer a call on her cell at that point, from either one of us.

Or would she?

I flipped to call history and tapped.
Six rings.
Voice mail.
No she wouldn't.

Chapter 76

Wednesday

About nine my cell chimed again. I'd left it on the kitchen counter when Spring's call sent me to the refrigerator for a beer. I sat for a moment to debate the phone call's potential worth versus the continued comfort of my recliner and the NBA playoff game.

The caller wasn't Spring. I knew that. I'd changed her ring tone to Pirates of the Caribbean earlier before I sat back down to watch the game.

Oh, what the hell. I lumbered up out of the recliner.

I reached the counter in time to see the screen displayed "missed call." I chided myself until I noticed the Caller ID was displayed as "private number." Was it the asshole of the prior two days?

I took the cell back to the NBA game and was just getting settled when it rang again.

Private number.

"Trench Coat."

"This the fat guy, Nathan Trench?"

"Might be. You the skinny tarred and feathered guy riding on that rail out of town?"

"Oh, a comedian."

I didn't reply. Left the line open.

"Question for you."

"Only one?"

"Still the comedian."

"You're going to say what you're going to say."

"You need to back off."

"That's not a question."

"Question is what they call *implied*."

"You been smellin' your own farts, asshole? Something else toxic? Maybe illegal white powder?"

"You shoudda never said that."

The connection terminated.

Third time evidently wasn't the charm.

I tossed the cell on the coffee table, motioned Zip from the far side of the room where he'd taken refuge when he'd ventured back from down the hall. He padded over beside the recliner where I scratched his ears and we watched the game.

< >   < >

Game was darn good, close, and playoff rough. I went to bed right after that, one of two tired puppies at my place – but I didn't sleep long. About half past midnight, Pirates woke me up.

"What the hell, Spring?" I said, plopping back down on the edge of my bed.

"Explorers. Three of them. Black."

"What the hell," I said, repeating myself. I was still asleep. I think I said, "You win them in a bunko game?"

"At the house."

"House? Whose?"

"You can't be that –"

"I got it. I got it."

I had. Where else would three Ford Explorers show up that late on a week night in Clear Lake City? Helm.

"What time? How many feds in each? You see a Buick four-door?"

"Whoa. Hard to function in the dark."

"Seriously?"

"Okay, only three Explorers."

"People – agents? How many?"

"Jocelyn, you hear that? I'm seeing nine fingers, Mr. T. You sure? Jocelyn is sure. She brought her dad's binocs. They are so way too big for her face but really awesome power, once you get the settings."

"Okay, thanks, Spring. What time did they arrive? Are they still there?"

"Maybe ten minutes ago. Less. I think there's one guy staying with each Explorer – right J? – and the rest went inside."

Should I run over there? Sure. I had to.

"Where are you two, exactly. Give me the address. What are you driving?"

"Three houses towards Space Center, across the street. Lots of shrubs."

"That's a bit close. What are you driving?"

"We left J's car over on the next block two hours ago."

I didn't know whether to be amazed or yell at them both.

Chapter 77

Wednesday

"You gals armed?" They were too young to carry, legally, in Texas, but I was where I'd believe almost anything when it came those two.

"J's dad's Binoculars," said Spring, "and Mom's digital movie camera. Wicked telephoto."

"*Armed*, I said. Guns?"

"You crazy?"

"Then get out of there."

I didn't get a response. I heard a shush and the line disconnected.

< >   < >

I turned on the bedroom light and dressed as fast as I could half asleep. Zip heard me and whined and whined. I had him on a short leash in the kitchen for training purposes. I'd have to take him outside to his long leash.

Awake and finally together enough to leave the house, keys and all, I heard Pirates calling again.

"Spring, you okay?"

"Sure. Why not?"

"You disconnected."

"Sorry about that. I put the phone in my back pocket for a sec, bumped into the dresser, and butt hung up on you."

Girls.

"Okay," I said. "What's happening now with the trucks? The people?"

"Not much. J gave me a turn with the binocs and there really wasn't much to see. Only one of the guys at the explorers is cute at all."

Crazy girls.

"Stay put. I'm on my way."

"You stay there. No room for guy your size behind these bushes."

"Okay. I'm on my way. Will park next to your car and we shall see."

"You can't."

"What the hell?"

"There's a driveway on either end. Made sure we could get away quick."

Smart girls.

"We came in Jocelyn's car."

"Okay, what is it?"

"Tiburon."

"That's a ski resort."

"That's Telluride. You should know that."

"Jocelyn's car – describe it."

"Hyundai two door. Kind of a turquoise ugly sporty. Five years old, minimum."

"What street?"

"The next one over."

"Which way?" There were parallel local streets on both sides of Helm.

"I don't remember. J, where's your car?"

I could hear a few mumbling and scratchy sounds as I got into the Forester and backed out of the garage.

"Mr. T., you there?" said Spring.

"Yes."

"J says we're leaving. The Explorer's all started engines and bunch of guys in dark warm-ups or something just came out of the house."

The line went dead.

I flipped the Z10 in my hand to call back, then stopped. The girls had to be running like crazy and wouldn't answer. I had to trust that the girls had some innate sleuthing skills and hadn't been taken from behind by guys connected with the Feds or a mob.

I'd hear from the girls soon enough.

Yes, I would. Yes, I would.

Chapter 78

Wednesday night

Driving west on NASA Pkwy., I was scared shitless, almost shaking. Hadn't heard from the girls. I guessed I need to go on up to the Helm St. area to be near where they had been but had expected to have heard from them already.

I about lost it when a new dark Ford Explorer pulled up to the light at Space Center Blvd. while I was entering the right turn lane to turn north. It took me a second to recognize the vehicle, there are so many SUVs in the Houston area.

I flinched when I registered Black Explorer. But was I being paranoid?

I passed within twenty-five feet of the Explorer as I turned, wanting to stare into the windows but wanting to hide as well. It was the middle of the night and the intersection's lighting was adequate but didn't afford any clues, so I got to hide.

What I did know was that the Explorer sat, its turn signal blinking in the proper direction, half way on the quickest route from Helm St. to my place in Seabrook.

There were lots of new Explorers in Clear Lake City – I kept telling myself. Lots of Explorers.

I ultimately decided that if the dark Explorer had a Fed or Mobster behind the wheel, he'd already know the Forester and its license plate and be coming up behind me in no time – I did the speed limit, 45mph.

< >   < >

Pirates rang.

"You all right?" I said in a rush, afraid the voice on the other end would be male and federal.

"Meet us at Denny's."

Relief! And confusion.

"Near Baybrook Mall? "

"No. Where Jocelyn used to work."

"Like I would know that? Are you two okay?"

"Yes. Of course. You worry too much."

"Denny's is fine, if I know which one – and you don't run out."

"Chill, Mr. T. Chill. The one off 146."

"There's not a Denny's in Seabrook."

"La Porte. At Fairmont Pkwy."

"Good choice. You there already?"

"Almost. We stopped at Wallyworld."

I wasn't even going to ask why. "On my way. At Bay Area and Space Center."

"We're good."

They had made a smart choice for two reasons. First, I assumed Jocelyn still had some friends there. Second was the location, only fifteen to twenty minutes away from Helm St., but in a whole 'nother world from Clear Lake City. I hoped the lot was well lit. I'd want to see the occupants of any Explorers.

< >   < >

Did you ever try to debrief a teenager?

Did you ever succeed in keeping a teenager on task?

In the Nav, we gave orders in a raised voice if we expected an order to be less than popular.

What did you do with teenage girls?

Kara would have told me.

I was half way through my Grand Slam breakfast when the girls' lack of attention to my questions set me off.

"Stop. Shut up a second. Both of you."

"What we do?" said Jocelyn.

"Yeah, what?" said Spring.

"Can I talk without interruption for a minute?"

Across the table from me, the two young heads turned toward each other. A series of facial twists followed by wide grins.

Spring said, bouncing around her hands held high, "Okay. Okay. We bad. We bad. We fun. We fun. But we bad. Bad. Bad. Say, J, what we give him, five minutes?"

"I'm good with that."

I used my napkin on my chin, then said, "You girls scared the bejesus out of me tonight."

I held up my hand, palm wide toward Spring. She was itchin' to talk.

"Now, I thank you for your efforts. I do. I see more power in you two than I would usually guess, so, thank you.

"That doesn't mean I'm happy with what you did. These bad guys that are messin' with your dad, whoever sent them, Spring, that entity is a monster and has some serious assets behind it. Money and people. You both could have been arrested, as adults, if the bad guys are government. Or you could have been injured, even killed if the bad guys were mob connected. Your futures could be trashed in one event."

I continued to look back and forth to each as I drew a sip of ice cold water.

"I've just met you both, true. And you two don't know me from Adam, true. Still, I give a damn. Okay, I care. Don't ask me why. I'm a guy. We're not good at explaining that."

I did the ice water sip thing again.

"So, now that I've let that out of the bag, I need for you two, one at a time, to tell me every little detail you can remember. Every one.

"When I hold my hand up, it means I can't write any faster and you need to go silent for a bit. Understood? And don't both talk at once."

Chapter 79

Thursday

I slept for three hours. That's all the time there was after debriefing Spring and Jocelyn.

The digital alarm made me less than a smiley face but I had work to do. First a shower, then I dove back into the Franklin mess.

I had taken on a client fourteen days back who said she was worried about the decline of Shrimp-Steak, Inc., figured skimming by her husband. She hired me to find out how her husband was taking cream off the top and where it was stored.

By that Thursday morning, it was clear she was actually after smut to fuel a favorable divorce decree. She had taken a lover and become cranky about the pace of my investigation, even though I'd told her at the outset that it could take months.

I'd take her money as long as she front loaded the cash.

As my second cup of coffee and I looked over my notes from Denny's, I became more confident about the accuracy of my take on Ben Franklin and Shrimp-Steak, Inc./Lake City Catering. There was a lot more going on than a restaurant business dropping in sales when the rest of the local restaurant industry was experiencing a boom. I couldn't prove it all but I was certain I was right.

Something bigger was in the kettle, lurking deep in the broth.

The thing that was going viral in my mind right then, the thing that was absolutely torqueing my jaw wasn't who was fronting the house on Helm St. and the Ford Explorers and the staff, whatever their true size. It had to be a Mafia or the Feds. Pick one. In many circles the players are interchangeable.

What was driving me nuts was simply, *Why*.

Why?

Whatever outfit / organization / political entity could detect and block wireless microphones immediately plus provide and staff Ford Explorers with crews of three at midnight had to have a *reason*.

It likely was a Very Big Why.

A great big monstrous W-h-y.

I had to find out *Why*. Viral and I do not share brain matter very long without an explosion – and my jaw was so tight, I had trouble sipping my coffee.

With luck I wouldn't get myself killed or arrested. Or anybody else.

< >   < >

8:31 AM. Candice came at me with fire and brimstone in her voice seconds after posted office hours began. I'd been in my chair a whole five minutes.

She omitted any nicety and plunged right into, "Seems to me if you're looking for evidence of infidelity, you would need to track my husband twenty-four seven, not just in the evenings, two days a week. I'm declining to pay for the four extra boys this evening. I may call off the entire student militia."

She had a valid point. Been nice if she'd been less circumspect in deferring my investigation into the whereabouts of skimmed dollars in favor of the latest installment of the Infidelity Files.

"Good morning, Candice. I have been mulling that over in my mind, as well. We will continue to need members of the student militia, primarily to assist with shadowing Ben twenty-four seven. Their hourly rate is much lower than mine."

"Yes. I suppose it would be more effective."

"Thank you. Do you want *any* spelunking on the matter of the skimmed profits?"

She coughed, twice, then said, "Of course I want you to find my money. At present my intuition says he's spending it on *her.*"

"Right. Might be able to trace the money path backwards – unless everything is paid in cash, of course."

No, I had not lost sight of the irony in cash skimming and Mrs. Candice Franklin's decision to pay me in cash.

"Yes, well, you will keep me informed at each step, will you not?"

"Absolutely, Candice."

"I must go. I have a –"

"One thing first."

"What is it?"

"Since I'm still looking for money traveling one way or the other, I think it would be a very big help to my investigation if you could get me a copy of that tax attorney's analysis you paid damn good money for."

"That won't be today. My schedule is full."

The connection terminated.

Had I hit a nerve? Did the report even exist?

Chapter 80

Thursday

I was waiting for a skip trace report to generate online, flipping my stick eraser up in the air and catching it with the same hand, and thinking about what else I might consider when I remembered the Helm St. download from Wednesday morning. I'd been so hassled with phone calls and trading the Honda Fit back in for a real car that I'd not played recordings four and five.

Where was it?

On your phone, dummy.

I located the folder and opened it.

Recording four began with static-like crackling, then a zero-beat adjusting tone like on the old military R-1 SSB receivers, followed by a guy talking in English but with an accent from hell. The overall tonal quality of the recording seemed much better than the sitcoms and I still couldn't understand a word

I checked the file and the recording had come from the front bedroom. I backed up the playback thirty seconds and listened again.

It was English all right, just not any regional accent I'd ever run across, even with all those characters in the Navy. If the guy had been Irish, I'd have called his speech a brogue. The guy on the recording sounded more like a long-term smoker who worked as a barker hawking the target rifles at a low budget county fair on a drunk afternoon. Loud, guttural, ugly, and pushy.

I listened to the end.

Maybe five intelligible words, none with any significance.

I went to recording number five.

Laughter. Two women complaining about mopping floors or something. I got the voices in another thirty seconds: "Laverne and Shirley." Crap. Damn.

But number four. Did I know any linguists? I did in Corpus Christi – well I had five or six years back. In Clear Lake. Maybe *islandgenius* knew one. Email attachments knew no geographic boundaries.

< >   < >

About the time I was wondering if Spring and Jocelyn had made it to school on time, my cell chimed and caller ID showed another stupid Private Number.

"Trench Coat Investigations. Good Morning," I said in my best Boston accent. I was a fan of Spenser and Hawk.

"Where are you?" said the Moog Synthesizer.

"You don't know? I'll bet you're a Fed. You should know"

No response

"Wait," I said, "You know where I am now, now that I've answered the phone – your buddy at NSA just told you."

The line disconnected.

I uttered an expletive deleted ... and remembered Jocelyn worked at Sonic,

< >   < >

Five minutes later something thudded against my closed office door. Shouting. Women. Another thud, then it popped open.

Allison Wilson with Lynnette in tow – no. Lynnette chasing Allison, a hand on my banker friend's right forearm, pulling it back.

"Sorry, Nate," said Lynnette. "I know today is major stress for you. I told Ms. Wilson here to wait while I checked –"

"Take your speech back to your desk. Nate and I have a long history, don't we, P. I. Man?" she said with a wink.

Women! Two teenagers was bad enough. Dealing with four females could be lethal. And how did Lynnette know that morning was unusual, stressed to the max?

"Ma'am, I'm paid to ensure privacy for our tenants. Until Mr. Trench tells –"

"I heard that, darling. How about you just go back to your roost," said Allison as she put her purse down on one chair and glided into the other. "We have important business. Run along."

"Allison, Lynnette's just doing her job. And I'm chained to a serious case right –"

"I've got great new low rates, Sugar, and lunch is gonna be on me, so –"

My cell broadcasted Pirates.

"I'm not going to lunch," I said. "Sorry. You'll have to leave. Client privacy," I waved the phone's screen at them. "Both of you. Out! Errr, thanks Lynnette."

That got me a wicked sneer from Allison, one of those "you'll be sorry looks." Lynnette ducked slightly, the cheek I could see turning pink around the crease of her small smile.

Chapter 81

Thursday

I keyed the Z10.
"Spring, aren't you supposed to be in class?"
"They're in a convoy."
The school?
"What's up – who's in a convoy."
"Explorers – but now there are four."
"What they hell are you doing?"
"What I do best."
Tailing. Had to be.
"Get the hell out of there."
"I'm – they're turning left onto Camino Real!"
The long talk I'd had with the two of them a few hours earlier at Denny's hadn't done any good.
"Left is a relevant word," I said. "Do you know which way would be mostly south? What street were they on?"
At that point I was pacing back and forth across my office, Z10 pressed all too firmly against my left ear.

"They just left El Dorado and now they're going towards your office!"

What the hell?

"How far back are you tailing," I said.

"I know how to do this."

"You've never tailed a Fed or Mafia."

"I'm going to have to pass them."

"You want your diploma presented through iron bars?"

"They're in the turning lane for Bay Area. No choice. They've stopped. I better not get in line with them."

"Which way?"

"Like they're going toward Lake."

"Clear Lake?"

"Yes, but the high school."

A sharp knock came at my office door.

Time to yell. "I'm busy. Slide a note under the door."

My door opened a bit slowly and Allison's best imitation of a Cheshire Cat entered."

"Ms. Wilson. Out. Now."

"Nate, I just wanted to –"

"Now!"

So much for low interest rates on business loans.

"You getting messed with at your office?" said Spring, laughing.

"Never mind. Where are you now?"

"Making a U-turn on El Camino, right near your office."

"Get out of here. Go home."

"The Explorers did turn. Watched in my rear view."

A wonder she didn't have a front collision.

"Spring. How can I get you to understand that –"

"Call you right back."

I was left with a dead connection and live anger. What could I do? I didn't have a sister to call and ask. Calling Candice would – no?

And where were the Feds heading – or whatever drove four Ford Explorers?

Chapter 82

Thursday

My cell chimed two minutes later.

"Spring, look, I need to get it across to you that –"

"They're turning south I think, like toward Nassau Bay but on Diana which doesn't go through, away from the library. Wait. Dammit."

Wait?

"There's only three Explorers," said Spring. "And I'm stuck at the light. Guy in front of me isn't turning."

"There were three at the house – hold it. You did tell me four a few minutes ago. What does that extra one look like?"

"They're quadruplets."

"Government issue. Great. Any idea where the other one is?"

"No. I was about two blocks behind when I first got back on Bay Area. Just now noticed."

A rhythmic but light knock. I knew that knock.

"Lynnette, I'm still in the middle of tension." I hadn't yelled so much in years.

My office door opened anyway, slowly, a very timid Lynnette sort of ducking her head in.

"I think you'll see this visitor, Mr. Trench."

"Not today, I don't have time. It's absolutely ...."

Lynnette had pushed the door wide open and stepped back into the hall.

A black-suited blonde crew cut of a middle linebacker who'd once had his nose broken strode into my office, the traditional two-pocket wallet of Federal Credentials held open in his extended right hand.

I got behind my desk and motioned him over.

The door clunked closed.

"Hey, super woman," I said into the Z10, "the other Explorer just walked in my office. Go home!"

I killed the call and reached for the creds.

Secret Service.

Secret Service?

"Umm, sit down, Agent Tor-*ville*. You want to see my Investigator's creds?"

"That won't be necessary," said Torville in a robust baritone.

He probably had a twenty-page file on me in his SUV, pdf copy in his phone.

"Mind if I call Lynnette for some water – you want anything?"

"Evans," said Torville, proving he could yell with the best of them."Tell reception to bring Mr. Trench a glass of water."

I heard a muffled "Done" from outside my office door.

So, there were two of them. Three per Explorer last night. The other agent was watching their ride.

"Thanks," I said. "How can I help you?"

Torville got up and walked over to the window.

What was it about that office of mine on El Camino Real? I've had two other public offices over the years, both with even larger windows and better views, and nobody ever went to stare out of either of those.

"Mr. Trench, actually I'm here to help you," he said to the glass.

Oh, I was believing that.

Not.

I held my tongue. Waited.

He took a while.

"We understand that you have been investigating the activities of a Benjamin Ivan Franklin."

I remained silent. Held still. Can you hold still while shaking in your boots?

The door opened. No knock. Evans set a glass of chilled water, I assumed from the water fountain near Lynnette's station, on my desk and placed a one-liter bottle of Dasani, unopened, in his boss's hand.

After Evans had left, shutting the door behind him, Torville said, "And your investigation has been rather extensive with widespread surveillance and the deployment of electronic detection measures.

"And we understand that your activities have been sponsored by a third party who is paying you rather handsomely, given your usual business receipts."

I felt a nod was in order so I gave him a quick one. He couldn't see it, was still looking out the window and down in the direction of the building's modest garden.

"And perhaps what you're doing is well within your license – except for attaching electronic transmitters to a private residence, of course."

He turned towards me, a small knowing smile on his rather large face. He wasn't any taller than me but he must have been two suit coats sizes larger. No gut.

I smiled back, I think.

He opened the Dasani. "I mean, anyone can park on any residential street in a public, ungated neighborhood and stare out the windshield – or have someone do it for them. We all have cellular communication devices these days."

He took a sip.

"No law against it," he said, "in most jurisdictions. You weren't the one who put those amateur transmitters on the Charger, were you? No, that's right. That was in the report. Mrs. Franklin most likely for that."

He took another sip, capped the bottle tight.

"So, what I'm here to communicate to you, Mr. Trench, is that your activities have impeded important activities of your government."

"I missed that memo, I guess. Do you have an extra copy?"

Okay, I should have kept my mouth shut. Just couldn't resist.

Torville slowly grew a smile, then, with a shallow nod, said, "Chief Trench, I have been briefed. Seems your personality is a bit unusual for geeks, former of senior enlisted personnel of the Naval Security Group, U. S. Navy retirees and such."

"Thank you, Agent Torville. But how is it you plan to help me – or is there more to your, shall we call it, overview?"

"Oh, there could be hours more. Since you're familiar with *need to know*, you won't feel left out on the rest of it, would that be fair to say?"

"I loved needing to know. It was like being asked to join the country club."

Okay, that one was plain dumb. I really did say it, though. No weapons were drawn and pointed at me, although I did glimpse

Agent Evans peeking in once as Torville talked and I listened. How had Evans managed to open it without a sound?

"So, Chief, we have an interest in Mr. Franklin and now we have an interest in you. We wish to work all this out. We don't see the need to involve local authorities, the media, or even your third party. You following me so far?"

I wasn't *certain* what he was asking me to say but I knew I wasn't going to like things going forward.

"Okay, Mr. Torville, I'm working on it. *And* I'm needing some clarification. I wish to cooperate, a proud veteran and all, but I need to understand clearly what it is you're asking. You know, spell out what you want me to do – or not do."

"I do believe we can work with a proud verteran."

"You're welcome. So, nuts and bolts, what's up?"

Torville and his bottle moved to my desk. He took the right chair. Barely fit.

"Mr. Trench, we'd like you to continue working for Mrs. Franklin but not have any contact, visual, telephonic, electronic, direct, indirect, cloud-based, written or otherwise with Mr. Benjamin Ivan Franklin."

Simple enough. I was supposed to lie to Candice.

Chapter 83

Thursday

"Okay, you want me to make Mrs. Franklin think I'm still investigating Mr. Franklin."

"Yes, but not go near him. Not contact him. Not communicate with anyone who has regular contact with him."

"Kinda hard to do my job, then, Mr. Torville. I'm not linked to NSG-NSA any more so I can't really investigate much without going near. About all I can do is check his credit report, some financial records, and matters of public record like liens and bankruptcy filings. You guys did such a good job of hiding much of Franklin's data and all of his metadata, I had to go with the physical monitoring stuff, the near stuff. Street leather. Mobile surveillance."

It was Torville's turn to stonewall, to sit there, say nothing.

I grew tired of his game in less than two minutes. "Look, I've just been doing my j-o-b. Mrs. Franklin is a bit difficult. You know that, so I'm going to need – is our conversation off the record?"

"Are you recording it?"

"No. I didn't have time to prepare for your arrival. I could, if you want – unless you're wired."

"I am and you know it," said Torville.

"I'll expect a copy of the transcript, same day," I said as I stared him down. Well, at least that's the face I gave him.

"You'll not receive an electronic file, Mr. Trench. You will not receive a typed transcript. We could of course follow protocol and take you into custody right now. Lose you in the system for a few weeks. Easy to do."

I bounced up out of my chair. "Weeks!"

"Please sit down."

"I haven't done anything –"

"Technically – literally – you have. You know it. Now sit down."

"This is a community property state. My client has a right to –"

"Please. We wish to avoid the drama. Don't you?"

I dropped into my chair, kicked my desk.

"Agent Torville, I'm not in the habit of making fraudulent representations to my clients. How long is this going to go on?"

He twiddled his thumbs, literally, for a good minute before saying, "Frankly, sir, we do not have a clearly defined timetable at this time."

"Your creds read Secret Service. Which are you really: FBI, ICE, DHS, ATF, CIA, DARPA, DIA?"

"Perhaps you need to research the current specified areas of federal agency responsibility."

That was it. That was the only information he gave me.

Later I recalled the United States Secret Service not only protected the President, it also had purview in federal financial crimes.

I didn't realize this at the time, so I kept after Agent Torville.

"What is it that you're trying to do? What's your mission?"

"You know I can't say."

"You'd better find a way."

"Mr. Trench, understand, you're not in a position to dictate terms."

"I'm a private citizen, Navy veteran, and –"

"And recallable to service for another four years and seven months."

That damn security clearance.

I kicked the other side of my desk, kicked my brain for wanting five thousand dollars a week, kicked Ben Franklin for not screwing around on his wife, and kicked Candice for being a bitch.

"Torville, lay it all out to me slowly. I need as long an explanation as you can give me."

He smiled. "Okay, let's suppose that ...."

He talked for maybe five minutes. Maybe it was ten. I don't remember. I'm pretty sure I didn't obtain any new information. It did occur to me as I sat there that the guy could write literary fiction – novels. He had a vivid imagination and lots of nice words which he poured all over very little information.

When I told him I'd think about it, I was informed that such was not one of my options.

When I asked for twenty-four hours, I was given five minutes.

Yeah, he was in charge.

He won.

I lost.

Chapter 84

Thursday

But I had a plan.

"Heya," I said, walking up to a back booth at Panera Bread. "Good to see y'all. Thanks for meeting me here." Federal agents were staked out, parked in Explorers, at my office and house.

"Hey, Trench, my B.F.F. is like not in the same universe as happy, right now."

"So, Bodyguard, I assume you drove; your mom's car?"

"You thinkin' I'm not good at instructions, Trench?"

That was exactly what I'd wanted. I knew the Feds had Spring's car on their radar. Would have Jocelyn's soon if they didn't already, but wouldn't come marching into a popular busy restaurant in the evening when the younger crowd would like nothing better than to have something to tap to Twitter, take photos of and post on Facebook.

"You take the batteries out of your phones?"

"Sprite, he's getting annoying."

"We're cool, Mr. T."

"Spring, did you watch for a tail?"

She looked too tired to see far. She gave me a nod with grunge on the side.

It was eight thirty and we were in the Panera franchise near the southern boundary of League City, well south of Clear Lake. I had checked and rechecked to see if I was being followed. Earlier I'd been dissatisfied with my visually scanning for devices under the Forester and had gone back inside for a signal detector and crawled under again.

"Here's my order flag," I said. "It's a black cherry smoothie. I'm gonna wash up."

< >   < >

Spring still looked more like Late November when I returned to the booth. Even Jocelyn seemed tired. I wondered if either of them had gotten any sleep.

"Rough day at Sonic?" I said.

"Not one I couldn't handle."

"Good, well thanks for driving down. Here's some bucks for your snacks and now I need you two to listen."

"Depends on what you got to say," said Jocelyn, smiling at the fifty I'd just handed her.

Spring waved her right hand in one of those "whatever" kinds of flutters.

"Okay," I said, "the Explorer at my office had at least two Feds in it. Two came into my office and one told me what's what."

I explained most of the Federal Visit. Since there wasn't really any information to tell, I could only drag it out for ten minutes. Then I delivered the punch line.

"So, Spring, you need to go have a serious chat with your dad. Maybe when he gets home this evening. Maybe follow him out in the morning and chat in a park, but away from your cars. And your phones. You work it out."

She gave me a gentle, if fatigued "thumbs up."

"But don't call him or text him or email him. I'm sure his stuff is being screened and retransmitted all over the planet. Yours will be, too, at least for a while, so figure your phone and your home are both being intercepted and monitored."

"Why they want to do that, the Feds?" said Jocelyn.

"That's what Spring is going to find out," I said, trying to smile.

Spring frowned, threw a still-wrapped straw at me. "You ever try to talk to the man?"

"Your dad? No. You know that."

I picked up the smoothie, sipped, said, "You wanted to be involved. Said you liked your dad more than your natural parent. Wanted to be appreciated for your chutzpah. For your mystery solving. Now's your chance to earn a rep."

"You tellin' us," said Jocelyn, "that we can't have any contact with Ben Franklin, even like with a camera?"

"I'm not telling you. The Feds are."

"Who the hell they think they – never mind."

"You think they know I was tailing my Dad," said Spring.

"Maybe not last month or the month before, but now, if you do, for sure."

"Did they see us last night?" said Spring.

"Don't know. I'm pretty sure they know you tailed the Explorers today. The agent I talked to, Torville with the Secret Service, didn't mention it. You'll need to remember that name."

"Whatever," said Spring.

"Why?" said Jocelyn.

"It's the only one I got – except for a flunky named Evans."

"Let him finish, J. I'm past exhausted."

"Okay, Spring," I said, "see if you can get your dad to understand you're not just a lucky guesser playing games. That you 'miss him' and maybe about how he's driven your mom to play outside the box. That you're his daughter and you all three live in the same house. But be damn sure you pay attention to what's going on around you. What's there. Who's there. What you maybe can't see."

"I'm too tired for this."

"Spring, dammit, the Feds got your dad on a short leash. So you need to go talk where you're sure the place isn't bugged, after you've asked him if he is."

"This is all so crazy," said Spring.

"Big brother is alive and well," said Jocelyn.

"Look, you two, what Spring gets to find out is two things. One, what the Feds have on your dad that caused him to cooperate. Two, why: what it is that he's spent the last year or so masquerading around for. What is the gig? What federal scheme has him on puppeteers strings? Who are they trying to catch?"

"It has been a year. Damn. This is crazy. Crazy. Crazy."

"Yes," I said, "and you get to hassle your dad for the truth."

"I so don't think that's going to be any fun. Are you sure he knows the truth?"

"No, but he does know what he knows – which is way more than we do. And y-o-u wanted to help. You're getting an inside peek at the raw side of finding the truth. Any problems with that?"

She squirmed and twisted on the seat for a bit, then said, "Awww, man."

"Look, he's your more favorite parent. You ever tell him that?"

"Man. Man. Man. You are so pushy the last so many hours. Damn."

"So, you agree?"

"She agrees," said Jocelyn, punching her best female friend's shoulder.

"Good, now neither one of you has an iPhone, right?"

"Androids, both," said Jocelyn. "We're graduating senior outcasts."

"Good. Whenever you know you're going to get near Mr. Franklin or Spring's house – like five miles is near – you need to take the battery out of your phone. Not just shut it off. Removing the battery is the only way to shut down the GPS-911 system. Removing the battery is the only way for the Feds to not be able to find you electronically."

"The feds aren't the cell phone company," said Jocelyn.

"No, they're not. But the Feds can gain access to your service almost instantly."

"It's like in the Bourne movies," said Spring. " He speaks true, J."

"For the most part," I said, "what you saw in the movies is representative of capabilities that are native to communications systems. It takes a lot of setup work to make all that data available instantly, though. The Feds have been messing with your dad for a year, so I'm sure they've covered all their bases by now."

Jocelyn groaned.

I said, "And don't forget, if you add in the Patriot Act, privacy is a ghost and you're toast."

Chapter 85

Friday

I didn't hear from Spring.

Chapter 86

Saturday

I didn't hear from Spring for two days.

Two ugly days.

Played hide and go seek with Candice – a major pain.

Mo Siddiqi thought I was crazy on Thursday evening. I had his guys park along what we had determined were the five optimum paths between the eight restaurants, not at the restaurants.

No one reported seeing the red Charger and I wasn't a bit surprised. No tellin' for sure if the Feds put a lock down on Ben Franklin that evening but I would have taken six-to-four odds on it.

I didn't meet with Candice on Friday – told her it was my turn to shadow Ben during daylight hours. She had other commitments Friday evening. Maybe she went on a date. No meeting with Candice, no lump of cash for reimbursement of the expenses I'd invoiced her for the week before. No five-grand retainer.

Zip was the happy one. I had more time to spend with him. He'd already graduated from Sailor's Skiff school.

Finally, just before dusk on Saturday evening, I got a call from Spring. Not a text. Not an email. A phone call from a pay phone. I almost let the untagged number go to voice mail.

We met a half hour later at the noisy Carl's Junior on El Dorado. That place never did seem to quiet down, but that made it a perfect meeting place. It was so busy on Saturday evenings, the racket masked any conversation from electronic monitoring. We both had taken the batteries out of our cells, of course.

Jocelyn didn't come along. Seemed Ben had made Spring promise she wouldn't reveal the explanations he made to her – and the inherent information – to anyone else but me.

I doubt Ben actually agreed to that. He'd never met me and any justification she could have given him for releasing information about the Feds to me would have compromised her mother. Spring was probably lying to both of us: she'd promised him she wouldn't tell anyone and promised me he said it was okay.

Maybe she was thanking me for trusting her to talk with her dad.

Maybe she was thanking me for not putting her dad in further danger.

Maybe she was protecting her mom.

I didn't know then. Can't say for sure now.

Chapter 87

Saturday

Spring and I had never done small talk – but we tried.

After just a couple of minutes, I couldn't stand the suspense. I said, "So, how did your dad get upside down with the Feds."

She gave me one of those *what are you asking me for* looks, then said, "Oh, it is such a dumb story."

"Dumb, stupid, or dumb, sad?"

"Some both ways. Get this. Dad was in business before he met my Mom."

"I think she told me he was doing catering when she met him."

"Before that."

"Well, sometime before that his first wife died."

"Exactly. And there was his son for him to take care of by himself."

"So he sold the business to have more time to take care of his boy."

"That's my guess."

"Good guy."

"Looking that way."

"So what went wrong?"

"He had a partner and they sold their company about a year after Dad's first wife died. He thought all taxes were paid with the profits from the sale. Partner, a guy named Derek, said he'd taken care of it."

"And you're telling me they were not."

"Exactly."

"So the Feds had a green light to twist his arm."

"Out of its socket. Damn. And married to Mom, I mean, she would so go ballistic if she knew."

"Seems the Feds could have landed on his head years before. You sure he's telling you the truth?"

"I asked that. Not 'cause I know much about taxes getting collected. Just seemed weird."

"What he say?"

"He's got no clue. He did mention something about a backlog."

My burger arrived and I took a bite. Spring shoved a long straw into her chocolate shake.

"How's your dad holding up to all this?"

She stirred ketchup before eating a fry, then said, "I think he's playing Hero Daddy to his little girl. Not admitting too much."

"Did he say how much the taxes amounted to?"

"Naw. Just his penalties for not paying are as much as the tax started out."

"Well, you're talking over twenty years. No wonder."

She seemed out of the loop on that point, waving her hands in mock surrender, so I shifted gears.

"Did he tell you why business is down at Steak-Shrimp?"

Spring shook her head. "My superior sleuthing skills tell me the Feds have a lot to do with that."

I thought the Feds might be the cause. But my problem was the reason.

"Did he say why the Feds were ruining his business?"

"I don't think they are. I mean, business looks the same as always when I'm around any of them."

"Wait, you just more or less agreed that business was down."

"That's what Dad is telling me is going on but I don't believe it."

"You don't believe him?"

"I believe him. I believe he is saying what the Feds are telling him to say."

"Okay, let's assume business is good. I guess I can tell you your mom had an accountant look at things."

"You serious? I wondered if *she* was taking money."

"What? Why?"

"Mr. T, I mean, I saw the wad of cash."

I had momentarily forgotten her telling me that. Must have been the lateness of her visit to my house in Seabrook.

"You mom thinks your dad is skimming – taking money, cash, out the back door every day or something. Steak-Shrimp's eight restaurants' numbers are all down when all the others in the Clear Lake have rebounded from the triple recession."

Was I doing no more than piling additional collateral damage on an eighteen year old daughter's head? If I was, she was hiding it better than I could have at eighteen.

"She's not the most fun woman for a wife but I know he's not got a mean bone in his body. Has trouble firing people. And I also know he's dungeon afraid of the I.R.S."

"How do you know? You're not exactly the age where parents begin bringing their children in on their finances."

"A feeling. I see his face flinch when he talks about taxes. Always has. He's like not into politics but he'll get mad about taxes one minute, then go crazy scared about not getting them in on time."

"Okay, you live with the man. He's your dad. I'll just go over this one other item."

"Shoot before I do."

"Now you sound like Jocelyn."

"Contagious, she is. What's your problem, Mr. T. ?"

"Your dad has no idea, no clue who or what or why the Feds are doing what they're doing?"

"I think he knows. I think he's going to do his best not to tell me any time soon."

Chapter 88

Saturday

I finished my burger and excused myself to the bathroom.

I returned to find Spring sipping on the milk shake straw and gazing out across El Dorado to about ten acres of undeveloped land.

"So, you and your dad are okay?"

"Yeah, I think so. He promised to talk more. He said there's a penalty, though."

"What's that?"

"I get to listen more."

We both laughed. We needed to.

"And you told him your mom hired me?"

"Yup."

I still didn't believe her.

"How much does he think your mom knows?"

"Not much."

"How can he buy that? I mean he knows the house on Helm is no secret, right?"

"Yes, but he thinks I followed him for fun one day."

"You're kidding."

"Well, maybe. Told him I had seen him coming up Space Center, so I'd tried to catch up and wave but got chicken when I saw him pull the Charger in that driveway."

Spring had surprised me, again. And there was more to come I found out.

"Is he going to talk with your mom?"

"I think that's gonna be another daughter-to-dad conversation."

"Are you going to talk with your mom, then?"

"Dunno. I think I need to tail her and find the boyfriend. You had a couple good points."

Another surprise.

I said, "Well, hurray for the home team."

"What? What is that?"

"Old baseball song. Forget it. What *you* going to do now? You got a whole life ahead of you. They say that in the movies."

She gave me one of those puh-leeze looks from the eighties.

"I'm thinking after I do the graduation ceremony gig the first week of June, I'll grab J and we'll take a trip, hop a flight or drive to where eighteen is legal drinking age and get legally toasted."

"And after that?"

She painted "annoyed" all over her face, shook her head, then said, "I'll get a good tan on Galveston's ugly sand. That'll take a couple weeks, maybe."

"And after that? "

"Special Agent."

She couldn't mean –

"You're not thinking of becoming a Fed, are you? Tell me you're not."

"Well, I was think –"

"Wait, you have to get a four-year degree first. Feds won't take you without a degree."

"Chill, Mr. T. Chill."

I nodded. Smiled after a sec, said, "Well, where – who with – is this special agent thing?"

"You, dummy."

"What? You give me a first-ever compliment, now you're saying I'm dumb?

"And I'll probably start U of H in the Fall."

"Good. What's your major going to be? Any idea?"

"Criminology. Figure I can help you out more that way."

"Spring, I've never even considered your helping me here. You begged on for your mom and dad. That's how you got in on things."

"You need help."

"Spring, I am not going to hire you. I don't need the help."

"Oh yes, you do."

"Spring, there's –"

"You do, man. You absolutely do."

I didn't know what to say.

THE END

Appendix

ALPHABET SOUP

Ingredients

AFSS	Air Force Security Service
ASA	Army Security Agency
ATF	Alcohol, Tobacco, Firearms & Explosives
CIA	Central Intelligence Agency
DARPA	Defense Advanced Research Projects Agency
DHS	Department of Homeland Security
DIA	Defense Intelligence Agency
FBI	Federal Bureau of Investigation
ICE	Immigration and Customs Enforcement
NSA	National Security Agency
NSG	Naval Security Group

Recipes

FISA	Foreign Intelligence Surveillance Act
PAT	Patriot Act

Resources

Electronic Frontier Foundation
https://www.eff.org/nsa-spying/timeline

next Trenchcoat's 1st chapter

COLLATERAL DAMAGE
Trenchcoat Investigation – Two
By
Chuck Emerson

*

Chapter 1 – Last Monday in April

*

I'm Nate Trench and my office opens weekdays at 8:30, even Mondays.

It's usually quiet until 9:30. Then folks stroll in looking for help finding someone – usually a person who's made them angry or left town owing them money.

I was in my office early on *that* Monday. Very early: 7:50.

My mind was deep into its office focus at 8:12 when I heard a light yet lively knock on my door. Lynnette's knock. She ran the front desk at the Executive Suites that my business, Trenchcoat Investigations, had called home for all five years.

Lynnette would escort folks down the hall to my office if she wasn't too busy – except she knew I didn't open until 8:30 so her knocking was unusual.

I wasn't open for business so I couldn't officially hear the knock, right?

Or did Lynnette want to visit or tell me something? She had snuck down the hall to chat the week before but we'd been interrupted by, you guessed it, work.

I waited to see if she knocked again.

Nothing in thirty seconds.

I resumed adding keystrokes to a report.

Half a minute later, I heard a commotion. Sounded like it had come from down the hall, maybe Lynnette's desk or the waiting area.

Thud and thud and thud.

A female screaming, expletives maybe.

So early on Monday. Not cool.

I stopped typing. Looked toward the door. No knock.

My cell chimed.

Executive suites phone number displayed.

"Hi, Lynnette," I said.

"Nate, I am so sorry. I know you're not open for another ten fifteen minutes. She won't take no for an answer. Told her you weren't open yet."

"It's a she? She have a name?"

"I've not seen her before and she didn't care to identify."

"How big is she?"

"Not big. A little tallish, maybe five-six, but not big."

"Well, I'll open five minutes early, come down and get her shortly."

As I tapped the Z-10 off, more thuds.

I darkened my monitor screens, then walked the five steps to my door. Waited.

More screaming.

I opened my office door and stuck my head out. Looking toward Lynnette's desk which was down the hall a bit and just around the corner, I said at twice my usual volume, "Do you have a warrant?"

A shriek.

Not what the woman wanted to hear.

Another thud.

"I'm coming, Ma'am. Just a moment."

I heard scuffling as I walked, then a high volume female discussion.

I knew.

I rounded the corner and laid eyes on Candice Faith Pence Franklin.

My client.

Made in the USA
Charleston, SC
10 August 2013